TRICKSTERS

N.L. MCLAUGHLIN

TWISTED SKY

To my Mom,
For all those nights, watching horror movies in the dark together

"Therε's something you need to understand about us tricksters...

We lie.

And we like to play with our food."

ONE

SURROUNDED by a blanket of sparkling stars, the full moon hung heavy in the midnight sky. On the ground, delicate shadows danced like specters between the skeletal limbs of desert plants. The earthy fragrance of wild sagebrush permeated the air.

Accompanied by the sound of gravel crunching beneath his boots, the young man made his way toward the small, back country gas station. Tonight was an important night. It was his chance to prove, for once and for all, that he was a grown member of the pack. To finally show his older brother Caleb that he was an equal. Two years had passed since his first turning, his acceptance as an adult member was long overdue. Forever relegated to the rear, under the watchful eyes of the others, he longed for a time when the pack trusted him enough to carry out important tasks. The gravity of this opportunity could not be overstated. What happened this night would dictate how the pack—how Caleb viewed him going forward.

Pax halted and surveyed his surroundings. Born and raised in the west Texas mountains, he could hardly imagine a more beautiful place to call home. As far as he was concerned, people could keep their cities to themselves. He much preferred the freedom of the

open desert. Only two visits to the city in nineteen years were suffi-
cient for him to realize it wasn't a place for someone like him. The
overwhelming smells and commotion made it unbearable.

He leaned forward to light a cigarette. As he gazed down at the
lighter, he exhaled a cloud of smoke and ran his thumb over the
emblem sculpted into the shell of polished bone. A perfect circle of
ancient runes surrounding four coyote paws. Of all his possessions,
this was the most cherished. Pax was never much of a collector or
keeper of things, but this small trinket held great importance to him.
This was the only item he kept that belonged to his father.

A lone coyote called out; Caleb was letting him know he was
nearby. Pax smiled and let out a howl, releasing a cloud of cigarette
smoke at the same time. A round of coyote chatter answered in kind.

He took another long drag from his cigarette, then pocketed the
lighter. It was time to stop fooling around and get down to business.
He picked up his pace and made his way to the gas station.

Standing in the shadows on the corner, he took a moment to
adjust to the blinding lights above and survey his surroundings.

Because of the late hour, all was quiet and calm. A blue SUV was
parked alongside a pump. The driver, a big, bearded man was
smoking a cigarette while holding the nozzle. He nodded his head
toward Pax, who reciprocated.

Pax rounded the corner of the building hoping for better options,
and was met with the sight of a red sports car sitting idle in a parking
slip. The owners of the vehicle were nowhere in sight, they must be
inside. The sound of a vehicle engine rumbling to life startled him.
He glanced over just in time to see the blue SUV pull out onto the
highway. As he watched the taillights disappear into the dark, Pax
finished his cigarette.

The double glass doors opened with a whoosh, blowing a gust of
artificial cold air into the night. Two young women stepped out,
nearly crashing into him, their arms laden with bags heavy with junk
food. A pretty redhead paused in front of him and gave him a once-
over. "Hello," she said.

Pax ran his fingers through his sandy blond hair and flashed his most charming smile. He cleared his throat and took a single step forward.

Once again, the doors slid open and out came another young woman, not as pretty as the other two, but still quite attractive. She rolled her eyes in disgust and sighed at her friends. "What did I tell you about picking up strays in the desert?" she scolded as she shoved the other two women toward the vehicle. "Do you wanna get murdered by a serial killer? Because this is how you get murdered by a serial killer."

"Come on, Nikki, don't be like that," said the redhead. "He's cute."

The one named Nikki eyed Pax. "Sorry Mr. Serial killer, I'm sure you're a lovely person, but you're gonna have to find other victims tonight," she said.

The redhead turned to Pax and made a pouty face. "Sorry, cutie, mom says no." She gave a shrug then climbed into the car.

"You're pathetic, Sarah," said the driver as she, too, climbed inside the vehicle.

The sound of laughter could be heard as the car backed out of the parking slip. Before the vehicle drove away, Sarah leaned out of the window. "Maybe next time," she called out, then blew a kiss at Pax. The women's laughter echoed as they sped away in a cloud of dust, leaving him alone under the bright fluorescent lights.

For the first time all night, doubt, followed by anxiety, crept into his thoughts. What if those girls were his only opportunity for the night? Why hadn't he spoken up sooner? Or at all? How was he going to explain this to Caleb? He couldn't stand the thought of seeing the look of disappointment on his brother's face.

As though the universe had heard his despair, a pair of headlights became visible on the horizon. Too small to be an eighteen-wheeler, and too large to be a regular passenger vehicle; it coasted along the highway, then slowly down the offramp and along the side road, heading toward the gas station.

Game on, thought Pax, as he prepared himself to put on a good show. This time, he would get it right.

As the vehicle approached, he could make out that it was an old model RV. The vehicle lumbered into the gas station, pulling up alongside a pump with the sound of squeaking brakes that reverberated throughout the hills.

A man climbed out of the driver's seat and stretched. Clean shaven and muscular, he surveyed the area, pausing briefly to study Pax. In the passenger seat, there was a woman digging through a bag on her lap.

With no other opportunities in sight, and eager to move forward with the night, Pax stepped off the curb and approached the man. A thousand conversation starters played out in his mind.

"Evenin'," he said in a friendly tone.

"Evenin'," replied the man. He shot a quick glance around the gas station. "Need a ride?"

Right to the chase, this made things a lot easier. He put on his best trustworthy country boy act and replied, "That obvious, huh?"

The man's lips curved upward in a smile. "Not much else you could want out here."

Pax nodded. "I don't need to go far. Just a few miles up the road."

He studied the man, noting his muscular build and the way he carried himself with quiet confidence. Everything about his mannerisms screamed military. Moving closer to the vehicle, Pax peered inside at the passenger. The woman with long, dark hair and trusting eyes rolled down her window and smiled at him. An infant cried from the back of the RV, followed by a slightly older child asking, "Who is it, momma?"

Pax's face broke into a sly grin. He returned his focus to the man.

"How'd you get all the way out here?" asked the man, his eyes darting around the barren landscape.

"I live about ten miles that way," replied Pax, pointing toward the hills.

A look of confusion swept across the man's face. "Then what are you doing here at this hour?"

"I had a little disagreement with my girl, sir," said Pax, doing his best to sound convincing. "She kicked me out of my truck and took off, and well, here I am." He bowed his head.

The woman let out a small chuckle. "You must have done something real bad to make her that angry," she said.

Pax peered up at the woman with his best impression of an innocent teen, and replied, "In all honesty, Ma'am, she knew what she was getting into when she hooked up with me." He winked at the man. "And for the record, I am an absolute gentleman."

The man let out a laugh. "I bet you are."

"My dad taught me to always be a gentleman," said Pax. "Lord rest his soul." He stared down at his boots for emphasis. "I wouldn't do anything to sully his memory."

The man's eyes grew soft. "Well, why don't you hop on in? We'll give you a ride home. As a dad myself, I wouldn't want my son out here alone at this hour. You can sort things out with your girl tomorrow."

"Thank you very much, sir," replied Pax, trying hard to stay in character. He strolled over to the side door and waited.

A moment later, the latch clicked, and the woman stood in the open doorway. She greeted him with a soft smile and said, "Come on in. Make yourself comfortable." She gestured for Pax to sit in the passenger's seat, then settled in beside the infant.

"Who's he momma?" asked a little girl sitting in a booster seat, her hair tied up in two pigtails. Clasped in her arms was a small brown rabbit that looked like it had seen better days. With a wary eye, she stared at Pax while twisting a soft ear in her tiny fingers.

The baby, who was strapped into the car seat, fussed, and arched its back.

"My name's Sherry," said the mom.

"I'm Chris," said the man as he climbed into the driver's seat and nodded in greeting.

"Pax," he replied. "Nice to meet y'all." He nodded toward the little girl. "And you too, miss."

The little girl stared suspiciously.

"That's Ella," said Sherry. "She doesn't take easily to new people. Don't worry about her. She'll warm up soon enough."

Pax winked at the girl, then set his focus to the infant in the car seat. "And who's this?"

With a smile on her face, Sherry picked up the child. "This little man is Liam." She settled him down on her lap and offered her breast.

"Pax," said Chris. "That's a good, honest name." He leaned forward and turned the key. The engine rumbled to life. "Alright son," he said. "Where am I going?"

"Head up the highway a few miles. I'll let you know where to turn off."

Chris nodded and pulled away from the station. "It sure is peaceful out here."

"That's the way we like it," replied Pax.

"What is it you do for work all the way out here?"

"My family owns a ranch. What about you folks? Y'all on vacation?"

"Chris is reporting for recruiting duty," said Sherry, her words dripping with pride. She took the baby from her breast, settled him on her shoulder and rubbed his back.

"Is that so?" asked Pax. "What branch?"

Chris cleared his throat and sat up straight. "Army. I'm heading to Midland to take on a recruiting position. You ever consider serving?"

"Me? Nah, my people ain't really a good fit for the military."

"That's too bad. There're a lot of perks to serving." Chris peered up at the night sky through the windshield. "There's an entire world filled with exotic places and interesting people to see."

"You mean besides all the women?" quipped Pax.

Sherry giggled in the back and shook her head.

"Turn off here," said Pax, pointing out the window.

Chris pulled off the highway and turned down the gravel road. "You mentioned your father passed. Does your mother run the ranch?"

"No sir, she died with my father. My older brother and I run it all now, my sister's a little too young to do much." A sense of melancholy settled in at the thought of his parents. Pax preferred not to think about his mom and dad, it only made him feel bad. He commanded himself to focus on the task at hand. They were almost there.

They drove in silence for three miles before Chris showed signs of suspicion. "You sure this is the way? It looks like there's nothing down here."

"Yes sir, I'm sure. We're comin' up on the gate now," said Pax calmly.

At the gate, Chris parked the RV. "Wow! This really is in the middle of nowhere! It's pretty though." He scanned the darkness. "I'm curious. What is it that your family does out here on the ranch?"

"Cattle," said Pax. He leaned back in the seat, taking in the final moments of calm in Chris's life. Too bad the foolish man had no idea what was about to happen.

"Well," said Chris. "It was nice meeting you, Pax. If you ever change your mind about serving, give me a shout." He held out a business card.

"That's not gonna happen," replied Pax, his tone serious. He stretched his jaw, revealing a mouthful of long, sharp, white teeth. His eyes shined with an icy blue glow.

Realization slowly dawned on Chris; his facial expression changed from apprehension to fear.

Pax didn't move, savoring the moment as they stared at one another in silence. The blissful ignorance of the innocents in the back of the RV ignited a rush of adrenaline that coursed throughout his body, his limbs twitched in anticipation.

When Chris attempted to move, Pax immediately lunged

forward and wrapped a clawed hand around the man's throat, holding him in his chair and inhibiting his breathing.

"Don't struggle," he hissed.

Despite the warning, the older man struggled against Pax's grip, but the trickster's strength and power were overwhelming. His face turned red from the lack of oxygen.

As soon as Sherry realized what was happening, she screamed, causing her children to respond with equal terror. When she moved to intervene on her husband's behalf, Pax lashed out with his free hand, knocking her to the floor.

"Try it again and I'll rip his throat out, then hang you with your children's entrails," he said with a vicious sneer.

Sherry obeyed with tears falling down her cheeks, choosing to curl up on the floor, close to the children, and cry. Restrained in their car seats, the children wailed.

"Please," begged Chris, tears pooling in his eyes. "Take me—just let my family go." His throat constricting with each word.

Pax let up some of the pressure on the man's throat. He leaned close enough to smell the fear emanating from his pores. "Whether they live, or die is up to you." He stared directly into the older man's eyes. "So, listen carefully."

Chris swallowed and gave a curt nod.

"Good man," said Pax. He released his grip and tapped Chris on the side of his face. "We're gonna play a little game. In a minute, I'm gonna let you and your family go." A wicked sneer played across his lips. "If you can get to the next town, you'll live to see another day. There's only one caveat." He reached down and pulled the keys from the ignition. "You're gonna have to do it on foot."

"Why?" stammered Chris. "Why are you doing this?"

A coyote's howl carried through the air.

"Because we prefer to hunt our meat," said Pax. "Enhances the flavor. You know?" He reached over to the glove box and flipped it open, exposing a handgun. "I figured you'd have one of these." He gave the gun to Chris, who refused to take it at first, remaining motionless. "Go on, you can take it. I want you to use it. It's best if you learn now that your toy won't do you much good."

With trembling hands, Chris took the gun.

The stunned silence was shattered by the deafening sound of a gunshot.

A searing pain erupted in Pax's shoulder; his ears rung. Hardly phased, he stretched his neck and popped his jaw, making room for his growing teeth. He raised a hand to his chest and retrieved the round, then held it high. The tiny metal object glinted in the moonlight. "Like I said, it ain't gonna do you much good." He dropped the bullet to the floor and rose to his feet. "If you head out that way," he said, pointing. "You'll come to the next town in about thirty miles."

Pax strolled over to the door, pausing in front of the sobbing woman. He stared down at her, breathing in her scent. The fear was intoxicating. He turned and swung the door open, allowing it to slam against the RV wall, then stepped out onto the ground. Banging his fist twice on the side of the vehicle, he bellowed, "Come on out. And make it quick."

With the toddler in his arms, Chris appeared in the doorway, while Sherry stood behind him, holding the baby closely.

"Well, stop dawdling," said Pax. "We ain't got all night. Get down here."

The couple did as they were told.

"Well, well, well," came a voice from the shadows. First to appear was Ezra, his wide smile and glistening teeth illuminated by the moonlight. Not far behind him were Bass, Izzy, and finally Caleb.

"I was beginning to think this night would be a bust," said Ezra.

"You and me both," said Bass. He locked eyes with Pax. "What do we have tonight?"

"A family pack," quipped Pax.

Caleb stepped forward and placed a hand on the teen's shoulder. "You did good, little brother."

Reveling in the compliment, Pax smiled. "Well," he said. "What are we waiting for?" He turned his attention to the terrified family.

The little girl buried her face against her father's chest, dropping her bunny as she whimpered.

Pax retrieved the toy and tucked it under the arm of the cowering child, then leaned close to Chris. "Run," he growled.

Without another word or prompt, the family took off running into the desert, leaving the pack behind.

While they waited, Izzy's soft, melodic voice counted down as she danced in anticipation. "Twenty-two, twenty-three, twenty-four, twenty-five." When she reached sixty, she turned to the group and said, "Ding, ding. Dinner time!"

The sound of shedding skin echoed around Pax as he and the others transformed. He was ready for the hunt. His excitement mounting, he let out a bone-chilling howl that pierced the stillness of the night. With a chorus of yips and howls, the others responded, then took off in a frenzy of excitement, following the scent of their prey.

TWO

THE INTERIOR of the van was filled with a thick cloud of smoke that hung heavily in the air, causing Ash's eyes to water. Coughing and waving her hands, she attempted to clear away some of the smoke, but it was useless. The entire van reeked of cheap weed. "Jesus!" she said. "It's a miracle you guys have any brain cells left."

Ben snickered and took another hit from the bong. "Brain cells?" He exhaled a plume of smoke. "What are these things you call brain cells?"

Snuggled up beside him on the rear bench seat, Jasmine giggled, twisting a lock of long, dark hair around a finger.

"You got a good point," said Hannah. "I'm getting hot boxed over here." She nodded toward Ash. "Open your window. We need to clear out some of this smoke."

Eyes burning, Ash nodded her head and rolled her window down, quietly berating herself for not thinking of that on her own.

A blast of warm desert air whipped through the compartment, lifting bits of trash like a tiny tornado, sending it swirling around the cabin.

After several attempts to push his unruly dark hair out of his face, Ben finally caved and pulled it all up into a bun knot.

Thankful for the fresh air, Ash leaned her head out the window and took a deep breath. Her long brown hair whipped wildly around her face. The clear blue sky was dotted with white fluffy clouds as the desert landscape scrolled by. The sun hung low on the horizon.

"Help me out, please," asked Hannah, one hand on the steering wheel, the other clenching a fistful of sandy blonde hair. "I need to get my hair tied up, so it doesn't take out one of my eyes."

Ash sunk back inside the van and took hold of the steering wheel while Hannah quickly pulled her hair into a messy bun.

"Okay, I got it," said Hannah, as she resumed control of the vehicle.

"We should plan on finding somewhere to stop for the night," said Ash. "I really don't want to set up a campsite in the dark."

"We got lights," teased Hannah.

"Lights or not," said Jasmine. "I'm with Ash." She stared out the window. "Besides, I'm getting hungry."

"My map shows a town called Sierra Diablo up the road a couple of miles," said Ben, staring at his phone. "We could stop, get some grub, then find a campsite somewhere nearby."

"The Davis Mountains are close," replied Ash. "My dad took my brother and I camping there when I was a kid." A wistful smile crossed her face at the memory. "We can reserve a campsite there for the night." She glanced around at the others. "Sound good?"

"I'm game," said Ben. "How about you?" he asked Jasmine, planting a peck on her cheek.

Jasmine sighed and leaned into him. "Sounds as good as anything else."

Ben returned his attention to his phone. "Bad news. It looks like the campsites are all booked." He pinched and moved the tiny screen. "The only sites available are on the backcountry trails." He peered up at Ash. "I'm gonna go out on a limb here and say no one's up for trekking into the wild to set up camp."

Ash wrinkled her nose and shook her head. "Um, hard, pass on that option," she replied with a chuckle.

"I'll search for something else," said Ben. "Maybe there's a hotel or another kind of camping spot nearby."

"Oh, a hotel would be nice!" said Jasmine excitedly. "Preferably, one with a hot tub."

"Wait," said Hannah. "Let me get this straight. If no one wants to camp, why did we bother to pack all this camping gear?"

"What can I say? We like to be prepared," said Ash. "Besides, the camping equipment is for the festival. Where we sleep until we get there is optional."

"So, according to the internet," said Ben. "This town, Sierra Diablo, has about two hundred people living in it. They also have an overzealous police force." He glanced up. "Apparently, a lot of famous people were busted for drugs while passing through."

"Oh, yeah?" asked Jasmine. "Anyone I would know?" She peered over his shoulder.

Ben scrolled through images of the celebrities. "Yeah, there's quite a few."

"Maybe we shouldn't stop there," said Hannah. "I don't really want to spend the night in a small-town jail because Ben has a bunch of weed on him."

"I don't have much left," he said, defensively. "Besides, the Feds aren't prosecuting weed possession anymore, so the odds aren't likely they'd do anything." He smiled. "And isn't Ash's brother a Texas Ranger?"

"Matt's up by DFW," replied Ash. "He wouldn't be much good for you down here with the local police."

"Ah, but I'm gonna bet you're wrong about that," he replied. "I have a feeling that if anything ever happened to his little sister, big brother would rush down here in no time with an entire Texas Ranger detachment in tow."

"I'm gonna have to agree with Ben," said Hannah. "Remember how he reacted when our rental car died in Los Angeles last year?"

Ash recalled the nightmare that was their trip to Los Angeles. Nothing went right. First, their rental overbooked, so their room was canceled without notice, then their car died in the middle of the freeway during rush hour. It was Matt who came through and salvaged the trip. He booked hotel rooms for them and even had a new rental sent out in record time. She would never forget how anxious he sounded when she called him for help. Ben was right, Matt would always be there for her.

"Come on," prodded Ben. "Don't tell me you're not intrigued. We'll just stop for an hour or so, then we'll be on our way."

"I'm in," said Jasmine.

"Of course you would be," teased Ash. "Your vote doesn't count because you always side with Ben."

"I'm in too," said Hannah.

Ash stared at her in shock.

"What?" Hannah shrugged. "I'm intrigued too."

"So, that's it then," said Ben. "It's settled. We're gonna make a pit stop in Sierra Diablo."

Ash sighed. "Okay, it's your hide."

"Just remember," warned Hannah. "The weed belongs to you." She peered through the mirror, locking eyes with Ben, who flashed an impish smile. "I've got plans for my future, and they don't involve doing time for possession."

"Just remember this later tonight when you're looking to get buzzed," replied Ben.

They exited the highway and turned down a narrow, paved road. Ash was sure they were heading the wrong way. After all, what town has a main road this narrow? A cursory check of the map told her they were on course, so she forced herself to relax.

"Is it just me, or is this the only paved road in town?" asked Ben, peering out the window as they rolled down the main road.

Ash followed his gaze. As far as she could tell, Ben was right. Apart from Main Street, all the other roads in town were gravel. "Interesting little place," she said quietly.

"Didn't you say you came here with your dad before?" asked Hannah.

"Not here," replied Ash, shaking her head. "We went camping at the Davis Mountains State Park." She pointed back in the direction they came. "We never stopped here."

"I can see why," said Hannah. She scanned the area. "I wonder what they do for fun around here."

"They probably hunt tourists," said Ben.

Jasmine slapped him on the arm. "Don't say that! This place is creepy enough."

Ben wrapped his arm around her shoulder. "It's okay, I won't let any cannibal townies get you." He laughed and ducked just in time to avoid being struck again.

One after another, dilapidated buildings scrolled by, all in various forms of decay. Ash wondered if anyone still lived in the town. She couldn't imagine who would choose to live in such run-down buildings.

Hannah pulled up in front of a small building. Years of exposure to the desert sun had blackened the wood siding, further adding to its decayed appearance. Here and there, the remnants of old posters dotted the facade like candy sprinkles on a birthday cake. A crooked sign hung above the open door that read Andy's Bar and Grill.

"Looks like this is our only option for dinner, unless someone else has any ideas," said Hannah.

Ash wrinkled her nose. She took in the area, noting the trio of old pickup trucks parked outside. At least there were other people around. It couldn't be that bad. She wondered if there would be anything edible inside the old, worn-down building. "What do y'all think?" she asked.

Ben shrugged. "We can check it out." He glanced out at the building. "Besides, some of the best food is made in dusty little holes in the wall."

Hannah scoffed. "Yeah, so is food poisoning."

"Well," said Ben, as he slid open the van door. "Food poisoning or not, I gotta take a piss." He hopped onto the road and held out his hand for Jasmine. "I'll bet the beer is nice and cold."

"Now you're speaking my language," laughed Jasmine.

"I'll settle for that," said Hannah as she slid out of the driver's seat.

A sense of unease settled deep inside Ash's bones as she climbed out of the van. She told herself that her negative attitude toward the town resulted from her being used to the safety and comfort of the suburbs. Not everyone could live in expensive subdivisions, surrounded by all the amenities of modern life. She glanced down the empty street, noting the small Sheriff's office. Although the building itself looked no different from the others, the sight of it put her nerves at ease. Lighten up, Ash, she commanded herself. Who would dare to attack a group of tourists with the police nearby? She peered up at the sky. A blanket of orange had replaced the clear blue. The sun was a bright red circle on the horizon.

With a final sigh of resignation, she reluctantly followed her friends inside.

THREE

HANNAH ENTERED the dimly lit bar, squinting her eyes as they adapted to the stark difference from outside. The air was heavy with the stench of stale whiskey, rancid beer, and old cigarette smoke. A garden variety country song blasted through the speakers that hung precariously from the copper tiled ceiling. A trio of elderly men sat along the bar. With their long beards and leathery faces, they were every bit the stereotype one would imagine finding in a place like this. Across the room, a group of more youthful individuals played pool. Set among the backdrop of the dusty little watering hole, the group stood out. She scrutinized their faces, not even one appeared to be older than thirty—a striking contrast to the crusty old fellas sitting hunched over the bar.

An attractive man with sandy blond hair leaned over the pool table, cue in hand. He paused briefly to glance up at the newcomers, locking eyes with Hannah. He winked and flashed a flirtatious smile, then struck the cue against a ball, all the while maintaining eye contact.

"Yo, earth to Hannah." Ben snapped his fingers in front of her face. "What do you want to drink?"

She narrowed her eyes to study the chalkboard menu of beers. "I don't know. I don't drink much beer." She turned to the bartender. "What do you recommend?"

The burly man grunted and pulled a toothpick from his lips. "I recommend y'all get back on the highway." He leaned over the bar and whispered, "This ain't no place for folks like yourself."

"Or you could," offered a smooth, male voice. "Pour everyone a round of whiskey." The blond man from the pool table appeared beside Hannah. "On me," he said.

The bartender drew back with a strange expression on his face; if Hannah didn't know better, she would have thought the old man was afraid of the young man. Of course, that would be absurd. What could anyone possibly fear from this attractive man? There was a strange vibe about the bartender, and she was relieved the stranger intervened.

"I'm Caleb," said the good-looking man.

His eyes were a spellbinding shade of pale blue. Hannah blushed and quickly looked away. "I'm sorry," she said, feeling the heat rise on her face. "I don't usually stare like that, but your eyes. They're such an amazing color." Once again, she locked eyes with him.

"All the better to see you with, my dear," replied Caleb with a thick Texas drawl. He smiled, revealing a set of flawless, bright white teeth. "But honestly, the eyes and hair are a gift from my mom."

A chill ran down Hannah's spine. Something about Caleb's mannerisms triggered a deep sense of something primal. Scarcely able to recall a time in her life when she felt this way, she had a hard time making sense of it. There was something about him that drew her in like a moth to a flame. His wild sandy blond hair highlighted the deep bronze color of his suntanned skin. His clothes were a mix of worn-out jeans and a clean, but not new T-shirt. A pair of well-seasoned cowboy boots rounded out the ensemble. Everything about this man screamed country boy. To say that she wasn't attracted to his unusual eyes and self-assured smile would be dishonest.

The bartender cleared his throat, interrupting the exchange. He lined up several shot glasses and poured whiskey in each one. When he finished, he moved to put the bottle back on the shelf, but Caleb stopped him by grabbing his wrist and snatching the bottle away. "Just put this on my tab," he said with a wink.

The old man gulped, gave a curt nod, and quickly pulled his arm back, rubbing it as though it had been burned.

"Why don't y'all come on over and join us at the pool table?" Caleb gestured toward the old timers huddled around the bar. "You may have already figured out that we don't get many visitors around here. Us folks under ninety need to stick together." He flashed another brilliant smile, leaning close to Hannah. "Besides, I can promise you, our company's much livelier." He wiggled the bottle in the air. "I'm offering good company and free liquor. What more could you ask for?"

"I'm always up for a round of pool and free drinks," said Ben.

Until that moment, Hannah had forgotten her friends were even there. She stole a glance past Caleb to find both Jasmine and Ash smirking. "Sure," she said with a shrug. "Why not? I'm in."

"Awesome!" said Caleb. "Come on then, let's get the introductions out of the way." As they approached, a woman with long dark hair finished her turn at the billiards, then gently rested her cue against the wall. She studied Hannah with cunning eyes, then flashed a sly grin and wrapped her arms around Caleb's waist, leaning her body into his.

A spark of jealousy ignited in Hannah, immediately followed by a deep sense of embarrassment over having misinterpreted her entire conversation with Caleb. This quickly morphed into confusion. She was sure he was flirting with her. Why would he flirt with her if his girlfriend was present? Did she completely misinterpret the whole interaction?

"We've got company tonight," Caleb said aloud. "This here is Hannah." He turned to the others. "I'm sorry, but I didn't get everyone else's names."

"My name's Ben." He wrapped his arm around Jasmine's

shoulder and pulled her forward. "This is my girlfriend, Jasmine. And the one hanging back is Ash."

"Greetings," said the raven-haired woman. Her piercing eyes once again settled on Hannah. "It's always great when we get some fresh blood in this town." She flashed a pleasant smile. "My name's Izzy."

The woman's beauty was beyond comparison to many women Hannah had ever seen. She carried herself with a level of confidence that most would find intimidating—it was almost predatory. A crimson tank top hugged tightly against her body, highlighting her athletic frame. Her hair was a thick cascade of dark brown locks that framed her bronzed skin. Her eyes were a vibrant amber brown, a literal golden version of Caleb's.

"The big goon with the beard over there is Bass," said Caleb. He took a step back from Izzy. "Bass, say hello to our new guests."

The big man nodded. He was a remarkable sight to behold, towering a full foot over the others. Muscular, with broad shoulders and veiny arms, his carefully maintained dark beard was a flawless match for his dark, wavy hair. Like the rest, his skin had a deep, bronze glow. The color of his eyes was identical to Izzy's amber hue.

Another man with short, dark hair stepped forward. A long, nasty scar, almost like a claw mark, extended from the corner of his left eye to his jaw. Even with the scar, he was still quite handsome. "I'm Ezra," he said with a small wave. He rubbed chalk onto his pool cue and peered up at the group. "It's always nice to have some fresh meat in this old town."

"Meat?" asked Hannah, a little taken aback by the peculiar choice of words. She gazed into his vibrant green eyes, trying to gauge what exactly he meant.

Caleb shook his head. "Ezra's never been great with words." He flashed a charismatic smile, as a ripple of snickers spread throughout the group. "Oh, and one more." He gestured toward a young man who had just exited the restroom. "This here is my little brother, Pax."

The young man approached with a swagger like that of his older brother. His eyes were the same pale blue; he could have been a younger clone. The family resemblance was remarkable between the two. Not only in appearance but also in charisma.

"My little brother here just celebrated his nineteenth birthday," said Caleb, beaming with pride. "Too bad y'all didn't come through that night. It was one hell of a party."

The younger man smirked.

Another round of chuckles erupted as the strange group shared an inside joke.

"Really?" asked Hannah. "It sounds like we missed a good time." She turned her attention to Caleb, and asked, "So, what is it y'all do around here for fun?"

"Besides hunt tourists?" he asked, with a sly chuckle.

A peculiar feeling stirred deep inside Hannah—something she had never felt before. Her pulse quickened; a tingling sensation coursed throughout her body.

"Okay, now that we've all made friends," said Caleb. "How about we get this party going? He raised the bottle high. "Here's to the most memorable night of your lives."

Hannah giggled and took the vessel from his hand. "That's mighty confident of you," she said, then took a sip.

Caleb's lips curled into a smirk. "Give us time, beautiful lady. I promise you; this will be the most exciting night of your lives."

FOUR

"NUMBER THREE," said Ezra. "In the left corner pocket." He tapped the edge of the table with his cue.

"Now that's some confidence right there," said Caleb. He lit a cigarette, took a long puff, then exhaled a thick cloud of smoke. "Tell you what. If you can do that, I'll buy you dinner."

Ezra snickered and stood upright. "I think dinner's already been sorted out. Now bet something you're willing to lose."

Caleb's face twisted into a vicious grin. "Name your price."

"That's easy. First choice," said Ezra.

"Hold up," interjected Pax. "I thought first choice was mine this time."

Caleb shook his head. "Nah, that was for your birthday. It ain't your birthday anymore, so now you're just a pleb like the rest of us."

Pax released a long sigh.

"What are you guys talking about?" asked Hannah. She rested against the edge of the table. "I'd add to the wager, if I knew what was going on." She flashed a coy smile and took a long sip of whiskey.

Caleb leaned close to the woman, breathing in the subtle scent of floral shampoo mixed with the cheap whiskey in her glass. "What's your favorite cut of meat?" he asked.

"Well," replied the pretty blonde. "What woman wouldn't appreciate a good prime rib?"

Barely able to hold back, he snickered. It would be insincere of him to deny that Hannah piqued his interest. But then again, at some point, they all sparked his curiosity. After all, if they didn't, it wouldn't be much fun. Notwithstanding her beauty, Hannah came off as very intelligent with a decent sense of humor. He glanced over at Izzy, who stood nearby, arms folded, with a sinister glare in her eyes. She couldn't possibly be jealous. She, of all people, had to know there was no other woman for him. Caleb sauntered over to her and wrapped his arm around her shoulder, then gave her a quick peck on the cheek.

Her body relaxed against his.

"Personally," said Jasmine. "I don't eat meat." She exaggerated a shiver. "I'll never understand how anyone can eat a poor, innocent animal."

"Well, that's where I agree with you," said Bass. "Which is why I only eat the ones who deserve it."

"How would you even know that?" asked Jasmine.

"For one," said Bass, moving nearer. "You only eat what you hunt yourself. From there, it's easy to see who deserves to go."

Jasmine rested her hands on her hips. "What would be an animal that deserves to go?"

"The weak," said Caleb, with a subtle sneer. "The slow, the stupid."

"That's just cruel," said Jasmine. "Here I was, thinking you were talking about predators."

"Predators can be slow and stupid," said Bass. "They can also be weak."

Jasmine scoffed. "That makes no sense."

Bass responded with a boisterous laugh.

"Nah," said Ben. "It's nature." He shrugged. "It happens every day."

"Ever been huntin'?" asked Caleb.

Ben nonchalantly responded, "A couple of times. When I was a kid, my uncle took me and my cousin deer hunting."

"That so? You bag any?" Caleb took a drag from his smoke and exhaled.

"Nah." Ben shook his head. "My cousin did, though."

"Too bad," said Ezra. "There ain't nothin' like the taste of fresh meat you bagged yourself." He chalked his cue. "I, for one, love the sweet flavor of a nice, plump young doe."

"I don't know," said Izzy, leaning into Caleb. "There's something about the meat of a strong young buck."

"I kinda prefer them lean and strong enough to put up a good fight," said Caleb. "Makes the meat tastier." Just thinking about meat fresh from the kill; the warm, salty blood mingling with the savory flavor of adrenaline-soaked flesh torn right from the bone, made Caleb's mouth water. His pulse quickened and his muscles twitched. He popped his jaw to accommodate his growing teeth, then willed the trickster to calm down.

"Y'all don't sound like you're talkin' about deer anymore," said Hannah, standing off to the side of the table.

Caleb turned his gaze toward the pretty woman. "Well, what else would we be talkin' about?"

Hannah shook her head and sighed. "You have got to be the strangest group we've met so far." She stared into his eyes.

"What?" teased Caleb, moving closer. "You tellin' me you don't like what you see?"

The blonde shifted her body uncomfortably as she glanced over at Izzy, who was busy pretending she wasn't paying attention. Hannah moved her eyes back to Caleb. "I wouldn't say that," she said.

Caleb gazed back at the woman; it was always too easy. A flirtatious smile here, a little whiskey there, and the inhibitions go right out the window. It was almost sad how simple prey could be. Sometimes he wanted more of a fight—it would be nice to have to use all his skills and ability. He always did like to play with his food.

"Do you guys know of any good places to camp around here?" asked Ben.

"Well, as luck would have it," replied Caleb. "We do." He glanced over at Ezra, who was fighting to hold back laughter.

"I'll draw you a map," said Ezra. He leaned the cue against the table and searched his pockets for a slip of paper.

"Here," said Pax, slamming a napkin against his chest.

Ezra blew a kiss to him, then pulled a pen from his pocket and leaned over the table, scratching out a rudimentary map. When he finished, he handed it over to Ben.

"Is this a public campsite or something?" asked Ben.

"No," said Caleb. "It's private land."

Concern swept across Ben's face.

"It's okay. We know the owners. They won't mind at all." With his most sincere expression, Caleb looked Ben in the eyes. "It's a perfect private camping spot."

"I just don't wanna get arrested or shot for trespassing," said Ben.

"Trust me when I say no one's gonna shoot at you," said Caleb.

"What do you think?" Ben asked the rest of his group.

They deliberated in silence, passing glances and nods around while Caleb patiently lit another smoke. Suburbanites were too easy. At least the country boys gave him a run for his money. A few had even managed to escape over the years. His personal promise was that anyone who made it to the next town over would be allowed to live. It's not like anyone would believe their rantings about a pack of wild coyote shapeshifters hunting the hillsides.

He watched the newcomers with a mix of amusement and disdain. Why were these types so simple? Their lifestyles made them soft and blind to the dangers that lurk all around them. They certainly were the meatiest, and he loved them for that, but they were also full of trust and naivete. Veal—that's what they were. Simpletons raised in pretty boxes, fattened up and weakened so someone like himself can come along and clean his teeth with their bones.

"Looks like we have a consensus," said Ben. "You swear the owners won't mind?"

"The owner's family goes way back in these parts," replied Caleb. "They don't mind at all."

"You know," said Ben. "I'm glad we stopped here after all. This was fun. If any of you ever find yourselves out in Phoenix, give me a shout. I'll show you around."

Caleb nodded in agreement. "Sounds good. You know, right before y'all came in, we were wondering what we were gonna do for entertainment tonight. Thanks for fillin' that void."

Ben nodded. "Okay then, before we head out, let's have one more round of drinks. Shall we? On me."

"Always up for free drinks, rare meat and wild women," replied Caleb with a wink.

FIVE

ASH POINTED toward an iron post gate. "Turn in here."

"You sure?" asked Ben, peering through the cloud of gravel dust that surrounded the van.

"It is according to the map," she replied, as she studied the tiny glowing screen. She hopped out of the vehicle, hesitant to let the door close, unable to shake the feeling of naked exposure as she scanned the surrounding desert. Her intuition was tingling with a deep sense of apprehension. "Maybe we should go back to the highway and find a hotel or something," she said.

Ben shook his head. "It's too late for that. I don't wanna drive all night. Besides, Caleb wouldn't have told us to camp here if it wasn't safe."

"Come on, Ash," said Jasmine safely inside the van. "Open the gate."

She shot one last glance around the area, then strolled to the gate. A shiny new chain was wrapped around a post, holding it closed, but there was no lock. A rusted metal sign hung precariously on the barbed wire fence. "Campers welcome. Keep gate closed." She turned to Ben and pointed to the sign.

He nodded and flashed an enthusiastic thumbs up.

After unwinding the chain, Ash stepped aside to let the van roll through, then quickly pushed the gate closed and put the chain back in place. Afterward, she wasted no time reclaiming her seat in the vehicle.

"For someone who was all about camping," teased Jasmine. "You sure are spooked."

"I didn't see you offering to go out there and open the gate," said Hannah.

Jasmine giggled. "Of course not. I'm not the outdoorsy one. I believe I've always been up front about being a five-star hotel kind of girl."

The van bounced and rattled along the winding driveway, stirring up dust and rocks along the way. The sound of its engine echoed off the surrounding hills. Ash watched through the side-view mirror as the gate disappeared behind a cloud of dust while her friends laughed drunkenly. At least someone was having a good time.

Sometimes she envied her friend's capacity to have fun no matter what was going on, or where they were. She was always too consumed with worry to truly have fun. It was as though her mind were hard-wired to fret constantly about potential dangers or whether they were moving toward a perilous situation. Fortunately, her worries and concerns were baseless. In the end, everyone would have a good time as the weekend or evening came to an end—everyone except Ash.

The van rolled to a squeaky stop. "Okay," said Ben. "Looks like this is the end of the line." He flung his door open and jumped out.

"Wow!" exclaimed Jasmine. "Caleb wasn't kidding. This really is secluded." She twirled around with her arms outstretched. "Woo!" she called out. "The sky is so beautiful. It's like standing under a blanket of twinkling lights."

"I don't think I've ever seen so many stars," said Hannah, staggering as she stared up at the night sky.

Ash swept her eyes around the dark, hilly desert scape, struggling to see the same beauty that held her friends in thrall. Try as she may, all she could see was a barren, desolate space. A blast of warm air carried the pungent odor of decaying flesh. She scrunched up her nose. "You smell that?" she asked anyone who would bother to listen.

"Smell what?" asked Ben, taking a deep whiff of the air.

"You can't smell that?"

He shook his head. "What's it smell like?"

"Like death." She inhaled deeply. "Like something's dead nearby."

He shrugged. "We're in the desert. Things die all the time out here."

His dismissive tone grated on her nerves. She watched as Jasmine and Hannah drunkenly collected wood for a fire, wondering how they could be so oblivious. How was it that the stench of something rotting nearby didn't affect them? What was wrong with her? Why couldn't she just be normal, like her friends? She tried to force herself to let it go and have some fun. After all, if no one else was worried, then she shouldn't be. Still, something didn't sit well with her. Was there something truly wrong or was this yet another instance where she worried over nonsense?

She thought back to when she first felt uneasy. The bar—Caleb and his friends. Their odd little inside jokes, and their ready smiles that never quite made it to their eyes. How Caleb studied Hannah— like a predator scoping out his prey.

Ash moved closer to Ben. "Was it me, or were those guys at the bar weird?"

"If you lived out here, wouldn't you be weird?" he replied, sarcastically.

"I suppose," she agreed. "But I don't know." She shook her head. "There was something off about them. Way more than the usual weirdo who lives in the middle of nowhere."

"I imagine a person has to be a little weird in order to stay in a place this far out," replied Ben. "I mean, it's not my vibe, but hey." He shrugged. "Who am I to judge?"

"I got a really weird feeling from Caleb," blurted Ash. "From all of them, actually, but he and his girlfriend were probably the creepiest."

"Look Ash," said Ben. "Whatever vibe you got from them, it's irrelevant. We had a few drinks in a dive bar with some desert dwelling locals. That's it. It's over. They went wherever the hell they go and we're out here." He spread his arms wide. "Prepping our campsite under the stars. No sign of the weird locals in sight." He leaned into the van and pulled out a sleeping bag. "Stop stressing about it. Neither you nor I will ever see Caleb and his group of weirdos again." He tossed another sleeping bag on the ground. "Now help me unpack." He nodded toward Jasmine and Hannah. "Those two are no help, so it's on you and me. The sooner we get camp set up, the sooner we can relax and have a good night."

Ben's desire to forget all about Caleb and his friends annoyed Ash, but she had to agree, he was right. Whatever she was feeling about the strange group was pointless. Odds were, they would never cross paths again. She should just file the whole encounter away as one of those odd meetups that she and her friends will laugh about years from now.

"What are you stressing about now?" asked Hannah.

"She got a weird vibe from Caleb," replied Ben. He took a knee in front of a makeshift fire ring that Hannah and Jasmine pulled together from rocks they found, then pulled out his lighter.

"Oh, weird vibe, huh?" Hannah giggled drunkenly. "Like what?"

Ash shook her head, not wanting to get into it with Hannah in her present state of mind.

Ben stacked tufts of dry grass underneath a pile of kindling. "She says he creeped her out."

"Seriously?"

Ash nodded sheepishly.

Hannah scoffed. "Well, I think he's hot."

"Is there a man out there who you don't think is hot?" teased Jasmine.

Hannah shoved her playfully. "All I'm saying is that I wouldn't be sad at all if he suddenly appeared." She laughed. "Minus his weird girlfriend, that is."

Ash was glad that someone else acknowledged the group's overall strangeness. "So, you agree they were creepy."

Hannah nodded and chuckled. "Yeah, I'll give you that one, she was strange. What was her name?"

"Izzy," responded Ben. He lit a small bundle of dried grass, then stuffed it under the pile of wood, and leaned close, blowing gently on the tiny flames.

"She seemed normal to me," said Jasmine. "Probably a little jealous of you flirting with her man."

"Nah," said Hannah. "She was being a bitch."

"I would be too if some out-of-town woman was all over my man like you were," said Jasmine. "Let's be honest, there's not a lot to choose from out here."

"I didn't see him protesting," said Hannah. "Did you?"

The whole conversation had veered in a direction that Ash didn't want. Her discomfort with the group at the bar extended far beyond who was sexually attracted to whom. There was something odd about their current situation.

An explosion of red and orange flames erupted in the fire ring, sending sparks flying into the cool night sky. Ben leaned back on his heels, admiring his handiwork, while Hannah and Jasmine twirled playfully, basking in the warm glow of the fire.

Thankful for the break in conversation, once again Ash found herself struggling with her feelings—wishing she could be more like her friends. Ben was right, whatever she thought about the locals, that whole episode was behind them. She really needed to learn how to be in the moment. Another blast of warm air brought the stench of rotting flesh, then, just as quickly, it was gone. She inhaled; the only scent was that of the wood burning in the fire. Determined to have a good time for once, Ash wrapped a cozy throw around her shoulders and joined her friends.

SIX

THE OLD HOUSE wasn't the same anymore. Once filled with laughter and love, it was now nothing more than a wooden structure of emptiness and melancholy. Jewel wandered through the empty rooms, each step she took causing the floorboards to creak and echo. She wasn't entirely certain when the others departed for town, as they didn't bother to inform her about their plans—she didn't really care; they were no longer people she cared about.

In the living room, she walked slowly past the collage of family photos, each frame filled with smiling faces frozen in time. A pang of sadness pierced her heart as she remembered how things used to be. Nostalgia hung over her like a heavy shroud as she recalled all the precious moments spent in this very room. Closing her eyes, she could almost hear the soft sound of her mother's voice telling her about the stories behind each photo.

The memory of her mother, with her serene smile and gentle touch, triggered a sudden, piercing pain in her chest. As she picked up the photograph of her parents, she felt a surge of nostalgia wash over her. Taken on their wedding day, the couple, full of youthful passion, smiled as they stared at each other. The warm desert sun shining on their tanned faces, highlighting the golden hair that was a hallmark of their family for generations. They were so young—her mother wasn't much older than Jewel was right now.

A tear slipped from her eye, splashing onto the glass. She wiped it away and studied the joyful faces of the young couple. Her heart ached to see them one more time—to sit in her mother's studio and talk with her. Jenny Riggs was the one person who could always make things better. No matter what was happening, Jewel never doubted that her momma could understand exactly how she was feeling. She would know how to manage the gnawing pain that seemed to radiate from every inch of Jewel's body. Her momma would know how to make her feel better. Most importantly, she would know how to quell the overwhelming desire to—.

It shouldn't be this way, thought Jewel as she struggled to hold back tears. Her mom and dad should still be alive.

Sadness gave way to anger that swelled in her heart. They left her —left her in the less than capable care of Caleb. Why him, of all people? Ever since his first turning, he had been cruel and self-centered, never considering the needs or feelings of others. He hardly acknowledged her, instead he went about his life only making time for Pax. There were times she was envious of their close relationship. She could never share the bond they had; after all, she was nothing like them.

She stared at a photo of her father and his younger brother Weston. Living with her uncle seemed like a more appealing option to her. Sure, he hadn't been around much after the death of her father and mother; his life was in Austin, far away from the desolate mountains of west Texas. Jewel wasn't entirely sure she would have been happy in such a busy place. But in all honesty, anything would have been better than staying in this lonely home with Caleb.

A stabbing pain shot through her jaw; her skin felt as though millions of tiny millipedes were crawling all over her. A wave of nausea crashed over her as she doubled over, wincing in pain. As soon as the sensations waned, she carefully placed the photograph back on the wall and moved away, knowing it was far from over. Her insides churned; every bone in her body cried out in pain as though they were broken. Waves of queasiness, lightheadedness, and revulsion crashed upon her like a relentless tide. She braced herself, waiting for the chaos to subside, wrapping her arms tightly around her trembling body, silently commanding her lungs to breathe through the pain.

The violent pain faded, leaving behind a steady, dull ache. With a sigh of relief, Jewel brushed her long, sandy blonde hair away from her sweaty face.

She left the living room behind, moving noiselessly up the stairs, and entered her old bedroom. The air in the room was stale, she didn't spend much time there anymore; not since Caleb took over the house and invited his friends to move in. It took her some time to locate her backpack, buried deep within the cluttered depths of her overstuffed closet.

As she made her way into the hallway, she couldn't help but pause and pick up a little red firetruck. A sentimental smile swept across her face as a stream of cherished memories flooded her mind of all the days she and Pax played together. Oh, how they fought over who got this little truck. They could never seem to resolve their issues without their momma stepping in to mediate. A tear escaped her eyes. She used to be so close to Pax, in fact, when they were young, they were inseparable.

That all changed after his first turning.

She missed the way it used to be. Caleb was always the older brother, but Pax was her best friend. All the warm summer nights they spent on the rooftop, staring up at constellations, counting the shooting stars. She wished she could go back in time and freeze it there forever. Why did things have to change? Why did people have to grow up? Why did people have to die? Mourning the loss of the life she once knew, she stuffed the tiny vehicle in her pack, then stepped into the hallway.

As Jewel stared down the hall, memories flooded her mind. She remembered all the nights when she would tiptoe from her own bed to the familiar warmth and safety of her parents' bed. They never ushered her back to her room, instead, both made space for the small child. She hadn't set foot in their bedroom since the accident. After Caleb took it over, as the head of the house, Jewel stayed away completely. That was when she moved all her important belongings upstairs to the attic.

A vast open space where she could go to be alone, the attic was her refuge. At one time, it was her momma's studio, a place where brushes danced on canvases and colors came to life.

Jewel had so many fond memories of the space—the entire room was filled with the echoes of laughter and sunlight streaming through the windows.

She climbed the stairs and stood in the center of the room. A bittersweet mix of sadness and joy washed over her as she glanced around. This was the only place left in the house that wasn't polluted by the scents and sounds of Caleb and his friends.

Her stomach growled. She hadn't been able to keep any food down for the past two days. If her momma was still alive, she would know why. Jenny would know what to do to make Jewel feel better. A stab of pain in her jaw caused her to cry out. The waves of discomfort were becoming more intense, and it took much longer for them to subside. Fear gripped her insides, refusing to let go until her body calmed down.

Outside, the distinct sound of tires rolling on the gravel road, made her heart skip a beat. They were back. She had hoped they would stay out longer, at least long enough to give her a good head start.

She wiped the sweat from her forehead, then pulled on her boots and grabbed her jacket. With barely any time remaining, Jewel quickly scanned the room before throwing her pack over her shoulder, dashing down the stairs, and out the back door.

SEVEN

CALEB HELD his glass high and said, "To the hunt!"

A chorus of shouts and whistles erupted, filling the air with excitement as the others toasted in celebration.

For Caleb, there was nothing more exhilarating than pursuing prey. The alluring scent of bitter panic ignited his senses and made him feel alive—powerful. Barely able to contain his excitement, he was itching to get started.

"How much time do we have left before we head out?" asked Ezra. He finished the whiskey in his glass and poured another.

"Bare minimum, we should give them enough time to set up their camp and get cozy," replied Caleb. "Maybe let the two girls sober up a bit." He snickered. "After all, they can't put up much of a fight if they're too drunk to run."

Across the rustic living room, Bass grunted in agreement.

Caleb stood before the massive, stony hearth, feeling the warmth radiating from the crackling fire, as he watched the red and blue flames paint a mesmerizing picture around the logs. He traced his hand along the rough edge mantel that was hewn from one solid piece of cedar wood, appreciating the artistry of his great, great grandfather, Elijah. He was just about Caleb's age when he built this house for his family.

The rustic farmstead, with its weathered wooden walls and creaky floorboards, might not be much to most people, but to Caleb, Pax, and Jewel, it was home. It was the only home they'd ever known.

Every corner of the house held a memory for Caleb, a silent reminder of the past. The notches on the pantry door frame were a visual record of all the Riggs children who were born and raised under this roof. The upstairs hallway was lined with worn and bowed wooden panels, evidence of years of children's hands sliding along the wall as they ran down the hall.

He recalled all the time spent huddled in front of the enormous fireplace with its hearth of stone. On frigid winter nights, bundled up in layers of warm blankets, he and his siblings would listen attentively to his grandpa's stories by the crackling fire.

Nostalgia washed over him as he fondly recalled the magical sight of snowflakes gently descending outside his bedroom window. His entire life had been spent on this land. Every memory from early childhood through adolescence to adulthood had taken place within these walls—or in the deep cave out back.

Tricksters were fierce and chaotic beings by nature. Their first turning was violent, uncontrollable, and excruciatingly painful. The young often found themselves consumed by a whirlwind of discomfort, adrenaline, and raw power. So much so, they had been known to turn on members of their own pack. It was for this reason alone that the first turning was always done under the close watch of an elder. For members of the Riggs family, that time was spent in the dark recesses of the cave.

After the first turning, it would be at least another year before the young could take part in a hunt. It took that long to learn to control their power.

The corners of Caleb's mouth turned up into a wistful smile as he thought back to his first hunt. Now that was something. Even now, he could feel the surge of absolute joy he experienced when his father, Eben, came to tell him it was time. The older man beamed with pride; his excitement almost equal to that of his teen son. Of course, Caleb's momma, Jenny, was nervous. She wanted to be there for her oldest son, but she had the little ones to care for.

The October air was crisp and cool when Caleb followed the pack to the old rest stop by the highway on the outskirts of town. The heavy moon cast its silver glow upon everything as far as the eye could see.

His body buzzed with excitement, like a tightly wound spring ready to be released. His hair and clothes were completely drenched in sweat, which was seeping from every pore. Every muscle was on fire, his senses had reached limits he never knew possible.

The soft sound of a small animal scurrying nearby, reached his ears, making him pause. He inhaled, easily picking up the scent of the little creature. Closing his eyes, he felt the dull ache of transformation coursing through his limbs.

For months after his first turning, Caleb trained himself to not only accept the pain, but to enjoy it. The tearing of flesh and cracking of bones were simply the path to supernatural power. It was a small price to pay. Caleb was never more alive than when he let loose the trickster.

"It's almost time, son," said Eben. "Best to prepare yourself. Remember, you need to keep your wits about you."

Caleb nodded nervously. "I'm ready."

Eben smiled. "I'm sure you are." He clapped a calloused hand on his son's shoulder. "Be mindful and keep your instincts under control."

They crouched low among the shrubs as a young couple several yards away was busy preparing their campsite. Soft laughter and playful banter wafted through the air. The campers blissfully unaware of the danger that encircled them.

A sharp, searing pain erupted in Caleb's jaw, causing him to clench his teeth and wince. The overwhelming sensation reverberated through his entire being, momentarily blurring his vision and filling his ears with a faint ringing sound. The metallic taste of blood flooded his mouth, accompanying the sharp ache that radiated from his jaw.

Eben stood nearby, watching. He offered no condolences, no words of calm. He knew his son was more than capable of going through the change alone.

The sound of splintering and cracking bones reverberated throughout Caleb's body. His teeth ached. A stabbing pain in his belly caused him to double over.

His spine shattered like a pack of firecrackers. One after another, he could feel each vertebrae pop and grow. His fingers curled in on themselves as his joints cracked and snapped. He watched as the bones in his fingers ruptured through his flesh, scattering droplets of blood everywhere. Sharp claws, a full inch long, extended from the tips of his fingers.

Pain exploded in his gut, causing him to lurch forward as his entire body took on a new form. Caleb tried to scream, but the only sound that came from his throat was a deep, guttural cry of agony.

The pain subsided as thick fur crawled out from each pore, no longer painful, his skin tingled with life. He climbed to his feet, feeling the full measure of his trickster body.

Electricity coursed through his veins, moving through every muscle, every nerve. He inhaled and let out a deep, excited howl. All around him, the rest of the pack called out in response.

This was Caleb's first hunt, so it was on him to signal the charge. The fledgling hunter made one last stretch to feel the power in his body, then leaped forward, bounding directly toward his prey.

From his earliest memory, Caleb dreamed of this night. He wanted to savor every moment, to enjoy every drop of blood, sweat and tears. When he descended upon the woman, she hardly could emit a scream before he had ripped out her throat. In a flash, the moment had ended. His part of the hunt was over. To be truthful, he felt underwhelmed. He expected so much more than this. Where was all the excitement? Where was the difficulty? This was easy—too easy. He wanted more. More pain, more fear, more blood.

All around him, the pack erupted in a raucous cry to celebrate his first kill. Caleb forced himself to join in the celebration, despite not feeling the same enthusiasm. As he fed with the pack, he pledged to take pleasure in the hunt going forward. To take his time and inflict the most amount of pain and terror. After all, the tastiest morsels were the ones marinated in stark, cold fear.

Izzy's soft arm wrapped around his waist. Caleb dragged himself out of his memories and planted a kiss on the side of her head.

"You're far away," she said.

He smiled. "Just spending a minute in the past."

Across the room, Ezra rubbed his hands together. "We about ready to head out?"

Bass rose to his feet and stretched, then popped his neck. "I know I'm ready."

"Well then," said Caleb. "I see no reason to waste any more time."

"She's gone!" shouted Pax, stumbling down the stairs. He came to an abrupt stop in the center of the large room. "She ain't here!"

"What are you talkin' about?" asked Caleb.

Pax raked his fingers through his hair. "Jewel. She ain't in her room."

"Yeah? So?" said Izzy. "She's probably in the attic."

Pax shook his head. "I checked. She ain't anywhere in the house." He stared nervously at Caleb.

"Son of a —!" Caleb slammed his fist against the giant mantle. "I knew she was up to something." He stormed over to Pax, standing nose to nose with the younger man. "Which is why I told you to keep a close eye on her."

"I did that," said Pax, defensively.

"Then why the hell is she missing?"

His younger brother shrugged helplessly.

The room became still, everyone waiting with bated breath to hear what Caleb wanted them to do.

His little sister had been a thorn in his side for far too long. Ever since their parents died, he did his best to see after the girl, but truth be told, he had no idea what he was doing with her. When puberty hit, he was lost. Thank God for Izzy. She stepped in and took Jewel under her wing, helping the girl navigate whatever it was that women had to navigate. Even so, Jewel still looked to Caleb as though he were a poor representation of their father. This enraged him. Playing nurse maid interfered directly with his hunting, which was all he wanted to do. It didn't help at all that the girl was downright intractable, which made things even more difficult.

He mulled over his options as he scratched his jaw. Maybe she needed some time on her own. After all, she can't get too far. Let the girl roam, maybe she'll clear her head.

He sighed. It was his duty to take care of Jewel, regardless of his feelings. He was the one in charge, there was no other choice than to put her needs ahead of his desires. Anger boiled in his belly.

Caleb turned to face the others. "Y'all go hunt." He nodded toward Pax. "We gotta search for Jewel."

"You sure?" asked Izzy.

"No, I'm not," he replied. "But I can't let her be out there doing whatever the hell it is she's up to. She's my responsibility."

"Alright, you heard the man," said Ezra, clapping his hands together.

Bass and Ezra bolted out of the doorway. By the time their feet hit the ground, they were already in full trickster form. Yipping and yapping with glee, they disappeared into the desert.

Izzy turned to Caleb. "I can help search for her."

He shook his head. "You go have fun," he replied. "Pax and I will find her. And when we do, we've got some talking to do. It's best we're alone for that."

EIGHT

"HEY ASH," said Hannah, wrapping a blanket tightly around her shoulders. Throw some more wood on the fire. I'm freezing." She mocked a shiver.

"Why are we keeping it so low, anyway?" asked Jasmine, as she cuddled up to Ben. "Hey Hannah, I bet a certain local country boy could help keep you warm."

Hannah laughed. "Let's just say that if he happened to wander into our campsite right now, I wouldn't turn him away." She turned her head toward the open desert that surrounded them. "You hear that? If you're out there waiting, now would be a good time."

Jasmine pointed up at the night sky. "The first shooting star tonight!"

Hannah closed her eyes and tilted her chin upward.

"Make sure you're specific about which blond country boy you want," warned Jasmine. "You might end up with the younger brother."

"I mean," replied Hannah. "That wouldn't be too bad."

Laughter exploded between the two.

Ash tossed what remained of the wood into the fire. She looked over the campsite and realized there was no more wood to be gathered nearby. A chill crept down her spine as she stared into the darkness beyond the light. If they wanted more wood, they would have to venture out away from the protection of the fire to find it.

"Alright, y'all," she announced. "It looks like we need to get more wood." She made eye contact with all three of her friends.

"You and Hannah can go," said Jasmine.

"Why us?" asked Hannah.

"Because we're busy," replied Jasmine. She snuggled Ben. "Besides, I'm not going out there. It's creepy."

"Fuck that!" shouted Hannah. "Ben's the dude, he can get the wood."

"Wow!" said Ben. "That's genuinely misandrist of you." He feigned shock.

"Aw, look at you," teased Hannah. "Learning big, new vocabulary words and using them in conversation." She tossed a pebble at him, hitting Jasmine instead, sparking a pebble toss battle between the two.

Ben sprang to his feet. "Y'all are gonna hurt someone. Cut it out." He peered down at Ash. "Looks like it's you and me."

Ash nodded. She didn't want to venture into the shadows, but if she had to, at least she had someone with her. "Alright Ben," she said, brushing her hands off. "Lead the way." She pulled her phone from her pocket and turned on the flashlight.

"Me?" he asked. "Why am I going first?"

"Because," she replied. "You heard Hannah, you're the man, so you get to go first." She cringed at her own words, secretly hoping he didn't argue.

Ben shook his head. "Y'all are something else, acting like your strong women, but the first sign of creepy darkness and you're all hiding behind the dude." He held his phone out in front of him, using the flashlight to illuminate his way. "Come on," he called over his shoulder. "Let's get this over with."

Ash followed closely behind him, being careful to avoid tripping on the spindly limbs of desert plants. The last thing she wanted was to fall and accidentally impale herself with one of these gnarly roots.

Ben suddenly halted, causing her to collide into his back.

She cast a glance upward at him. "Why are we stopping?"

"I don't know about you, but I haven't caught sight of anything sizable enough to be worth our while to carry back," said Ben. "You see anything?"

Ash shook her head. "It looks like all the wood that could be used for a fire has already been scavenged."

"Well, Caleb told us that lots of folks camp out here," said Ben.

"Yeah, he did." She held her phone aloft and scanned the area. As far as the eye could see, there was only barren scrub, rocks, and dirt. For the first time since they came to this place, she was keenly aware of the silence all around them. "You hear that?"

"Hear what?" He shook his head. "I don't hear anything."

"That's just it," she replied. "There's nothing. No crickets, owls, frogs, nothing."

"Well, it is the middle of the night," he said. "And we're in the middle of nowhere."

"I don't know how much time you've spent camping, but the middle of nowhere is usually pretty loud." She shook her head. "This ain't normal."

"You're just making yourself paranoid. It's the desert. It's too dry for frogs." He tilted his chin toward the sky. "There're no trees where an owl could perch." He looked down at Ash. "Don't get yourself too worked up."

"Then where are all the crickets?" she blurted. "If there're no frogs, why are there no crickets?" She stared directly at him. "Shouldn't the lack of predators mean there'd be in abundance of prey out here?"

Ben exhaled loudly. "I'm not letting you freak me out." He backed away from her, holding his phone high, looking closely in search of something. "You see that?" he asked.

"See what?" Ash stared in the direction of his light beam as she moved closer. "It looks like it might be a tree."

"That's what I think," said Ben. "I bet there'll be wood over there." He tugged her arm. "Come on, let's go check it out."

High in the mountains, a lonely coyote called out, followed by random responses from a few more.

"There's your wildlife," said Ben.

"Sounds like there's a pack nearby," said Ash, nervously.

"They're way off," said Ben. "They don't pose a threat. Besides, most coyotes do their best to avoid contact with humans."

She nodded; he was right, she had never seen a coyote that wanted to be close to people. Wherever the pack was hunting, Ash and her friends weren't in peril. She picked her way along, doing her best to follow Ben's footsteps as precisely as possible until they made it to the tree.

"Now this is what I'm talkin' about!" exclaimed Ben. He bent down and scooped up a broken limb. "Come on, there's lots of wood scattered around here. Gather a bunch so we can get back to the others."

Ash hurried to collect a full load of large and small pieces of wood. As her arms grew heavy, her mood lightened at the thought of going back to the safety of the fire. She sighed, considering how foolish it was to believe that a bunch of burning logs would protect her. Her arms full, she glanced over at Ben, who had taken off his shirt and was using it as a sack.

"Anything to avoid another trek out here," he quipped.

"Are we ready to head back?" she asked, trying not to appear as anxious as she felt.

"Yeah," he replied. "I think I've got about all I can carry. You all set?"

Ash was more than ready to get back to the campsite. She gazed into the surrounding darkness; something didn't feel right. Every nerve in her body tingled. "Let's go," she said aloud.

It appeared as if the trek back was taking forever. She knew this was just her mind manipulating her. Why on earth did they have to wander so far away? Of course, she knew why, but for some reason, the simple dialog in her mind made her feel better. The fire flickered up ahead, growing larger as she approached. With each step, her mood lifted, her sense of well-being grew.

"There you are," said Jasmine, as Ash and Ben stepped into the light. "I was about ready to go search for y'all." She took some of the wood from Ben and carried it over to the fire.

"We had to go out further than we thought," said Ben.

"This area's been picked clean of firewood," said Ash.

Jasmine shrugged. "Caleb said lots of folks camp out here."

"That's what I told her," said Ben. He jabbed a thumb toward Ash. "Our girl here is feeling a little spooked by this place."

"Really?" asked Jasmine. "It's just a campsite."

Hannah gazed up at the sky and said, "I think it's pretty out here."

Jasmine scoffed. "You're just hoping a star is gonna make your wish come true."

"Yes," replied Hannah, laughing. "That's exactly what I'm doing."

Ash disregarded them and went about placing more wood on the fire. Let them make fun of her, she didn't care. She couldn't quite place her feelings about this place. Why did she feel so uneasy? If she couldn't explain it to herself, how was she ever going to explain it to the others? In her gut she knew there was something wrong. Unfortunately, she lacked the means to describe it in a way that didn't make her sound like a person with irrational beliefs. Any attempt to get the others to understand would be futile.

"Did you hear that?" Hannah jumped to her feet and spun around, leaning forward to stare into the dark.

Wiping her hands on her thighs, Ash stood up and strained her ears to listen. She heard what she thought was a faint rustling sound, as though something was running through the brush just beyond the light. "I think I hear something," she said.

"Aw, come on," said Ben. "No more."

"What gives now?" asked Jasmine.

"She's creeped out," replied Ben. "First it's too quiet and now there's a creepy sound."

"It's not just me," argued Ash. "Hannah heard it too."

Hannah raised a finger to her lips. "Shh!"

A little smirk played on Ash's lips, thankful, for once, that someone else was feeling as though something was off.

Ben sighed loudly and raked his fingers through his hair.

Hannah took a careful step closer to the edge of the light.

The rustling grew louder, confirming that they were not hearing things. Something was out there, and it was moving toward them. Ash reached out to grab hold of Hannah and pull her back.

The shadows moved as the sound grew louder. A teenage girl burst from the brush and stepped into the light. Covered in scrapes and bruises, her long blonde hair cascading over her shoulders, wild and unkempt. Her face was a mask of fear.

"Please help me," she cried, as she stumbled closer.

"Hold up, right there," ordered Ben, stepping forward, placing his body between the girl and the others. "Stay right there."

The girl froze in place, her entire body trembled. She glanced around, locking eyes with Ash. "Please," she whined.

A feeling of protection washed over Ash. Whoever this girl was, she was a kid, and she was scared. She needed their help, not their scrutiny. "It's okay. She's just a kid."

Ben didn't budge, so Ash stepped forward.

"What's your name, sweetie," she asked, taking another step closer to the teen. A strong hand landed firmly on her shoulder, pulling her back within Ben's reach. She shrugged him off and approached the girl.

"My name's Ash," she said softly. "That's Ben, Hannah and Jasmine."

The girl wrapped her arms around herself and shivered. "Please get me out of here," she whispered.

NINE

A SINGLE HOWL pierced through the hills, causing the girl to jump and frantically scan the darkness. "Please," she begged. "We have to leave." Tears flowed from her eyes; her entire body trembled.

Hannah reached out. "You're safe now," she said. "You're with us." She moved within a foot of the girl, who took a slight step back. Worried that if she moved any closer, the girl might run away, Hannah remained still.

"Where did you come from?" asked Ben. "Is someone following you?"

At the sound of his voice, the girl flinched, then turned to face him. Suddenly her face went pale, she lurched forward and threw up, causing Hannah to turn away, lest she end up doing the same. Mercifully, it didn't take long before it was over. A little steadier, the teen wiped her mouth with the back of her hand and swept her hair away from her face.

Hannah pulled a clean bandana from her pocket and handed it over. "Here," she said.

Jasmine spoke up, "What's your name, sweetie?"

The girl stopped messing with her sweaty hair and glanced around the group. "Jewel," she responded, hesitantly.

"Well, hello Jewel," said Hannah. "That's a pretty name." She leaned forward. "You're safe with us."

Fidgeting with the bandana, Jewel kept a watchful eye on the area surrounding the camp. She didn't appear to be afraid of the group, but something in the shadows scared the living hell out of her. Her eyes settled once more on Hannah; a fresh cascade of tears streamed down her cheeks. "Can you please get me out of here?"

"Sure, sure, we can do that," replied Ben. He pivoted to face Jasmine and said, "Let's get everything packed up."

As the others hastily cleaned up the campsite, Hannah stood near Jewel, doing her best to calm the teen. The poor thing was a wreck. Her long blonde hair was a rat's nest of sweaty tangles and debris as though she had run through every bit of wild brush. Tiny scratches littered her arms, hands, and face, even her t-shirt was torn. Clearly something had scared her so much that she ran blindly through the desert, alone—in the dark, to get away. But from where? Hannah searched the area, there were no lights as far as they eye could see. She reflected on the drive out to this isolated spot and how all signs of civilization vanished a few miles back.

"Jewel," said Hannah. "Where did you come from?"

A coyote howled. The girl shrieked and sprinted for the van. "We have to go now!" she shouted.

Right before she could leap inside the van, Ben caught her around the waist, pulling her away from the vehicle. A shrill scream erupted from the teen, echoing off the surrounding hills as she struggled against him, trying desperately to get free.

"Ben!" shouted Ash.

Jasmine stood there in shock, with her hands over her mouth.

Hannah approached. "It's okay," she said. "Ben, let her go!"

Before he could release her, Jewel reared up and slammed the back of her head into his face. Blood exploded from his nose as he shoved her away. "Son of a—," he hissed through clenched teeth.

"Let me see," said Jasmine.

The girl took full advantage of the moment of confusion and jumped into the van, burrowing beneath the sleeping bags.

"Get out of there!" shouted Jasmine.

"It's okay," said Hannah.

"No, it's not!" hollered Jasmine. She pointed at the pile of trembling sleeping bags. "That crazy bitch just hurt Ben. She is not getting in our van."

"She's scared—"

"I don't fucking care! I'm scared too!" Jasmine placed her hands on her hips. "She gets the fuck out of the van, or it doesn't move."

"It's okay," said Ben, attempting to calm his girlfriend. "I'm okay." He blotted blood from his nose. "I was the stupid one for grabbing her. She's obviously been traumatized by something."

The pile of sleeping bags stopped trembling and was now swaying rhythmically back and forth. Hidden beneath, Jewel muttered incoherent words under her breath.

"Do you not see what I see?" asked Hannah. "She's messed up." She turned to Ben and Jasmine. "We can't leave her."

"We're not," replied Ben.

Jasmine reeled around on him. "What the hell do you mean?"

"Hannah's right," he said. "We need to get her some help."

"I can't believe you." Jasmine folded her arms. "After what she did, you still want to help her?"

Ben shook his head. "We have to. It's the right thing to do. She's a kid." He pointed inside the van. "She can't be more than fifteen." He took Jasmine by the hand and pulled her closer. "Come on, this kid needs our help."

Jasmine sighed. "Okay. But if she flips out again, we're leaving her by the side of the road. We can go into town and tell them where we left her. Got it?"

Hannah shook her head and said, "That's cruel."

"It's okay," said Ben. "I think she'll be fine once we start driving."

"Do y'all hear that?" asked Ash, standing by the fire. She had already extinguished the flames with water and was busy kicking up sand to make sure the flames were out.

"Jesus, Ash," cursed Ben. "Not this again."

Ash pressed a finger to her lips. "Shh, shh. Listen."

"I don't hear anything," said Ben. He stalked over to stand beside her.

"What are you listening for?" asked Jasmine, her voice growing more panicked."

A profound sense of discomfort took hold of Hannah. Every instinct she had told her they needed to leave right away. "Come on guys," she said aloud. "Let's just get out of here."

Ash held up her hand.

"Okay, I heard that," said Ben.

"I told you!" shouted Ash.

"What?" asked Jasmine, inching nearer to the van. "What do you hear?"

Every hair on Hannah's body stood on end. Inside the van, Jewel pleaded to leave, tunneling deeper into the sleeping bags until only a sprig of her hair was visible.

"Y'all, let's get out of here," said Hannah.

Ben stepped closer to a cluster of shrubs.

"Get back!" hissed Jasmine.

Ash made a motion toward him with her hand.

The brush trembled. A dark shadow reached out and took hold of Ben's arm. He cried out in pain and shock, then vanished among the wild desert scrub.

Ash turned and ran for the van.

"Ben!" screamed Jasmine as she lurched forward.

Hannah seized her arm, hoping to prevent her from running straight into the brush after him. A coyote howled, followed by another and then another. They were surrounded.

Inside the van, Jewel screamed.

"We need to go now!" shouted Ash.

"We're not leaving him!" cried Jasmine.

Hannah was torn. She wanted to go after Ben. To see if they could save him, but she knew there was little they could do. They had no weapons.

Once more, the shrubs rustled, sending a shiver down her spine. Whatever had taken Ben was coming for them. Ash was already in the van, struggling with the keys. Hannah shoved and prodded Jasmine, trying to coax her into the vehicle.

"Ben!" screamed Jasmine. "Oh my god!"

Hannah swiveled just in time to see Ben stumble from the brush, his legs giving way as he fell to the ground. Covered in blood, his shirt was torn to shreds. His right hand clutching firmly to his left arm—a bloody stump where the hand used to be. The crimson liquid gushed out, pooling into the sand.

In the shadows, just beyond view, coyotes cackled. It was almost as though they were laughing—as though this was all just a sick, twisted game. Impossible. Hannah shook her head. They're just animals. Animals don't hunt for fun. She shifted her attention back to Ben, who was growing increasingly pale by the second. Shoving herself under one of his arms, while Jasmine took the other, the two of them were able to carry him to the van. Quickly and as softly as possible, they placed him inside. As soon as Jasmine joined him, Hannah slammed the side door closed and hastily jumped into the passenger seat. They were already peeling down the gravel driveway before she could even close her door.

TEN

IN THE RED glow of her taillights, Ash caught a quick glimpse of a large coyote through the rear-view mirror. It was massive, making her question if it was a coyote at all. She had never heard of one being so big. As she sped down the winding driveway, she watched in awe as the giant beast kept pace with the van. How was this possible? No animal could keep up with a fast-moving vehicle. She floored the gas pedal, trying to put more distance between the van and the beast. As the monster receded into a cloud of gravel dust, she breathed a sigh of relief. The gate came into view.

"Ash, slow down!" shouted Hannah.

There was no way Ash was going to climb out of the safety of the van to open the gate. She pressed the gas pedal to the floor and hoped for the best. The van crashed through the gate as though it were made of toothpicks. With a sharp twist of the steering wheel, they were back out onto the gravel road.

"What the hell was that?" cried Jasmine from the back seat. Beside her, Ben sat sprawled out, blood gushing from his hand.

"Somebody help me!" screamed Jasmine. "He's gonna bleed out!"

"I got it," said Hannah. She turned to Ash. "Please slow down."

Ash lifted her foot from the pedal, watching through the mirror for any sign of the giant beast. Unable to see anything back there, she finally accepted that they had left the creature behind.

Ben moaned in agony.

Ash tried to crane her head around to see what was going on back there but was unable to see beyond Hannah. "How is he?" she asked.

"He's fucking bleeding out!" shouted Jasmine. "He's gonna die!"

The smack of Hannah's hand on Jasmine's face reverberated around the van's cabin.

A hush set in, giving Ash the opportunity to hear Jewel muttering somewhere in the back. She had completely forgotten about the girl.

"Hannah," said Ash, doing her best to keep one eye on the road and the other on the group behind her. "Is he gonna be okay?"

"I don't know," replied Hannah. "I put a tourniquet around his arm and wrapped what's left of his hand in clean gauze. It's already soaked through. I can't stop the bleeding." She leaned closer to Ash and whispered, "That thing bit his hand clean off. I've never heard of a coyote doing something like that to a grown man. Have you?"

Ash shook her head in response. "Did you see how big it was? I've never seen one so big before."

"Tricksters. Tricksters. Tricksters," cried Jewel, huddled deep under the sleeping bags, her voice raising with each word.

"Shut the hell up!" shouted Jasmine.

An eerie chuckle erupted from Jewel. She pulled back the sleeping bags and stared at Jasmine with hysterical eyes. "They got your scent. They're not gonna stop." More ominous laughter.

The girl's behavior, at that moment, gave Ash the creeps. This was all too confusing. Where did Jewel come from? What are the chances she would accidentally stumble into their campsite? What the hell was that beast? Was it a coyote? What the hell did Jewel mean when she called them tricksters? Was that thing chasing her? Did she lead it directly to them?

"Look out!" screamed Hannah.

55

Ash glanced out the windshield just in time to see the giant beast standing in the middle of the road. Its face was a horrifying mask of snarling fury with a mouth full of long, sharp teeth. It reared up on its hind legs, standing well over six feet tall. The beast locked its glowing eyes on Ash, sending an icy shiver down her spine. This was no ordinary animal. It appeared to possess human intelligence.

She kept her foot heavy on the gas pedal, refusing to slow down. The van was heading straight for the animal. She didn't think she could run it over; its size alone would surely destroy the vehicle. As she sped up and drove forward, she hoped the beast would move.

"What are you doing?" asked Hannah.

"It's gotta jump out of the way!"

Hannah clutched the handle above her window and pushed herself against the seat, bracing for impact.

The beast's massive head rose toward the sky, unleashing a deafening howl as the van approached with reckless speed.

"It's not moving!" shouted Hannah.

Less than seven yards from the monster, Ash twisted the steering wheel, sending the van, with all its occupants, careening into a dried-out riverbed. Jasmine and Hannah's screams filled her ears as the vehicle bumped and jostled over rocks, kicking up plumes of dirt before crashing to a stop.

Headlights buried in the embankment; the red light of the taillights cast an eerie glow behind them.

"What the hell was that?" demanded Jasmine, lifting herself from the floor.

"Shh," ordered Ash. She strained to listen for any sign of the beast.

"We've got to get out of here," whispered Hannah.

"And go where?" demanded Ash. "I don't even know where we are anymore." She shook her head. "And that thing is still out there."

Outside the van, a band of coyotes yipped. They were surrounded.

"What are those things?" asked Hannah.

"They look like coyotes." Ash shook her head. "But they're way too big and smart."

"Coyotes don't stand on their hind legs like a man," said Hannah.

"That's because they're not coyotes," whispered Jewel, somehow still hidden among the sleeping bags.

"Then what are they?" asked Jasmine, clearly at her wit's end with the girl.

Jewel sat upright. "They're tricksters." She gnawed at her dirty nails.

"You're gonna have to be more specific than that," said Ash, her patience also wearing thin for the strange young girl.

Jewel's eyes glistened with fresh tears. Her lips trembled as she remained silent.

"Whatever they are, they don't want us. They want her," said Jasmine, her tone resolute. "They were chasing her." She stared at Jewel. "I say we let them have her."

"No, no, no!" wailed Jewel, shaking her head wildly.

"Everybody be quiet!" shouted Ash. "Arguing isn't helping us." She stared at Hannah, hoping she had something to add. After a period of uncomfortable silence, she turned back to the girl. "Jewel," she said, doing her best to mask her own fear. "How do you know about these tricksters?"

"Everyone in these parts know what they are," whispered Jewel. Tears streamed down her cheeks and snot flowed from her nose. "They're monsters." She reached out a bony hand and grabbed hold of Ash's arm. "You can't let them catch us."

Ash struggled to control the urge to snatch her arm away. She didn't know if she believed Jewel or not. At this point, she was unsure about everything. The only thing she knew for sure was that she didn't want to stick around and find out if the girl was telling the truth.

Something massive slammed against the side of the van, causing it to sway. Jasmine and Jewel screamed. Another huge object collided with the opposite side of the van, followed by a deep, throaty growl.

Jasmine sobbed, tears streaming down her face. "What are we gonna do?"

Ben lifted his good hand and gently stroked her long hair. He whispered, "It's gonna be okay, Babe."

Ash studied him long and hard. His clothes were soaked in his own blood, his face had a ghostly hue.

"You have to run," he said weakly.

"Run?" asked Jasmine. "Where? They're out there."

Ben struggled to sit up. He locked eyes with Ash. "I'll distract them. When I do, you'll all run."

Jasmine shook her head. "No, no, no," she said. "I'm not leaving you."

His lips curled into a passive smile. He leaned forward and placed a gentle kiss on Jasmine's forehead. "I need you to get to safety. If I don't do this, you'll never get away."

Ash didn't want to accept what she was hearing, but deep down inside, she knew Ben was right, they needed a distraction. Her heart mirrored Jasmine's pleas, but her head told her it was the only way.

One of the creatures slammed into the side of the van. The sound of digging and scratching filled her ears. They needed to do something fast.

Ash turned to Hannah. "What's your opinion?"

Eyes filled with tears, Hannah sighed, the expression on her face told Ash that she too agreed there was no other way. She opened her mouth to speak.

"No!" shouted Jasmine hysterically. "We are not leaving him!" She wiped her face with her sleeve. "If you want to leave, then go. I'm staying right here."

Jasmine's resolve was a major issue. As much as Ash hated the idea of leaving Ben behind, she hated the idea of leaving Jasmine with him even more. Outside the van, howls erupted, followed by loud scratching sounds on metal. Something big sniffed loudly through the crack of the door, followed by another round of joyful yips.

"It's okay, Jaz," said Ben, as he held her close. "I'll be fine. You go with the others. I'll catch up."

The crimson pool had grown so large, Ash wondered how Ben was still conscious. His breathing was labored, and his color was bad. The phrase, dead man walking, came to her mind. "How are we going to do that?" she asked.

"I'll crack the door," said Ben. "Not a lot, just enough for them to get a whiff, and think they can get in that way." He nodded toward the driver's side door. "When they're distracted, y'all will sneak out through that window and head for help."

"What if they follow?" asked Hannah. "What if they figure it out and they follow?"

"They're animals," replied Ben. "There's no figuring it out. At least not right away." He paused long enough to take several deep breaths. "Besides, I'll still be in here, so they'll think they have all of us trapped."

Jewel burst into a fit of terrified laughter, startling everyone. "They'll know," she said.

"Someone shut her up!" shouted Jasmine.

Ash had to agree, now was not the time for anymore of Jewel's insanity. She had no intention of dying in the middle of nowhere at the hands of a bunch of supposed tricksters—whatever that was. She fixed her eyes on Ben. Something in his expression told her he wasn't planning on joining them. She inhaled, struggling to contain her emotions, then said, "Okay, Ben. I'm ready when you are."

He shifted his body. "When I crack the door open, you're gonna open your window. It's gotta happen at the same time."

Ash nodded.

"Let's hope that they'll be so preoccupied," said Ben, "they won't hear the window open." He took several labored breaths. "Ash, you and Jewel are gonna be the first out." He turned to Jasmine. "You and Hannah are gonna be next."

Jasmine opened her mouth to speak, but Ben quickly placed a

finger on her lips. "Shh," he said. "Just do what I say. I'll bring up the rear right behind you."

Tears flowing down her cheeks, she nodded.

"When you get outside," he said. "You run and keep on running. Don't stop until you make it to safety."

Silence.

"Jaz," said Ben. "Get up there with Hannah." He turned to Jewel. "You get up there with Ash."

Without protest, both Jewel and Jasmine did as they were told.

Ash waited nervously for his signal with her finger on the window control. Tension hung heavy in the air. She had doubts that this plan would work, but, lacking any alternatives, she had no other choice than to hope for the best.

While everyone got into position, Ben counted down quietly. He got to one, inhaled, and gently undid the latch on the door. Almost immediately, maniacal scratching and sniffing erupted. The door moaned on its hinges as the van wobbled back and forth.

Ash pressed the button, and the window slid open.

"Go!" mouthed Ben.

The scratching outside the door grew louder, accompanied by a deep, low growl.

Ash quietly slipped through the window, then reached her hand out for Jewel. As soon as the girl hit the ground, they took off through the brush, running as hard and as fast as their legs could carry them.

Thorny desert flora lashed out at her ankles, tearing her clothes, and slicing her skin. With Jewel's hand firmly in hers, Ash rushed through the darkness. She strained to listen, fearful that, any moment she would hear the telltale sign of one of those monsters crashing behind them.

Her thoughts and fears were disrupted by the sound of a blood-curdling scream. A man's scream—Ben.

Ash froze; her heart skipped a beat. The screams continued. She didn't have to see what was happening, to know that the pack was tearing her friend apart. Terror threatened to overwhelm her. She pulled out her phone, her fingers instinctively hitting the emergency contact, to call Matt. If she could only hear his voice, everything would be okay.

No signal.

A tidal wave of despair washed over her. She was alone. There would be no help from big brother this time. Cut off from the outside world, Ash and her friends were completely on their own.

She searched the darkness, realizing, for the first time, that Hannah and Jasmine were nowhere to be found. No, no, no, no, this can't be happening. Where the hell were they? She strained to listen for the slightest whimper from either Hannah or Jasmine, but aside from Ben's screams, there were no sounds.

Suddenly, the screams stopped, replaced by the joyous sounds of the pack celebrating their kill. Silence descended, shaking Ash from her thoughts. If they didn't continue to run, they would be next. She told herself that her best course of action was to get to safety and bring help to find Hannah and Jasmine. She uttered a quiet prayer for her friends, then held Jewel's hand and led her through the desert.

ELEVEN

BEN FOUND it difficult to sit upright. Each beat of his heart served as a reminder of the precious time slipping away from him. His eyelids were heavy; maintaining consciousness was a struggle. The agonizing truth settled in his soul—there was no way he was getting out of this alive. He gazed at Jasmine as she struggled to wrap his wrist, doing her best to appear strong, but he knew better. Her face was an open book.

Beautiful Jasmine. It pained him to see her this way. His heart ached at the thought of her being alone.

Outside, the pack crept closer. He could hear them sniffing through the door. It won't be long before they figure out how to get inside. He had to devise a plan—a means to ensure the safety of the others—of Jasmine. Of course, he knew there was only one way to do this. The hard part was to get the others on board.

Ben breathed in deeply, feeling the feebleness in his bones. He made eye contact with Ash, silently begging her to play along with his plan.

Jasmine was near hysterical, crying uncontrollably while screaming she would not leave him.

He kissed her forehead, pausing for a moment to breathe in the subtle scent of her floral shampoo. Was there an afterlife? He wondered. And if so, would he miss the feeling of her soft skin against his? Would his heart ache for her? He pulled away and gazed into her eyes, doing his best to maintain a casual smile. Oh, how he loved those big, brown eyes. His heart grieved for the future they would no longer share.

A cloak of silence hung heavy inside the van; each person deep in their own thoughts. Ben waited with patience for them to process exactly what he was offering to do.

Outside the van, the digging and scratching grew more frenzied. The time was up. If there was any chance of Jaz and the others getting out of this alive, they needed to move now.

He watched as Ash turned to Hannah. "What's your opinion?" she asked, seeking confirmation. It was apparent, she had already made up her mind.

Good old Ash, always pragmatic. For once, he was thankful for the one-character flaw that would drive him crazy any other time. There were no other options.

Hannah sighed, she didn't have to say it, Ben already knew she agreed.

"No!" shouted Jasmine hysterically. "We are not leaving him!" She wiped her face. "If you want to leave, then go. I'm staying." She grabbed hold of his arm, causing Ben to cry out in pain.

Howls pierced the night, the eerie sound of claws on the side door filled the van, followed by sniffing and another round of yips. Those beasts were enjoying every minute of this.

"It's okay, Babe," said Ben. With his remaining hand, he held her close. He turned to Ash and Hannah and laid out his plan for escape. There were no guarantees that it would work, but they had to try something.

Jewel erupted into a fit of terrified laughter. "They'll know."

"Someone shut her up!" shouted Jasmine, clearly at her wits end.

Ben's patience was wearing thin, say nothing for his lifeline. The world around him was growing dimmer by the second. They didn't have time for any of this. Those things were going to get inside. If he didn't get these girls out of the van, they didn't have a fighting chance of survival. So, he did what he had to do—the one thing he vowed he would never do. He lied to Jasmine. He told her he would be right behind her.

He put on his best face and was able to convince Jaz to go along with his plan.

Once everyone was positioned, Ben took a deep breath, and said a silent prayer for the strength to handle what was to come. He cracked the door open. Right away, the creatures scratched and clawed. He could smell the blood on their breath—his blood. The door moaned on its hinges. It wouldn't hold much longer. To buy as much time as possible for the girls, he tried to keep the door steady by using his legs as a wedge. The frenzied beasts outside were strong. As he watched the girls slip through the window, he could feel his strength waning. He closed his eyes and willed himself to hang on— he needed to buy as much time as possible.

The door slid, and the van rocked. Ben's leg muscles weakened, he fished his pocketknife from his blood-soaked pants, chuckling to himself at how pitifully small it was. This was it, he was about to go down, fighting some weird mythical beasts called tricksters, with a stupid little pocketknife. Ten-year-old him would be proud.

He held the small weapon aloft, fully aware that it would do little harm against his opponents. If this was the end, he would cause at least one beast injury before he breathed his last breath. He couldn't help but wonder if this is what warriors of old felt when their time came upon them. He pulled his legs away from the door and leaned back, waiting.

Heart pounding against his rib cage, time stood still. There was a moment of absolute silence, then the door was completely torn off the side of the van. It hurled into the air as though it were nothing more than a piece of cardboard. The beast that stood before him was terrifying to behold.

The head of a coyote, its enormous body larger than any man he had ever seen. It leered at him and leaned into the cabin. Saliva dripping from its mouthful of razor-sharp, white teeth. Two more creatures were present behind it, all equally terrifying, though varying in size. The monster snarled and moved so close to Ben; its nose brushed against his cheek. He closed his eyes and prayed for strength. With all his remaining energy, he thrust the tiny pocketknife directly into the glowing eye of the creature.

The beast shrieked in pain and retreated, struggling to dislodge the object from his face.

Proud of his last act of resistance, Ben smiled.

One of the slighter ones leaned into the van, licking his face with its long tongue.

He recoiled in disgust and averted his gaze.

With a throaty growl the creature lunged forward and snatched Ben's leg, forcefully pulling him onto the rough, rocky terrain. With a painful thud, his head collided with the rocky ground, feeling the impact reverberate throughout his body.

The pack fell upon him. Sharp claws and long, white teeth slashed and tore away at his flesh. A man cried out in agony; he thought the voice sounded familiar but couldn't place it. It took him a moment to realize the screams were his own. As he slipped into unconsciousness, Ben clung to the belief that Jaz and the others were a safe distance away.

TWELVE

HANNAH PUSHED Jasmine through the window first, fully aware of the fact that, given the slightest chance, Jasmine would try to wait for Ben. Who could blame her? After all, this was the man she loved, it only made sense she would want to be certain he too was safe.

When Ben came up with his plan, Hannah knew right away, that he had no intention of following. The chances of him being able to, even if he wanted to, were slim. A shared glance between the two confirmed her thoughts. He was doing what was necessary for the benefit of everyone and required Hannah's help to ensure Jasmine's safety. It was her duty to see that his sacrifice wasn't in vain.

As she crept through the window, she glanced over her shoulder and nodded a farewell to him. He nodded his head in encouragement and remained steadfast in place, straining to hold the door, as a sharp, lethal claw poked through the gap.

Hannah hit the ground and seized Jasmine's hand.

"Wait," Jasmine said in a low voice, pulling her hand back. "Ben."

Each second wasted was the difference between life and death. Ben wasn't coming. Hannah knew if she said those words aloud,

Jasmine would probably jump right back into the van. That wasn't what Ben would want. No matter what happened, she owed it to him to honor his wish.

"He'll be right behind us," said Hannah. "He has to hold the door a little longer before letting it go." Once again, she grabbed hold of Jasmine's hand. "Now come on."

At first, Jasmine fought against her, but the sound of scraping metal interrupted their stalemate.

Hannah seized the opportunity and forcefully led Jasmine through the brush, hoping they were headed in the same direction Ash and Jewel had gone. Since she was the last person out, she didn't have the benefit of seeing which way they ran, and Jasmine was too busy worrying about Ben to have paid attention. With no path to pursue, Hannah had to rely on her intuition, so with Jasmine in tow, she sprinted into the wilderness.

They got quite a distance away when the most gut-wrenching scream she had ever heard erupted into the night. It was Ben. The pack had gotten to him. His screams echoed for what seemed to be forever, sadly drowning out the sounds of Jasmine's own screams, followed by her cries of anguish.

At first, Jasmine tried to turn around and run back, only to be tackled by Hannah. "Ben!" she screamed.

Covering Jasmine's mouth with her hand, Hannah was terrified that the screams would alert the pack. "Stop it, stop it. They'll know where we are."

Jasmine writhed against her.

"Do you want Ben's sacrifice to be in vain?" she hissed through clenched teeth.

Those words appeared to be enough to calm Jasmine. She gave up struggling and remained still. Confident that she wouldn't try to run off, Hannah climbed to her feet and held out her hand for her friend.

"Ben," cried Jasmine. Tears poured down her cheeks, mixing with the dirt from the desert floor.

Hannah hugged her friend tightly, unable to comprehend the heartache she must be feeling. "I know," she said softly.

The pack broke out into a round of celebration. It was over. Ben was dead.

With a strong resolve, Hannah lifted Jasmine's chin to stare her in the eyes. "We have to go."

Jasmine swallowed and, after a quick, mournful glance back toward the van, she wiped her face, and nodded.

That was all the encouragement Hannah needed. She gripped Jasmine's hand tightly and darted into the darkness with only one aim in mind—get as far away from the pack as possible. She prayed wherever Ash and Jewel were; they were doing the same.

They ran blindly through the desert. Hannah had no idea where they were. For all she knew, they could be heading in the wrong direction. She came to a halt and looked around. They needed to get their bearings before going any farther, so she took out her phone, only to find that there was no signal. Of course, that would be the case. After all, they were in the middle of nowhere. She remembered the map feature worked regardless of signal strength. With a sigh of relief, she opened the app.

At first, nothing appeared on her screen except a grid. "Come on, please, please, please," she whispered.

A few feet away, Jasmine paced back and forth with her hands atop her head.

Hannah stared down at the tiny screen, willing it to show something she could use. A square filled in, followed by the rest. At the center of everything, a small blue dot marked the spot where they stood. She pinched the screen to see what was around. Not much. She slid left, nothing but a whole bunch of nothing. She slid right, scrolling slowly, hoping that she would come across something. Anything.

A road appeared on the screen. Finally, something that gave her hope. She continued in that direction and came across the highway; the town was just beyond that.

Her heart raced as hope buzzed throughout her body. "Jaz," she said excitedly. "Come here."

"Anything?" asked Jasmine, peering down at the phone.

Hannah pointed. "If we head that way, we'll come to a road. After that's the town, and help."

Jasmine scanned the darkness. "I don't see any lights." She turned to Hannah. "Shouldn't we see them if a town is that way?"

"It's probably too far away," responded Hannah, hoping that was it.

"So, what?" asked Jasmine. "We head toward the highway and get help in the town?"

Hannah nodded. "It's our best bet."

A sorrowful expression washed over Jasmine's face. She stared back in the direction they just came. "His scream," she choked. Tears streamed down her cheeks.

Unable to think of anything to say, Hannah wrapped her arms around Jasmine and, once again, comforted her. There was no doubt Ben was dead. He gave his life so they could live.

When Jasmine's sobs subsided, Hannah pulled away and said, "It's time to go."

Jasmine wiped her face, leaving grubby streaks of mud on her cheeks. She sniffled and rubbed her hands on her thighs.

Hand in hand and determined to find help, they made their way through the dark.

THIRTEEN

A HEAVINESS SETTLED in Jasmine's chest, a deep ache within. She couldn't determine whether it was due to all the running or losing Ben. Her lungs were on fire. In an effort to calm her racing pulse, she rested her hands atop her head and paced in circles. Whenever she paused her steps, she would lean on her knees, fighting to stay upright. She was unsure whether she was exhausted or having a panic attack.

A few feet away, Hannah was busy pulling up the map on her phone.

Jasmine hadn't given one thought of their phones since the entire ordeal began. She pulled hers from her pocket, quickly swiping away the wallpaper photo of her and Ben, feeling a piercing pain in her heart. Her eyes stung with hot tears. There was no signal. She muttered a curse under her breath and tucked the gadget away.

"Anything?" she asked.

Hannah pointed. "There's a road that way. After that's the town and help."

Jasmine wanted to argue—to question Hannah's decisions, but she knew her friend was right. There weren't many options available to them. And Ben would want her to get to safety—to survive this nightmare.

Ben.

A torrent of happy memories flooded her mind. Fresh tears sprung forth, cascading down her cheeks. A deep sense of loss and despair threatened to overwhelm her. She struggled to breathe. He was gone. How was she going to move on without him? It had only been a few minutes, and she already could hardly function because of the void she felt growing inside. Was life even worth living without him?

She longed to go back the way they came and let the beasts take her, at least that way she would be with him again. Even if there was no afterlife, she wouldn't feel the heartache of loss anymore. That alone made it more tempting.

Jasmine shook her head. That's not what Ben would want. He didn't sacrifice his life, so she could turn around and end hers. After taking a deep breath, she calmed her nerves and resolved that she would not let him down. She was determined not to squander his sacrifice. They were going to find that town and get the authorities. The men with guns and badges would come and hunt the tricksters down, killing them all like the wild animals they were. Yes, that was the only way to honor Ben's sacrifice.

"It's time to go," said Hannah, softly.

Jasmine nodded. She was ready.

"This way," said Hannah.

Trekking along the uneven terrain was far more complicated in the dark. They couldn't take more than a few steps without encountering another rock or shrub, causing them to stumble or feel the pain of scraped skin. The desert plants seemed to be solely focused on causing harm with their sharp needles and thorny branches. Come to think of it, that seemed to be the purpose of everything in this hellscape. She never liked the desert—until an hour ago, she never had a good reason.

Somewhere far away, a coyote howled. The pack of demons were back on the trail. An icy chill ran down her spine. A shock of pure adrenaline coursed throughout her body.

Hannah halted and placed a finger to her lips. From this point on, they needed to be quiet and swift.

They made their way across a dried riverbed, navigating over loose rocks and through a small cluster of trees. Somewhere along the way, Jasmine got a pebble in her shoe. Initially, she tried to resist acknowledging its existence, but eventually, it came to feel as though she was running on broken glass. She had to stop and remove it before it made it impossible to walk.

She placed her hand against the trunk of a tree for support, only to feel a sharp pinch.

"Shit!" She yanked her hand back, cursing. A tiny bead of blood formed in her palm. "Dammit! Is there anything in this place that doesn't want to kill us?" A brand-new wave of despair crashed over her, threatening to erase every ounce of courage and resolve she had.

"Let me see," said Hannah. She pulled her phone out and used the flashlight to inspect the wound. "You'll live," she said.

"Not if this place has anything to say about it," quipped Jasmine, not really intending to be humorous.

"Do you need something to wrap it?"

Jasmine shook her head.

"Good," replied Hannah. "Because I don't have anything but what I'm wearing." She looked down at herself. "And that isn't very clean at the moment." She scrunched her face in thought. "I could really go for a shot of whiskey right now," she said wistfully.

"If Ben were here, he'd already have a joint lit up," replied Jasmine.

A mournful expression spread across Hannah's face, echoing Jasmine's emotions.

Despair once again settled heavily in her heart. Jasmine shoved it away. She redirected her attention to Hannah. "You ready?"

Hannah opened the map on her phone. After a few pinches and

pulls, she peered up at Jasmine. "It looks like the road is just a couple miles away. We're almost there."

Finally, a bit of good news. Just a couple of miles to cover and they would be safe. All she had to do was keep it together for a little while longer.

A round of howls echoed in the darkness. The pack was much closer now, yet still far enough away to ensure the girls' safety as long as they continued to move.

With more determination, the duo pushed through the gnarly trees and emerged into the open desert. Jasmine felt vulnerable because of the lack of cover, but at least she didn't have to worry about any thorny trees. They ran, as fast as their exhausted legs could carry them, tripping and stumbling on loose rocks and the occasional prickly pear.

The coyotes called out again; it sounded as though they were right behind them.

The iron grip of terror tightened around Jasmine's heart like a vise. She pushed herself to run faster. Her leg muscles screamed in pain; every breath was a hot fire in her lungs. Her heart threatened to pound its way right out of her rib cage. She had to stop.

They stumbled upon a ravine, another dry riverbed. How did the animals and plants survive out here with no water?

A round of yips and yaps broke out from behind. The pack was closing in on them.

Jasmine took a momentary break to scan the area. She could see nothing.

"Come on!" shouted Hannah, stretching her hand along the ravine wall, searching for something to hold on to. "Climb!"

Jasmine snapped out of it and set her focus on the wall before her. It was about fourteen feet tall. As an avid climber, she had scaled much taller obstacles than this. This shouldn't be too difficult.

A deep, low growl came from behind her, sending a shiver down her spine. When she glanced back, she was met with the menacing gaze of a large coyote, inching its way toward her. As she stared on in horror, another beast emerged, followed by yet another. Its head stained red from blood.

"Jasmine!" yelled Hannah. She had already made it to the top and was reaching down to help.

In the ravine, the tricksters closed in around her.

As she looked into their demonic eyes, she detected a glimmer of wicked delight. Panic exploded in her chest. She made a frantic effort to climb up the wall, her palms scraping against the rough surface. Behind her, a chorus of cackles erupted.

The pack was already celebrating.

"Fuck you!" she shouted over her shoulder.

"Climb!" screamed Hannah, stretching herself as far as she could without falling. "Please Jaz. Climb!"

Jasmine's heart pounded in her chest as she inched closer to her goal, climbing another foot. Adrenaline surged throughout her body. She reached out for Hannah, feeling the gentle brush of her fingertips.

The tricksters stood directly below her, waiting.

She stretched. A glimmer of hope sparked in her chest as Hannah's hand clasped around her wrist. She was gonna make it. Jasmine thrashed and scrambled her way toward the top. Just a little more to go. A burst of euphoric power flowed through her body, rejuvenating every muscle; she was almost there.

An intense pain erupted on her left leg, followed by a flush of warmth. Hannah shouted something, but Jasmine couldn't make out exactly what she said. Her heartbeat slowed. Another piercing pain, only this one was on her right. She realized she could no longer feel her legs. She shivered. A sudden urge to sleep threatened to overwhelm her.

"Don't look down!" shouted Hannah, her face red and covered in tears.

But Jasmine looked down, just in time to see the large trickster swallow a bloody piece of flesh.

The beast licked its jaws and peered up at her, hungrily.

Jasmine glanced down at her legs, but they weren't there. Both were missing from the knee down. She let out a piercing scream.

Hannah pulled. "Jaz, please!" she begged.

Below her, the giant trickster with the bloody face crouched, preparing to leap. Its muzzle was splattered with dark scarlet stains, as it bared a mouthful of razor-sharp, white teeth. It launched.

A quiet sense of resolve settled upon Jasmine as she realized she wouldn't make it after all. Despair and acceptance settled in; poor Ben, he sacrificed his life for nothing. She peered up at Hannah, who was sobbing uncontrollably.

"It's okay," she said, hoping her friend would have the strength to keep running.

The giant beast came into her view as he bit down on her arm, severing it from her body at the elbow.

Jasmine fell to the ground in a daze, barely able to hear Hannah's screams from above.

The pack hovered over her, taking their time. Another round of celebratory yips filled the air. They moved closer, sniffing and lapping at her blood. Jasmine closed her eyes, willing herself to drift off into slumber. She could feel her body being pulled left and right—felt the sensation of strong jaws gripping her flesh, but there was no pain. She smiled at the prospect of seeing Ben again, then darkness settled in.

FOURTEEN

"JAZ!" screamed Hannah. She scurried back from the ledge, unable to comprehend what just happened. They killed her! They killed Jasmine! That massive creature leaped higher than Hannah thought possible. All she could do was stare in horror as the monster's massive teeth bit down on Jasmine's arm, severing it from her body. It happened so quickly—there was no time to react. The sensation of her friend's hand in hers, still lingered in her muscle memory, she looked down. Her scream echoed through the darkness upon the horrifying discovery that she was still clutching the severed arm. She flung the bloody limb as far away as possible, then vomited the entire contents of her stomach.

In the gorge below, Jasmine's screams turned into a volley of celebratory yips and howls from the pack.

Frozen by fear, Hannah struggled to pull her mind together. She had to run. The pack was busy, she could hear their noisy eating below. Once again, her stomach flipped; she leaned over and spilled out whatever remained in her belly, onto the rocky ground. She searched the area, unable to decide which direction to take, fighting against the urge to sit right there and wallow in her fear and misery.

What was the point in running? It was only a matter of time before the beasts hunted her down and ate her, too.

She crawled to the ledge and peered down into the ravine. The scene below was worse than any nightmare she could ever envision. Three giant, blood covered monsters hovered over what remained of one of her best friends. A crimson river flowed out beneath their feet as they feasted on Jasmine, one bite at a time. One of the beasts turned its massive head upward and gazed into Hannah's eyes. A shiver ran down her spine as she stared into the gold, glowing eyes of the animal. It was grinning, she was sure of that. Her mind told her that was impossible, but deep in her soul, she knew the creature was completely wicked.

If she was planning to run, now was the time to do it. Every muscle in her body trembled uncontrollably as she climbed to her feet. After taking a moment to orient herself, Hannah took off running. The road couldn't be much farther ahead, she was sure of it.

Howls erupted behind her, the pack was finished with Jasmine and had reset their focus on her. She quickened her pace. Her legs trembled, threatening to give way beneath her. She tumbled over a fallen tree limb and crashed to the rocky ground. Gravel lacerated the soft flesh of her palms and cheek. A sudden, searing pain in her ankle, prompted her to check for any visible damage. Already swollen, a purple hue settled in and grew progressively darker with each passing second. Her heart filled with despair. How was she going to run with a sprained ankle?

Behind her, the pack howled. They were drawing nearer. A steely resolve settled upon her. If they wanted her, they were gonna have to work for it. She rose to her feet, sending a wave of searing pain up her leg from her ankle, causing her to stumble.

Move, move, move, she willed herself. Each step was excruciating as she hobbled along in the dark, at first slowly, but gradually, picking up her pace.

Up ahead, what appeared to be headlights crawled along in a straight line. The road! She made it to the road! At first, Hannah was convinced it was a fabrication of her imagination. Something she manifested with her agitated, pain-wracked mind. She blinked and shook her head, but the lights continued to move along slowly. Mustering all the strength that remained in her body, she stumbled toward the lights. Just a few more yards. Keep moving, keep moving, keep moving, she repeated over and over.

An ominous growl crept up behind her. Hannah could almost feel the creature's hot breath against her neck. Stifling a scream, she pushed forward. The road was right in front of her. Waving her hands frantically over her head, she hobbled out into the center of the blacktop.

"Stop! Please stop!" she cried.

The truck slowed down, its engine rumbling softly as it rolled closer.

Hannah stood firm in the headlights, nervously glancing around at the darkness. She was certain that the pack lurked just beyond the glow of the lights.

The truck came to a squeaky stop.

"Please help me," she cried, limping closer to the vehicle.

Both the passenger and driver side doors flung open, and two men climbed out. Hannah raised her hand above her eyes, squinting to see past the blinding glare of the headlights.

"Hannah?" said a familiar voice.

Relief swept over her. She knew that voice. "Oh my God! Caleb!" She staggered toward him, tumbling into his sturdy arms.

"What the hell are you—," he said.

"We have to go! We have to go now!"

She could hear the creatures sniffing the air all around them. They didn't have time for explanations; they needed to get out of there. She was sure the beasts were about to strike.

Caleb carried her to the passenger side of the truck and helped her inside. As soon as she was situated, Pax climbed in and closed the door.

From the safety of the truck's cab, she watched in anticipation as

Caleb strolled around the front of the truck. From the looks of it, he was taking his time. That had to be her imagination. At the door, he hesitated and stared out into the darkness. A strange expression on his face.

"Caleb, get inside!" she shouted, genuinely terrified for his safety. Now was not the time for him to show off. She didn't want the tricksters to get him, too.

He climbed inside the cab and slammed his door shut. "It's okay," he said. "We got you."

Hannah's heart pounded in her chest, her lungs could barely function. The pain in her ankle gave way to a wave of complete exhaustion as every muscle in her body surrendered at the same time. She rested her head against Caleb's shoulder and closed her eyes.

The truck rolled forward, then halted. She lifted her head and stared out through the windshield at the three beasts standing in the center of the road. The big one stood up on its haunches, howled, then dropped back down on all fours. Something about it changed. It tilted its head in what seemed to be a nod, then all three of the creatures ran off into the darkness.

Relief washed over Hannah. It was over. She survived. She was safe. Every ounce of energy in her body was spent. Unable to fight it any longer, she surrendered to slumber, knowing that she was safe in the care of Caleb.

FIFTEEN

"WHERE THE HELL DID SHE GO?" Caleb mumbled in a rage. Every minute squandered searching for Jewel added fuel to his anger. He spent his entire life priding himself on being an understanding older brother, but that girl pushed his patience to the limit. It was almost as though it was her private mission to drive him insane.

As he drove slowly on back country roads, his mind drifted to all the mischief she had caused over the past several months. Jewel certainly wasn't the brightest bulb in the shed. The girl was always wandering around in her own world, unconcerned with anyone else around her. She'd done some stupid things before, but this was on a whole new level. What was she thinking? Stupid child. When he found her, he was gonna teach her a lesson that she would never forget. This was the last time she pulled her shit.

"Any sign over there?" he asked.

"Nah," said Pax. "Why do you suppose she ran away? I mean, she's never done anything like this before."

Caleb shook his head. Pax was right, this stunt was more extreme than any of her previous stunts. Where the hell did she think she was gonna run away to? Did she really think the human world would welcome her with open arms? He let out a deep breath and rubbed the stubble on his chin. "Has she said anything to you lately?"

"Nothing out of the usual," replied Pax. He looked at Caleb. "Just her typical whiny stuff." He swallowed and stared out the window. "Think she's getting close to her time?"

The first turning! Caleb did some quick calculations in his head, acknowledging that all the pieces meshed. How could he be so blind? "I think you might have hit the nail on the head, little brother," he replied. "Apparently, girls mature faster than us." He shifted in his seat. "If it's true, and she's comin' into her first turning, we better find her quick. There's no telling what damage she could do when the frenzy hits."

A coyote called out from the hills. Caleb perked up his ears; he could recognize Izzy's call from anywhere. He listened as Ezra called back, followed by the deep bellow of Bass. At least someone was out here having fun. He envied his friends. They didn't have any family drama to deal with. No younger sisters doing stupid shit—disrupting their lives or getting in the way of their fun.

When he finally found Jewel, he was going to make damn sure she paid for this.

Caleb turned the truck down the old highway. Window down, he drew in a deep breath, letting the trickster inside analyze all the scents, hoping to pick up any sign of Jewel. Sage, dirt, mesquite, something dead. He sniffed the air; it was a small animal, and it had been dead for at least a week. A soft breeze brought a familiar scent. Caleb hit the brakes, bringing the truck to a complete stop. He stuck his head out of the window and inhaled. The scent was faint, but he was positive it belonged to his sister.

"You smell that?" he asked.

Pax sniffed the air and nodded. "She's been through here."

"That's what I thought," said Caleb. He glanced around in the darkness. "She ain't here anymore."

"She might be heading toward town," said Pax.

Caleb had already thought of that. "Nah," he replied. "She's not that dumb. She knows there ain't a single person in town who would help her." He scratched his chin. "But she would head for the interstate. A young girl would have no problem hitchin' a ride at this late hour."

He turned the truck around and was just about to hit the gas when another scent wafted into his nostrils. Blood—fresh blood, heavy with the enticing aroma of fear.

Pax smacked his arm to get his attention and gestured out the window. Caleb looked up, following his brother's gaze.

Hannah staggered out into the middle of the road. In the glare of the headlights, she stumbled toward them, her arms flailing over her head as she cried for help. Covered in blood, her eyes were wild with fear and panic.

Caleb laughed. "Well, damn. Looks like we might get to have some fun tonight after all."

"What about Jewel?" asked Pax. "We gotta get to her before she gets to the highway."

"Hang with me little brother. We can do both." Caleb rolled forward, bringing the truck to a full stop about six feet from the terrified woman. She raised a hand above her eyes.

From the cab, he watched the relief wash over her. The stupid girl thought she found help. He threw the truck into park and climbed out.

"Hannah?" he called out.

"Oh my God! Caleb!" She limped closer.

The trusting woman fell into his open arms.

"We have to go! We have to go now!" she sobbed into his chest.

He breathed in, taking in the irresistible aroma of her fear. There really was no better scent. His mouth watered. The urge to sink his teeth into her throat was strong. Ah, but where's the fun in that? It's far better to let them marinate in their fear. He escorted her to the truck and guided her inside, exchanging a mischievous smirk with Pax as the younger man climbed in and closed the door.

Caleb made his way back around to the driver's side, pausing momentarily to lock eyes with Izzy hovering in the dark.

"Caleb, get inside!" cried Hannah, genuinely terrified for him.

How adorable, she was worried for his safety. Oh, if she only knew, he thought as he climbed inside the truck. "It's okay," he said. It took every ounce of self-control for him to say those words with a straight face.

His trickster ears could hear her heart pounding against her rib cage. She leaned her head against his shoulder and closed her eyes. The cab was filled with her scent. Caleb could hardly wait to taste her.

He rolled the truck a few feet ahead, then halted, peering out through the windshield at Izzy, Ezra, and Bass. From where he sat, Caleb could see Bass had suffered a nasty injury to his eye, though now healed, the blood that stained his fur told the story. That was the thing about their kind. Tricksters were damn near impossible to kill. You could injure them, sometimes good enough to put them out of commission for a few days. But killing them, now that was a different story. That took a lot more effort and frankly, most humans didn't have the wherewithal to pull it off.

Bass stood up on his hind legs and howled, then he dropped to his feet, chuffed, and gave a quick nod to Caleb, who nodded back.

Sorry, buddy, thought Caleb. Looks like this one is all mine.

His friends turned their attention to the rest of their quarry, vanishing into the desert, no doubt following the trail left behind.

In the truck, Hannah once again rested her head on his shoulder and quickly fell asleep. It would appear as though his presence gave her a sense of security. He stifled a laugh. Stupid girl.

SIXTEEN

THE PARCHED WILDERNESS WAS NEVER-ENDING. The more they pushed themselves, the less progress they seemed to make. Were they running in circles? Hope was slipping away. Ash slowed her pace, every muscle in her body was ready to surrender. She had to take a break, to catch her breath and possibly figure out where they were. Resting her hands on her hips, she paced in a wide circle; her chest rising and falling as she gasped for air. Sweat saturated her clothes, making her hair cling to her face and the back of her neck.

Crouching down with her arms resting on her knees, her eyes fixed on Jewel. The girl wasn't out of breath at all. In fact, she showed no signs of physical stress. She certainly didn't appear as though she was running for her life from a rabid pack of wild beasts. Envy filled Ash's mind as she thought how wonderful it must be to be young and healthy. If only she had that kind of energy, they would be in town already.

"How are you holding up?" she asked, between gasps for air.

Jewel nodded, keeping her gaze fixed on the blackness behind them. "I'm fine."

Ash stood upright. Her heart rate was finally normalizing. She looked out in the direction that Jewel was staring. "I think Hannah and Jasmine made it." She winced at the unsure sound of her own voice, aware that she was trying to convince herself. If she just said those words out loud, the universe would hear them and make it true.

"The man didn't," said Jewel, a foreboding tone in her voice.

Sadness settled in Ash's heart at the mere thought of poor Ben. "He did what he had to do. He was too weak to run." She struggled to keep from crying. "Those things made sure of that."

Jewel signaled her agreement with a solemn nod. "Is that a common thing? For a man to sacrifice himself for the people he cares about?"

What an odd question to ask, thought Ash. "I suppose it is," she replied. "I mean, I'd give my life if it meant I could save the life of someone I loved. Wouldn't you?"

The girl shrugged in response. "But that's not what you did."

"What the hell does that mean?" asked Ash, angrily. "And fuck you for saying that." She raked her fingers through her sweaty hair. The whole nightmare in the van played out in her mind. Ben's ashen face, the way his body trembled with weakness from the slightest exertion. His hand. And all the blood. The sound of his screams of agony echoing throughout the valley. She wondered if she could ever think of him without hearing that sound.

"I-I'm sorry," stammered Jewel. "I didn't mean to upset you."

Ash studied the young teen standing beside her. Who was she? Where did she come from? How did she end up in the middle of nowhere? A sense of doubt emerged since the first time seeing the girl.

"Jewel," she said. "How did you end up out here? How do you know so much about these tricksters?"

At the mention of the word trickster, Jewel flinched. Her eyes darted to the darkness, then back at Ash. She shifted her weight from one foot to the other while her fingers fiddled nervously with a lock of her hair.

"Did you hear me?" demanded Ash. "I'm gonna need you to be

honest with me." She pointed behind them. "My friend is dead, and the others are God only knows where." She stared hard at the girl. "I'm not taking another step with you until you come clean. What do you know about these things, and how do you know it?"

Jewel fidgeted, her eyes darting around nervously.

Ash was done messing around. She needed answers. "Well? How did you end up out here?"

"I live here," blurted Jewel.

"I need you to be more specific," said Ash.

The girl swallowed. "This is my home. I grew up here."

Confusion was on the verge of transforming into rage. The way this girl was coughing up answers was like interrogating a criminal. "So, did you take a wrong turn out here?"

Jewel shook her head. "No." She pointed toward the hills behind them. "My house is up there."

"Why didn't you say something?" demanded Ash. "We could have run to your house and gotten help."

"There's no help to be found up there," said Jewel, moving her head frantically.

"What about your parents?"

"They're dead."

Ash gasped and stared at the young girl, immediately over-whelmed with regret for being suspicious. She let her own fear get the best of her. After everything they just went through, here she was, harassing an already traumatized kid. She pictured the poor thing witnessing her parents die at the hands of those beasts, the same way Ben just died. No wonder Jewel was too petrified to think clearly. No wonder she was running around in the dark, lost and alone. The poor thing was probably in shock. Ash wrapped her arms around the teen and pulled her in for a hug. "Don't worry anymore," she said. "We're gonna get out of here together." She pulled away and gazed into the teen's eyes. "I promise you, we're gonna get out of here."

Tears streamed down Jewel's cheeks. "I just want to leave."

"I know, I know," said Ash. "I do too."

Jewel wiped her cheeks with a filthy sleeve. Her face went white, then she clasped a hand over her mouth, and then turned away and threw up.

Poor thing thought Ash, being a teenage girl was enough of a struggle on its own, let alone having something as horrific as this happen. What if the girl had no other family—no one to take care of her? When this was all over, maybe she could convince Matt to take Jewel in and care for her. Of course, that would mean Ash would have to move back home to Texas, something she would have never considered twenty-four hours ago. After everything she'd been through in the past hour, she could think of nothing she wanted more to than walk through the front door of her old childhood home. Jewel would be happy there. With Matt's help, they could help the girl navigate through the trauma she just suffered through.

Plans aside, there were questions that needed immediate answers. Ash needed to know exactly what they were up against. She waited for Jewel to compose herself, it was obvious the stress of this whole nightmare was wearing on her. "What do you know about those things?" she asked. "What are they?"

"They're people who turn into coyotes," replied Jewel.

Ash could hardly believe her ears. "What? Like werewolves? That's impossible!" She saw those things, and they most certainly weren't people—they were animals. Large, feral, and terrifying but definitely animals. "There's no such thing." She scoffed. "People can't turn into animals."

"Tricksters can."

"No, they can't." Ash had had enough of this fantastical bullshit. She reeled on the girl. "The things that attacked us were animals. Giant animals that I've never seen before, but they were still animals. They were not men."

Jewel stared, unblinking.

Ash exhaled and cast her eyes up at the sky. "Okay, let's say you're right. These things are people who turn into coyotes. It's not even a full moon."

"They don't need a full moon," replied Jewel. "They can change whenever they want."

Ash struggled to wrap her brain around what Jewel was saying. On the surface, it was the easiest explanation for the creatures she saw. But everyone knew all those horror movie creatures weren't real. There was no such thing as werewolves or tricksters or whatever the hell the things were that Jewel was describing. But what if she was telling the truth? What if those things really were what she said? What if there really was such a thing as a trickster and she and her friends had stumbled right into their lair?

"I'm not lying," cried the girl. "They're men who turn into coyotes. Tricksters. They're feral beasts who take pleasure in hunting humans."

Ash thought back to the beasts she saw. Their sheer size, the way one of them stood on two legs—like a man. A very large man. Its eyes —the cunning way it stared directly into her eyes. She gasped and shifted her gaze to Jewel.

"Okay, let's say that these things are tricksters," she said. "Then they must have a weakness or two. What are they?"

Jewel shook her head.

"Sunlight?" offered Ash. No, no, no, that was vampires. She snapped her fingers. "Silver bullets!"

"Bullets in the right place, at the right time could kill anything," offered Jewel. "They don't have to be silver."

"Good point," agreed Ash. "Either way, they're not immortal. Right?" She spoke rapidly, all the while pacing in a circle. "If they're human-like, then they have weaknesses. We just need to find those."

Coyote chatter echoed through the hills, startling Ash.

Jewel cried out, trembling. "We need to keep going. We need to get to the highway."

The girl was right. It was pointless to try to figure out how to kill these creatures as long as they were out here in the middle of nowhere. They had no weapons, and they had no protection. Out here, they were exposed; just prey, waiting for the slaughter. They needed to get to somewhere safe. They needed to get to the town.

Ash pushed Jewel ahead of her. "Come on, this way!"

SEVENTEEN

THE TRUCK HIT A POTHOLE; jolting Hannah awake. She didn't mean to fall asleep. Her body must have shut down as soon as she felt she was out of danger. Lifting her head and rubbing her eyes, she asked, "Where are we?"

Silence.

She fixed her eyes on Caleb. Something about his demeanor was deeply unsettling. Whether it was the unusual shimmer in his eyes or his change of posture, she wasn't sure. All the tiny hairs on the back of her arms stood erect. She glanced back and forth between Pax and Caleb. "Are we heading to town?"

There was no reply from either, instead both continued staring out their windows as though they were scanning the area for something.

"Caleb!" shouted Hannah. "Why are we going so slow? Are we heading to town?" She shoved him. "Answer me!"

The truck came to a creaky stop. He turned his gaze toward her, his eyes moving with deliberate slowness.

"I want to go to town," said Hannah, surprised at how weak her voice sounded. Every cell in her body told her she was in danger, but there was nothing she could do. She was sandwiched between the two of them. A tempest of fear and confusion brewed inside her.

"She ain't gettin' it," said Pax.

Something in his tone made her snap her head in his direction. His face was different, more angular—almost cruel. His lips were curled into a wicked smirk, as he stared at her with glowing eyes.

"Yeah," said Caleb. "She seems to be a little slow on the uptake."

Hannah shifted her gaze to Caleb.

He stared directly into her eyes. "I'm only gonna tell you this once," he said menacingly. "Keep your mouth shut and behave, and we might keep you around for a little while." His lips curled into a sneer, revealing a mouth full of sharp teeth.

Before she could stop herself, Hannah blurted, "Your teeth."

Caleb chuckled softly. "All the better to eat you with, my dear," he said in a sing-song voice.

A primal sense of terror rose from Hannah's belly. Her heart fluttered in her chest, beating like a panic-stricken rabbit who had found itself face to face with a fierce predator. Her breath came in short bursts, she could feel her lungs struggling for oxygen.

A low-pitched growl sounded on her other side. Hannah resisted the temptation to turn and look, already terrified of what she would discover if she did. The weight of realization bore down on her, filling her with fear. She stared, wild-eyed and frozen, at Caleb.

He placed a rough hand against the back of her head and pulled her into him.

The feeling of his hot breath against her neck triggered a guttural feeling of disgust. Hannah recoiled, pushing against his grip, but it had no impact. Her entire body trembled in fear.

Caleb inhaled and let out a low moan. He pulled away and scowled, then with one sudden motion, he slammed her head into the dashboard.

Stars erupted in her vision. Her face exploded in pain. Hannah struggled to fight back, but she was no match for his strength. Her sight was shaded crimson red as blood poured into her eyes from the open wound on her forehead. She blinked and swallowed. "Please," she begged.

"Don't worry," said Caleb. "We ain't gonna kill you." He slammed her head against the dash one more time. "Not yet anyway."

Maniacal laughter broke out on both sides of her. As the world grew dark, she realized the sound she heard was not the snickering of two men. It was more savage—like the gleeful yips of a pair of coyotes.

EIGHTEEN

"HOLD ON," wheezed Ash. She stopped running and paced in a circle with her hands atop her head. The fire in her lungs burned more intensely with each breath. Her heart seemed ready to jump right out of her chest. The muscles in her legs quivered and ached.

She reached into her pocket and discovered that sometime during their run, her phone had fallen out. They had no means of navigation, and calling for help was out of the question. "God dammit," she cursed. How could she be so stupid? That was her only lifeline. Her only way to connect to the outside world—to reach Matt.

Ash scanned the ground, knowing full well the effort was futile. She struggled to recall when she had seen it last. She remembered stopping at the old rest stop several miles back. That was the last time she could recall holding the device in her hand. Fighting back tears, she resigned herself to relying solely on her memory of the map from here on out.

She surveyed the surroundings, looking for any sign of the pack. Nothing. She breathed a sigh of relief. It had to have been at least two miles since they crossed the old highway. If her calculations were correct, they should be very close to the interstate.

"Come on," cried Jewel. "We have to keep going." She pointed. "The highway is right over that rise."

Ash was in no state to run the rest of the way; she was certain that if she tried, she would collapse before ever getting close. "I can't run anymore." She studied the young girl. Once again, questioning how the teen wasn't fatigued? How could she have run as far as they did and not even break a sweat?

"Would you rather be dead?" asked Jewel.

The harshness of the girl's tone shook Ash into reality. Jewel was right, if she didn't keep going, all their effort was for nothing. They were almost there. She just had to push herself a little more. The town wasn't very far away. She placed her hands on her hips and took deep breaths to calm her racing pulse.

"Okay," said Ash. "I think I'm ready."

Jewel nodded and ran toward the rise.

Ash did her best to keep up, but as soon as she hit the hill, her strength waned, and she lost all momentum. On her hands and knees, she inched her way to the top of the sandy hill.

The young girl was right. The interstate spread out before them.

Ash had never been so happy to see a highway in her life. She glanced left, then right. Not a single vehicle in sight. She lifted her head to the sky and cursed this area of the country for being so desolate. No more road trips for her—and she was never going camping again. Across the highway, the lights of the town lit up the sky. Hope filled her heart.

"Come on," she said, taking hold of Jewel's hand and gently tugging her toward the road.

The young girl pulled back. "No," she said, shaking her head.

"Look, Jewel," said Ash. "Our only hope is to get help in the town."

The teen shook her head.

Ash clutched the girl's wrist and pulled, but Jewel yanked her hand away and stepped back out of reach.

"What are you doing?" demanded Ash. Anger swelled inside at the young girl, who didn't seem to fully understand their situation.

"I'm not going!" shouted Jewel. "I want to stay here and wait for a car or truck to come by."

Ash could hardly believe what she was hearing. She shook her head. "Are you crazy? What if those things come along?"

The girl said nothing.

There was no time for this foolishness. Ash stared long and hard at Jewel, suddenly realizing that there was no way she was going to convince the girl to go with her. As much as she wanted to save the teen, Ash was the only hope for her friends. She needed to put them first.

"Okay," she said calmly. "I want you to stay right here." She pointed to the town. "I'm gonna get some help. Do you think you can stay put and wait for me to come back?"

Jewel nodded slowly.

"Whatever you do," warned Ash. "Do not go running back into the desert. Stay here and when I have help, we'll come by and pick you up."

Don't go," pleaded the girl, tears streaming down her face.

"I have to," replied Ash. "My friends need me to get help. I'll come back for you." She backed away, leaving the teen alone on the edge of the highway. Despite feeling guilty, she knew the girl had left her with no other alternative. She turned and ran toward the town.

Streetlights buzzed overhead, casting a dim glow of yellow light upon the empty street. Ash shuffled wearily down the center of the road, feeling a sense of isolation and fear. Her steps echoed off the buildings. There wasn't a single person in sight. She passed the bar they visited earlier; it was closed. The Sheriff's office loomed up ahead. The lights were on, and someone was moving around inside. Hope surged in her chest, giving her a much-needed rush of adrenaline, which she used to run toward the small building

Ash stormed into the office, momentarily blinded by the light. "Help!" she screamed.

Startled, the Sheriff stood up, mouth agape, and stared at her. He stepped around his desk and approached her just in time to catch her as she collapsed into his arms.

"It's okay," he said calmly. "You're safe."

"My friends," cried Ash, unable to get any more words out.

The Sheriff nodded. "Let's get you a seat and you can tell me all about it."

"We need to help them," she croaked.

"And we will," he replied. "But if you pass out, I'll have no one to tell me where they are." He guided Ash to a chair beside his desk and helped her to sit down. "Stay here. I'll get you something to drink."

Ash wanted to stand up and demand he help her now, but her body refused to budge. Every muscle trembled with fatigue. Her face was drenched in tears.

The Sheriff returned with a bottle of water. He handed it to her, then leaned against the edge of his desk. "Go on, drink that down. You need to hydrate."

She held the bottle to her lips and drank deeply, letting the cool water flow into her body, soothing her parched throat. Before she realized it, she had downed every drop.

"That's a girl," said the Sheriff. "Now, you wanna tell me what's going on?"

Ash nodded. "Jewel. We have to go get her. She's out by the highway. We ran all the way here. I don't know where my friends are." She peered up at the older man. "Please help them." She broke down into uncontrollable sobs.

Her head spun, she remembered feeling this way once, long ago, when she had a bout of vertigo. A cold sweat broke out along her forehead. Was she having a heart attack? Why was she suddenly so dizzy and sleepy at the same time? She glanced down at the empty bottle in her hand. Oh god! She'd been drugged. Panic flooded her mind, but she couldn't move from the chair. She looked up at the Sheriff with teary eyes. "Why?"

He shook his head. "Nothing personal, it's just the way of things. I'm sorry for you and your friends that it had to turn out like this."

Ash's body slumped, falling out of the chair, and hitting the floor with a solid thump, then everything was gone.

NINETEEN

CALEB FINISHED TYING the last knot, giving the cord a tug to ensure the girl was secure. "At least we got something out of this night," he said as he brushed a lock of her hair away from her face. He studied the unconscious young woman hog-tied in the bed of his truck. She sure was a pretty one. Were it not for the unfortunate circumstance of wandering into his domain, she would have had a nice life for herself. Maybe even got married and had a few kids.

"You gettin' soft on this one?" asked Pax.

"Not even close," he replied.

The younger brother jumped from the bed of the truck. "You ever wonder why it is we don't ever feel bad for any of them?"

"Do you feel bad when you eat a burger?" asked Caleb. "Or a thick, juicy steak? Do you think any of them feel bad when they do? He caressed Hannah's soft cheek. "Nah, they may look the same as us, but they ain't anything close. To folks like us, they're just another prey animal." He jumped out of the truck bed, landing softly on the ground. "A source of entertainment, if you will."

Pax nodded in agreement. "We ready to get back out there and find Jewel?"

Caleb sighed. "Yeah, we might as well."

"You sound like you don't want her to come home," said Pax. "She's family. I mean, sure, she's been a pain in the ass lately, but she's still our little sister. Besides, Mom and Dad would want us to stay together."

The reminder of his parents was like a stab to his heart. "I suppose you're right," replied Caleb. "You know, as much as I hate to admit it, things would be a lot easier if we let her go." He shook his head. "But we can't do that. She wouldn't know how to function in the world and, frankly, the world wouldn't know what to do with her." He stared at his younger brother.

"Then we better find her," said Pax. "She needs us. Especially right now."

The kid was right. Even though Caleb was angry at his little sister's behavior, she was still his sister—his blood. It was his responsibility to take care of his younger siblings. He just wished Jewel didn't make it so difficult.

Deep inside, he yearned to go back to the way things were a few years ago, when their parents were alive—when their family was whole. Life was far less complicated when being the older brother meant you were the admired one. The one who taught the younger siblings how to sneak out at night or steal an extra snack from the cupboard. Memories of his childhood rushed into his mind. He remembered the day Pax was born, followed a few years later by Jewel. She was such a devotee of Caleb back then, always following him around. The girl would do anything he told her to do. His lips curled into a wistful smile as he pictured her little face peering up at him with those big, innocent eyes.

This whole responsible family elder gig was lousy. He wasn't their father—he knew it and so did they. He never wanted to be the patriarch of the family. That was his father's job. The obligation was foisted on him against his will. Caleb remembered how he felt when he finally realized his new role in the family. Angry and resentful, he distanced himself from his younger siblings and became someone completely different. He drank a lot and was quick to anger, spending nearly every night hunting along the highway.

He wasn't proud of that period of his life. Fortunately, it was a short-lived experience. Alas, it was just long enough to leave a lasting scar on his relationship with Jewel. Pax bounced back right away. Jewel; not so much. The poor girl was a wreck. In hindsight, she lost more than her parents; she lost her older brother too—the one family member besides her parents who she should have been able to count on.

Growing into adulthood was difficult for everyone, it was even more so for their kind. Caleb recalled what it was like experiencing the change for the first time, how chaotic and terrifying it was. The strength, the rush of sensations, the hunger—the pain. It was hard enough for him, he could only imagine how difficult it must be for a young woman. They had so many other issues to deal with moving into adulthood. The poor girl just needs patience and understanding. She needed her older brother.

"So, are we heading back out to the old highway?" asked Pax.

Caleb loathed admitting it, but he didn't know where the best place to search would be. When he caught a scent back at the old highway, he was sure they were on the right track. But then it was gone, making him wonder if he had caught it at all.

Come to think of it, he remembered catching Jewel's scent after that. It was in the truck, shortly after picking up Hannah, while she lay with her head against his shoulder.

A wave of shock surged through him. He hopped back into the truck bed and leaned over the unconscious woman, sniffing. Jewel—her subtle scent invaded the fibers of Hannah's clothes unmistakably.

"Come here!" he said. "Give her a good sniff and tell me what you smell."

Pax sprang into the truck bed and leaned close to Hannah. He inhaled. "Jewel." He gazed up at Caleb. "She was with them."

Caleb nodded. "Probably still is."

"Well, what are we waiting for?" asked Pax excitedly.

"Let's go," said Caleb, feeling optimistic for the first time all night ever since he found out his sister had run away.

They sped down the long gravel road, kicking up a cloud of dust and sand in their wake. The entire time, Caleb's mind swirled with all the ways he would be different toward his little sister once they got her home. He would finally be the big brother she deserved.

His thoughts were interrupted by the sudden sound of Sheriff Ramirez's voice squawking from the handheld radio in the glove box.

"Caleb," the voice popped. "If you're out there, answer me Goddammit."

What the hell did the old man want now?

Pax flipped open the glove box and offered the radio to Caleb.

Annoyed, he snatched the device and held it up to his face. "Yeah," he said into the microphone, in no mood for niceties. There was no great love or respect between the townspeople and Caleb's pack. Theirs was an uneasy truce. The implicit understanding was that the townsfolk would turn a blind eye, and as a result, the pack wouldn't hunt any resident of the town.

"Where the hell are you?" asked the Sheriff.

Caleb's frustration was mounting. Who did this pathetic old man think he was talking to him in such a way? He pushed back the urge to put the radio away, opting instead to ask simply, "Is there a reason you're calling me?"

The Sheriff scoffed. "You and your people are out there making a huge mess of things." He paused. "You're not keeping your end of the bargain."

"Look, old man," replied Caleb.

"No! You look!" shouted the Sheriff. "Get your ass down to my station and clean up your mess. Now!"

Anger erupted like a volcano. "Don't you ever talk to me like that!" yelled Caleb. "I can show up to your seedy little shack right now and rip your cancerous lungs right out of your pathetic body!"

Pax took hold of the radio. "Sheriff," he said. "Why don't you tell me what this is all about."

Caleb was boiling with anger, his hands gripping the steering wheel so tight, it was a wonder it didn't break apart.

"A girl came into my station looking for help." The radio crackled with feedback.

"Just one?" asked Pax.

The Sheriff keyed the handset but didn't respond right away. "Just get your asses down here and get her out of my office."

"We're on our way now," replied Pax. He keyed the handset and spoke, "Was Jewel with her?"

"No," responded the Sheriff, harshly.

Pax gave Caleb a brief glance. "We'll be right there," he responded into the handset, then he put the radio away.

"Dammit!" Caleb yelled, hitting the steering wheel.

"Jewel would know better than to go to Ramirez for help," said Pax. "It makes sense she wasn't with the girl."

"Then we still have a chance of bumping into her on our way to town," said Caleb. With that thought in mind, he pushed the gas pedal to the floor. He had a hunch that his little sister would try to catch a ride out of town on the highway. So he took the less direct route along the access road. "Keep your eyes open," he said, as the on-ramp to the interstate came into view.

Caleb leaned out his window and stared into the shadows. His human eyes weren't so good at spying things that wanted to be hidden, but his trickster eyes were more than capable. Summoning his inner beast forward, he could feel his eyesight grow stronger. Blades of grass and the spindly arms of tree branches cast tiny shadows that danced in the moonlight. A slight movement caught his eye.

He stopped the truck and called out the window. "Come on out, girl," he said, doing his best to mask his frustration. "You know we ain't got time for these bullshit games anymore."

Silence.

Caleb studied the shrub; a vague form crouched low inside.

"Alright Jewel, now, I'm gonna count to ten. If your ass ain't out here by the end, I'm gonna go in there and drag you out by your hair." He waited for a response.

Nothing. No movement, not even a sound.

"One," he counted. "Two."

The shadowy figure shifted slightly.

"Three."

"Four." Caleb let out a deep breath; this girl was as headstrong as he was. This wasn't going the way he hoped. Time for a new approach. He climbed out of the truck and stepped cautiously toward the shrub.

"Jewel, darlin'," he said softly. "This ain't the way." He crouched down close enough to pick up her scent. He sniffed the air. Something about his little sister had changed—was still changing. He could smell her fear mingling with the scent of change.

No more messing around. It was time for him to step up and be the big brother she needed. Caleb sat on the ground and crossed his legs. "How many times do you think we played hide and go seek when we were kids?" he asked, not expecting a response. "You were real good at hiding."

"No, I wasn't," blurted Jewel, her voice filled with sorrow.

Caleb smiled as the memories of his little sister swam forward in his mind.

"You always knew," said Jewel. "You knew where I was hiding before the game even started." She sniffled. "You only pretended that you couldn't find me." She moved close enough for him to see her face—blotchy, red, and covered in grime.

"I haven't been the best brother lately," said Caleb. "But I'm here now." He offered his hand.

Pax, standing close by, said, "We both are."

"It's gonna be okay," said Caleb.

Jewel's delicate hand reached out from the shrub and clasped his, allowing him to help her to her feet. As soon as she emerged from hiding, she fell into his arms and sobbed.

Determined to give his little sister all the space she needed; Caleb waited until she was finished crying. He was in no hurry—not any longer.

Jewel drew back and gazed up at him with red, puffy eyes. Even with all the swollen redness surrounding them, he could see the tell-tale sign of a subtle pale glow.

"You're in for an interesting night little sister," he said, smiling gently. "We best get you home." He guided her to the truck. "We got one quick stop to make first though," he said, as he climbed into the driver's seat.

TWENTY

"WHAT THE HELL took you so long?" demanded the Sheriff.

"We had some family matters to attend to," replied Caleb, doing his best to control his temper with the old man.

"I called you almost an hour ago."

Caleb nodded. "I'm aware."

"This isn't a game," hollered the Sheriff. "I told you to get over here right away, not an hour later."

With great speed, Caleb wrapped a clawed hand around Ramirez's throat, following through with enough force to slam the man against the wall. He bared his teeth and used just the right amount of force to raise him off the ground, all the while restricting airflow. The sound of the Sheriff's feet skidding on the tile floor, in search of support, was a delight to Caleb's ears.

Sheriff Ramirez was not his favorite townie. Truth is, he didn't really have one. In his eyes, the locals' worth depended solely on their commitment to keeping the pack's secret. Other than that, they were nothing more than tasty morsels in reserve. He let the man struggle for a bit while he weighed his options. Should he dispatch the old creep now and be done with him forever? Or should he let him go this time, with a single warning to never speak to him like that again.

Saliva dripped from the corners of Ramirez's mouth, his face turned red, and his eyes bulged in a mix of terror and lack of oxygen.

With a hateful sneer, Caleb let go, leaving the man to slump to the floor. He lowered himself to gaze into Ramirez's eyes. "Never make the mistake again that you and I are on the same level."

The Sheriff stared up at him and nodded. When he regained his composure, he climbed to his feet and led Caleb to a small, cluttered office. The girl lay unconscious, spread out upon a worn-out leather sofa. The stink of many decades' worth of cigars and body odor permeated the tiny room. Caleb wrinkled his nose. Sometimes the stench of humans made him wish his kind didn't have such a keen sense of smell.

"You and your people need to be more careful," said the Sheriff. Quickly realizing his tone, he corrected himself. "I mean, this one nearly got away."

"But she didn't," replied Caleb. "You made sure of that."

The old man shook his head. "I don't like being a part of this."

"You'll do your part," hissed Caleb. "Nothing more, and nothing less." He stared directly into the Sheriff's eyes. "The pack is the only reason you even have a job."

Sheriff Ramirez grabbed hold of Caleb's arm. "I'm serious. This is the third time in as many months where your people let things spill over into town."

"We cleaned it up," said Caleb, fighting back the urge to rip the old man's heart from his chest while it was still beating.

"Only after I called you!"

Caleb was done dealing with the Sheriff, he turned and walked closer to the sofa, ready to pick up the girl.

But the old man wasn't finished. Once again, he placed his hands on Caleb and tried to pull him back to face him. "Now you listen to me!" he shouted; his face red with impotent rage. "This town isn't here to run cover for you and your pack of mutants."

Rage ignited, turning Caleb's vision red. He spun around and leered menacingly over the Sheriff; the pungent odor of sweat and stale liquor assaulted his senses.

"No!" he said through sharp teeth protruding from his snarling lips. "You listen to me!" Caleb poked a clawed finger at the old man's chest. "The only reason you and this town are still here is to run cover for the pack." He paused long enough to enjoy the sound of the Sheriff's racing heart and the intoxicating aroma of his fear. 'You're gonna continue to hold up your end of the bargain, or all bets are off. Do you know what I mean by that?"

Ramirez didn't respond, instead he stepped back and stared with his lips quivering as though he would burst into tears at any moment.

"Good," said Caleb as he allowed his teeth to return to normal. "And Sheriff." He paused for emphasis. "Don't you ever use the term mutants to describe me or any member of my pack again." He locked eyes with the old man. "It'll be the last thing you ever do. Are we clear?"

The old man nodded. "I just don't think—"

"I don't care what you think," said Caleb, with a sneer. "No one cares what you think. You do what you're told, and nothing more."

Ramirez opened his mouth to speak again.

The old man was determined to get his point across, so Caleb decided to let him dig his grave. "Alright, just spit it out And make it quick, I've got more important things to do right now." He crossed his arms and waited.

"There's a lot of growth coming to the state," said the Sheriff.

"And?" Caleb's patience was wearing thin.

"And," said Ramirez. "It's only a matter of time before more people venture out here."

A malevolent sneer spread across Caleb's face. "All the more hunting for us."

The Sheriff shook his head and licked his lips nervously. "And what are you gonna do when the disappearances end up bringing the

Feds down here? You know, the state is one thing—the Feds—" He wiped his sweaty palms on his thighs.

Caleb hadn't considered that notion before. It certainly was a valid concern. What would the pack do if the area was suddenly flooded with Feds? He chuckled under his breath. It would certainly make for a wild and bloody time.

"Go ahead, laugh about it," said the Sheriff. "If you have a death wish for the pack, then that's on you." He stepped back. "I, for one, refuse to pay for the things you and your kin have done."

"Is that your way of telling me you'll turn on us?" asked Caleb.

The Sheriff shook his head nervously. "All I'm saying is I don't intend to go to prison."

Caleb nodded. "Duly noted." He glared at the old man. "When the time comes, I promise you, I'll make damn sure you never make it to prison."

Ramirez swallowed and backed away, leaving the cramped office.

On the sofa, the girl moaned and shifted her body, but never awakened. Caleb hovered over her, studying her features, breathing in her scent. He tossed her limp body over his shoulder, then walked out into the main room, where he found Ramirez pouring himself a tall glass of whiskey.

"Be seeing you around Sheriff," said Caleb on his way out the door. "Say hello to the wife for me." He paused and smirked. "The kiddos too. Maybe I'll drop by and pay a visit the next time the grand-kids are visiting. Kids really like me." He didn't need to see the old man's face to know his reaction. Without another word, he stepped out onto the street, letting the door swing closed behind him.

TWENTY-ONE

HANNAH REGAINED consciousness back in town, just in time to witness Caleb unceremoniously throw Ash into the truck beside her. Hands and legs tied behind her back, she could do nothing more than stare in terror at her unconscious friend and whisper repeatedly, "Ash! Ash! Wake up! Please!"

The truck's engine turned off.

She struggled against her restraints, the throbbing pain in her head making it difficult to think. A sudden wave of nausea washed over her as the world spun in a dizzying blur. She closed her eyes and took a deep breath, waiting for the sensation to fade.

With a forceful thud, the tailgate slammed down, sending vibrations throughout her body. She opened her eyes and watched Ash's lifeless body slide out of view. Panic exploded. She screamed and cried out for help, but the only response was the gleeful laughter of a band of coyotes.

Caleb climbed into the truck and squatted down in front of her. "Well, hello there, sleeping beauty. Hope you're feeling well rested." He took out a long hunting knife and held it up.

Hannah flinched but couldn't move away.

"Oh, don't worry," he said. "I ain't gonna hurt you with this." He reached behind her and cut the rope, then leaned back on his heels and stared. "Go on," he said. "You can sit up."

Wary at first, Hannah sat up and leaned back against the truck bed wall. Her hands and feet tingled from the surge of blood flow. "Where are we?" she asked, rubbing her wrist. "Where did you take Ash?"

Caleb regarded her with a cold eye. "We're home," he replied. "At least my home."

Her senses were overwhelmed with confusion. "Why?" asked Hannah. She quickly scanned the group who gathered around the truck, recognizing every one of them from the bar in town. "Where's Ash?"

"She's not your worry anymore," said Caleb.

What did he mean by that? Was Ash dead like Ben and Jasmine? What happened to Jewel? Was there a connection between the creatures who assaulted them and these people? Tears flowed down her cheeks. "Please," she begged. "Please let me go."

Caleb stared at her with cold, calculating eyes. "You're in luck. Because, that's exactly what I'm gonna do." He jumped to the ground. "Hurry up!" he hollered, banging on the tailgate. "We don't have all night."

Hannah scanned the area as she climbed out of the truck. An impressive old farmhouse stood before her, set among a backdrop of rocky mountains. Off to the side, a large, red barn stood with its giant doors wide open. The people from the bar formed a circle around her. She turned around to face Caleb. "I want to go home."

"We're gonna play a little game first," said Caleb. He moved close —too close.

"I don't want to play a game," said Hannah, taking a step back. She spun around only to find herself face to face with Pax, who was grinning wildly with a mouth full of razor-sharp teeth.

"That's the thing, sweetheart," said Caleb. "You don't have a choice."

Panic and confusion overwhelmed her. She struggled to tame her racing heart. "Why are you doing this?"

"Now, now calm down," said Caleb. "You gotta pay attention." He stared at her with a menacing glow in his eyes. "Because this part's real important. It determines whether or not you make it home."

The mere mention of going home stirred a small flame of hope within her. Hannah wiped her face and sniffled.

"Good girl." Caleb pointed. "About thirty miles that way is the next town." He took a step back. "If you can make it there by sunrise, we'll let you live. If you don't, well," he said with a playful wink. "Let's just say we gave you a fightin' chance."

A low-pitched growl reverberated behind her. Hannah resisted the temptation to turn around as the terror of awareness settled in. She couldn't tear her eyes away from Caleb, frozen in awe as wild hairs sprouted along his jawline and spread across his face. His canines stretched past his bottom lip.

All around her, the others were changing, too. Coarse tan fur covered their bodies. Powerful muscles rippled in their arms and through their chests.

The icy fingers of panic gripped her lungs, making it difficult to breathe. This can't be happening. Her logical mind tried to dismiss it as unreal—a hallucination, while her primal instincts screamed in terror.

Behind her, she heard a low, menacing snarl that sent shivers down her spine.

Caleb leaned close to her. "Move!" he growled.

Hannah's heart raced as she started running, her body instantly responding with a surge of power, driving her toward the hope of escape. Desperate for cover, she ran into the woods, the sound of her footsteps echoing through the trees. Pulse racing, she leaned her back against the trunk of an old oak tree. Not a trace of the pack could be found, the only sound resonating was the peaceful trickle of a nearby stream. She licked her parched lips and scanned the darkness. Nothing. The water beckoned her. She crept along, her footsteps barely audible, until she reached the edge of a narrow river. After a quick scan of the area, she swiftly lowered herself to the ground, grabbed a handful of the cool water, and drank eagerly.

Behind her, she heard the sudden snap of a twig. Before she could react, a powerful hand grabbed the back of her head and thrust her face first into the water.

She fought in vain to free herself from the monster's grip, but the creature was too strong. Helpless and tired of fighting, Hannah stopped struggling and readied herself to inhale one final time, filling her lungs with the cold water. The creature pulled her from the water and flung her to the ground. Gasping for air, she scooted backward, coming to a stop against a tree.

The pack stood in a ring around her.

"Fuck you!" she choked, defiantly.

The beasts yipped gleefully, their eyes glowing bright in the darkness.

She had no more tears left—no more fear. Too weak to walk, Hannah rolled over and dragged herself along the ground, one handful of rocky dirt at a time. She could hear the slow footfalls of the pack behind her, their chuffs and growls serving as a constant reminder of their presence. To them, this was nothing more than a playful game.

Hannah came to a halt. She rolled onto her back and peered up at her stalkers. There was no more fight left in her body. She gazed up at the twinkling stars overhead, listening to the soothing sound of the river, and prayed for a swift end.

Her eyes focused on a solitary creature that emerged into her field of vision. As it studied her, its amber eyes glowed with an intense, burning hatred.

"What are you waiting for, bitch?" asked Hannah.

With a snarl, the beast exposed its teeth and pounced. There was a sharp tear of pain, followed by warmth as blood gushed from her throat. Hannah closed her eyes and let herself go.

TWENTY-TWO

DRIP, drip, drip.

Ash opened her eyes to the rhythmic sound of water droplets echoing off the damp cave walls. The air was filled with the scent of dirt, rock, and something metallic. She sat up and wiped the sand from her face. Darkness enveloped her. A muted groan came from somewhere close. Too frightened to investigate, she scooted backward until she reached a solid rock wall then pulled her legs close and wrapped her arms around them.

A flame sparked to life, illuminating Caleb's face. Ash watched him warily through a set of rusty iron bars.

He ignited two torches on both sides of the wall then seated himself on a wooden stool. "How're you feelin'?" he asked, regarding her with a heartless glare.

Ash kept a safe distance from the bars and pressed her back against the wall. Her body was weak from exhaustion, and her head throbbed. She rubbed her temples.

"This'll help flush out the drugs that're makin' your head hurt," he said, holding a bottle of water through the bars.

She didn't move.

Caleb nodded and pulled the bottle back, then twisted off the cap, and drank deeply. "Well, your loss, I suppose." He closed the bottle and placed it on the ground at his feet, then leaned forward with his elbows on his knees. "You're probably wondering why I brought you here," he said playfully.

"Where are my friends?" blurted Ash.

Caleb sighed and shook his head. "Unfortunately, they didn't make it. My friends saw to that." He stared at Ash with glowing eyes. "It wasn't all them though. Lucky for me, Hannah brought herself right to me. Musta been fate." He licked his lips. "She was an impressive woman. A tasty morsel, for sure."

His words triggered a flurry of emotions, of which fear, and sorrow were only two. "Why?" she croaked.

"It's nothing personal." He stared coldly into her eyes. "It's just the way of things. We gotta eat, just like everyone else."

"What are you?" she asked, though deep inside she didn't want to know the answer to that question.

Caleb sat upright. "Good question." He tapped his chin. "Let's see. Where to begin? You know what a shapeshifter is?" He waited for her to respond, when she didn't, he continued. "There're lots of us out there. You'd be surprised to find out just how many. In fact, it'd blow your mind if you knew how many celebrities and politicians are among my kind." He took another drink of water. "Me and my pack are tricksters. We don't transform into wolves; our ancestors went a different route." He smiled. "The coyote route." He waved his hand. "It's much more suitable for this area of the country."

Tricksters. That was what Jewel called them. Jewel. For the first time since waking up, Ash remembered the girl. The thought that she may have made it to safety gave her a tiny bit of solace.

Something shifted in the dark recess of the cave. Ash moved her gaze, trying to discern what the shadowy form hovering in the corner was. Every cell in her body screamed at her to run, but she had nowhere to go. There was no way out. She peered up at Caleb. "Please let me go," she begged.

He shook his head and released a weary breath.

"Please. I won't tell anyone about you."

"Now that's a useless offer. I mean, if I keep you in here, you ain't gonna tell anyone, anyway." He leaned forward, sporting a wicked grin. "Even you have to admit, there ain't any potential advantage for me to let you go."

Panic seized her brain. She tried to formulate a discussion but couldn't string together a complete thought. In utter defeat, she placed her forehead atop her knees and wept.

"Now, now, now," said Caleb. "Don't cry. Consider this an honor."

Ash picked up her head and wiped her face. Honor? What the hell was he talking about? Since when was it an honor to die alone and cold in a dank cave in the middle of God knows where?

"You see, Ash," said Caleb. "Most of the lore surrounding our kind is wrong. We don't need a full moon. There's no difference between silver bullets and the regular kind. They're both useless." He paused. "Oh, and we're not made, we're born this way." His eyes glowed in the dark. His teeth grew frighteningly long, protruding from his mouth. "We start out like everyone else; I suppose. Ordinary children with a keen sense of smell and a craving for raw meat. Then we grow." He took another drink from the water bottle. "During puberty, we change. One could say we come into our own."

He held the bottle of water through the bars, this time Ash grabbed hold of it and quickly gulped down the entire contents.

"Feel a little better now?" he asked.

She didn't respond, merely opting to stare, unblinking at the terrifying spectacle that sat before her.

Caleb chuckled. "I can see you're still wondering what the hell is going on. Allow me to enlighten you." He stood up and pulled one of the lit torches from the wall. "When the trickster comes out for the first time, it's a sight to behold. The unbearable pain, the euphoric strength—the insatiable need to feed. Some younglings have tried to eat anything in sight. And I mean anything. Their own family members included. Ezra can attest to that." He ran his finger down the side of his face for emphasis.

He lifted the torch high. "You remember Jewel?"

Ash startled at the sound of the girl's name rolling off his lips. Her heart filled with rage. "Wasn't it enough that you killed her family?"

Confusion swept across his face, followed by a malicious smile. "Oh Ash, you really are clueless. Aren't you?" He laughed demonically, then stopped abruptly and sneered at her. "I am Jewel's family," he stated with a deep, monstrous tone.

The heap in the corner moaned as it shifted ever so slightly in the shadows.

"She's my baby sister," said Caleb. "Which brings me to why you're here and not a chunk of meat that I pick from between my teeth." He leaned against the bars. "Jewel's comin' into her own. Tonight—right now, in fact. Lucky you. Y'all arrived just in time to be a part of it all."

More moans and shuffling. The dark shadow in the corner grew as it moved closer to Ash.

Caleb held the torch aloft, illuminating the entire cell.

It was Jewel! For a split second, Ash felt relief at the sight of the girl, then just as quickly horror washed over her.

"My little sister is changing for the first time." Caleb smiled proudly, showing off a mouthful of long, sharp teeth. "And you have the privilege of being her first."

Jewel's moans turned into low growls. The sickening sound of cracking bones bounced off the walls. Ash jumped to her feet and pressed her back against the wall as she watched the girl's horrific transformation. Coarse hair sprouted all over the teen's body, her clothes fell away in tattered pieces as her limbs contorted into a new shape. Sharp white teeth grew from her elongated jaw.

Ash shrieked in fear as the beast turned and stared directly at her with cunning, ice-blue eyes. It let out a howl so loud that it threatened to burst her eardrums.

Caleb laughed.

The creature prowled closer to Ash, sniffing the air, and frothing at the maw.

"That's right, little sister," encouraged Caleb. "That's the sweet scent of fear. Take it in."

The beast stretched, then lunged forward. Ash let out a final scream, then the world plunged into darkness.

TWENTY-THREE
TWO WEEKS LATER

"SO, explain to me why we're going alone instead of with the whole department?" asked Troy. He tossed a duffle bag into the back of the old gray jeep. "I mean, we got no backup. And as far as I can tell, no one in the department even knows we're going down there."

Matt let out a frustrated sigh. "We've been over this. They don't believe something's wrong," he replied. "The Captain gave me some bullshit about adults getting away from it all. He said it's too early for any sort of investigation. So, they're not gonna do anything." He stopped on his way back into the house. "If you don't want to come along, I'm okay with that. There's a good possibility that we could be in hot water if the Captain finds out we went against his orders to stand down and wait." He paused and waited for a response, when none came, he continued. "Ash is the only family I have left. She's out there and I need to find her."

"What if the Captain's right?" asked Troy. "What if she is staying away intentionally and, for whatever reason, wants to be left alone?"

Matt shook his head. "She's not. She wouldn't do that." He turned to walk away. "I can do this all on my own. You don't have to come along," he said over his shoulder.

Troy followed him inside the house and grabbed another bag. "Like that's even an option," he said. "We've been through too much together. Besides, I can think of at least four times you needed me to pull your ass out of trouble." He flashed a bright smile. "And little Ash is the kid sister I never had. If something happened to her, it affects me too."

Matt lowered his head, realizing he wasn't giving his best friend a chance. He and Troy had been inseparable since middle school when Troy's family moved in next door. He could hardly recall an adolescent memory that didn't involve him. "I'm sorry, man," he said. "My head hasn't been right since she disappeared."

"I totally understand," replied Troy. "And you're not wrong for being worried. How long has it been since you heard from her?"

"A little over two weeks," replied Matt. He shook his head. "She's never been out of touch with me for more than a day or two. That's how I know something happened." Just thinking of Ash sent a wave of anxiety coursing through his body. There was no way his sister would go off by herself and not let him know. They were too close for that. Something was terribly wrong; he could feel it in his bones. He learned long ago to trust his gut with certain matters. Their family's track record for longevity was less than impressive. When Matt was a senior in high school, a convenience store robbery gone awry took the life of his father. Cancer snatched his mother away in the middle of his junior year of college.

Troy grabbed hold of another bag and followed Matt to the jeep. "So, how do we know where to start looking?"

"Her credit card statement came in yesterday," replied Matt. "It shows activity all the way from Arizona, through New Mexico and into Texas." He tossed his bag inside the vehicle and brushed off his hands. "The last charge was at some dive bar in Sierra Diablo."

"Hold up," said Troy. "You ain't draggin' me to that town where all those sightings happened of the kids with the black eyes. Are you?"

"No, that's not where we're headed," said Matt. "Although we will pass through there on the way." He chuckled softly, knowing his best friend hated everything supernatural. It was a chore to even get him outside on Halloween, let alone visit haunted houses, and horror movies were a definite no-go.

Troy stared. "There ain't no way we can bypass it completely?" He waited for Matt to respond. "Please tell me we're not gonna drive right through the center of the creepy town."

"We're not driving through the center," replied Matt. "We're just gonna pass through a small portion of it."

Troy scoffed. "Because that makes it better."

"Makes what better?" asked Sam, as she sauntered up with a backpack slung over her shoulder." Behind her, Lauren wrestled with two giant suitcases.

"What are you doing here?" asked Matt.

Sam tossed her backpack in the jeep then turned to face him. She planted a kiss on his cheek. "I thought that was obvious. We're coming along with you."

Matt shook his head in protest.

"Shh," she said, placing a soft finger against his lips. "It's not up for debate." She gazed into his eyes. "We're coming with you and that's that."

"What the hell do you have in these things?" asked Troy as he hefted one of Lauren's suitcases. "You know we're not gonna be staying at any four-star resorts or anything. In fact," he said, turning around to face her. "We're probably gonna be spending most of our time roughing' it."

"I'm just bringing the necessities," said Lauren. "I wanted to be prepared for all possibilities." She glanced around. "So, why all the secrecy? Sam says y'all are taking a leave of absence to do this behind your captain's back. How come the Texas Rangers aren't investigating this? I mean, aren't they supposed to be law enforcement?"

"I tried," replied Matt. "Leadership says there's no reason for them to get involved, let alone allot any manpower."

"They don't investigate criminal cases anymore?" asked Sam.

"How is a missing person not something they would at least investigate?"

"I asked the same questions," said Matt. "All I got for answers was that the Rangers don't bother with missing persons cases. They kept telling me there was no evidence of foul play. That Ash probably just wants to be on her own for a while. The Captain made it sound like I was the reason she disappeared; like I was some sort of overbearing family member that she needed to get away from."

"They're not even looking into it?" asked Sam.

"They told me to let the local law enforcement handle it."

"And what did the local PD have to say?"

"Nothing." He exhaled loudly. "Big fat nothing. Honestly though, after talking to Sheriff Ramirez over the phone, I got the distinct impression that he was hiding something." He locked eyes with Sam. "He knows something, and I'm gonna find out what that is."

"You mean we're gonna find out," she said, as she pulled her long, dark hair up into a ponytail.

"So, where are we going?" asked Lauren, as she opened the door to the jeep.

"West Texas," replied Matt. "A hole in the wall town called Sierra Diablo."

"Oh! Devil's mountain! I like the name!" squealed Lauren, excitedly. "Is that the place where the black-eyed children are?"

"No," replied Matt. "The town you're thinking of is Toyah. We're going to Sierra Diablo, it's further to the south and west."

"Yes!" said Lauren, as she jumped into the jeep and closed the door. She leaned out the window and asked, "Can we make a detour in Toyah?"

"No!" shouted Troy, climbing into the passenger side of the vehicle.

Lauren pushed out her bottom lip. "Oh, come on, just a quick drive through?"

"I said, no!" stated Troy.

"Come on," she taunted. "Where's your sense of adventure?"

"It's right where it needs to be, a healthy distance from all things involving ghosts or supernatural creatures."

Sam laughed and gave Matt a kiss on the cheek. "Like it or not, we're along for the ride." She slapped him on the butt, then winked and climbed into the vehicle.

Matt performed a quick mental check of the gear he loaded and what he thought they might need. Then he locked the front door to his house and climbed into the driver's seat.

TWENTY-FOUR

TRAFFIC LEAVING the metroplex was the typical North Texas congested mess of cars, trucks, work vans and delivery vehicles. A never-ending parade of people all needing to get somewhere in a hurry—all trapped in the same stop-and-go chaos. This was the part of driving that he loathed.

His friends appeared to be unaware of the traffic. They were far more concerned with switching radio stations and having minor arguments about what music to listen to. He envied them.

The City of Fort Worth loomed large up ahead. As Matt realized his traffic nightmare was coming to an end, a wave of relief flooded through him. Little by little, the traffic dispersed as vehicles exited on their way to their destinations. After what seemed like an eternity, he was finally cruising along on the interstate; the city receding in his rear-view mirror. The road stretched out before him; he could finally drive the way he preferred—about ten to twenty miles above the speed limit.

Before his eyes, the landscape transformed from dense suburban sprawl, to small, rural homes set back along narrow gravel driveways. Short, dense mesquite trees grew wild in clusters behind rusty barbed wire fencing that barely held back the cows munching away on the grass.

Matt rolled down his window and inhaled, taking in the scent of warm, desert air. If things were different, he would enjoy this part of the road trip, but this wasn't that kind of trip. He was not here to have fun.

The miles turned to hours, as it does when driving through Texas. Mountains rose far ahead in the distance. Gone were the cows and the occasional tiny farmhouse, and in their place was nothing but miles of unforgiving desert.

It had been years since Matt explored this part of the state, even then, he never ventured as far south as Sierra Diablo. Texas was large, but the vast emptiness of this region of the state was shocking even to the most seasoned traveler. Most of the towns were no longer what you could even call a town. The number of run-down and boarded-up buildings surpassed the amount of dilapidated huts that seemed to have people living in them. He couldn't help but wonder, who exactly would want to live in such a desolate place?

"Oh, look!" shouted Lauren, pointing to a road sign. "Toyah!"

"Keep on driving," said Troy.

"You sure?" teased Matt. "Not even a little run through town?" He flashed a toothy grin.

Troy glared at him.

"Aw Troy," said Lauren. "Don't worry, I'll protect you."

Matt turned the steering wheel, pretending as though he was taking the exit.

"I mean it, man," warned Troy with a shake of his head. "If you take that exit, I'm gonna have to beat your ass."

A round of laughter erupted in the jeep as Matt continued along the highway.

It was late afternoon when a sign finally came into view that read, Sierra Diablo, five miles. His backside was numb after hours of sitting in one spot. Matt shifted in his seat, then quickly realized that he shouldn't have moved, since all it did was make him even more uncomfortable. The exit appeared up ahead.

Relieved that the long drive was ending, he turned off the highway and turned down what was supposed to be the main street. From what he could see, it was the only paved road in the entire town. The dive bar that was the last charge on Ash's card loomed up ahead. From what he could tell, it was the only establishment in the entire place that was still in business. The Sheriff's station was situated just beyond that. He drove past the bar and parked in front of the run-down building.

"This town has creepy vibes all over it," said Lauren as she hugged herself tightly.

"Is that coming from the person who nearly pitched a fit when we didn't stop in Toyah?" teased Troy.

Lauren responded by sticking her tongue out at him.

"It doesn't look like anybody's home," said Sam as she sidled up alongside Matt.

The office, like everything in this area of the state, looked as though it hadn't been used for a long time. But Matt had spoken to the Sheriff less than two days ago. He knew the man was here somewhere.

He approached the door and tried the handle. It was locked. The windows were covered in so much dirt; it was impossible to see anything inside. Of course, it would be his luck that he would arrive after hours. Matt turned to his friends. "Well," he said. Looks like the office is closed for the day."

"Were they expecting you?" asked Sam.

"No," he replied, shaking his head. When he spoke with the Sheriff last time, he intentionally refrained from sharing any information about a visit. He wanted Ramirez to think he believed everything he was being told. He wanted to catch the man off guard.

"So, now what?" asked Lauren. "Do we try to call the Sheriff, or do we wait until tomorrow?"

"Looks like the bar is the only thing open," said Matt. "Let's go check it out." He stepped onto the road. "That's the one place I know for sure Ash visited."

"I'm always up for a cold beer," said Troy.

"After all that driving," said Lauren. "I could use the ladies' room." She laughed. "And then a cold beer."

Matt opted to leave the jeep parked in front of the office in case the Sheriff returned while they were at the bar. There wasn't much happening in this lifeless place, so it was a good bet that the Sheriff would know where to find them.

The air in the bar reeked of stale tobacco, rancid alcohol, and mold, making Matt's nose itch. The bartender was a burly man, exactly the sort you would imagine working in a place like this. A trio of dusty patrons sat at one end of the bar, shrouded in a cloud of cigarette smoke. At the other end of the bar sat a giant beast of a man, seemingly alone, drinking a beer. A set of leather work gloves sat atop the bar in front of him. Unlike all the other patrons in the bar, the giant man couldn't be older than thirty. He never looked up, nor did he take note of the strangers who walked in.

"Hi," said Lauren, cheerfully.

The bartender nodded slowly.

She tapped the bar top with her long fingernails. "Um, where's the—"

The rough man pointed to a door in the far corner.

Lauren smiled, then spun around and headed toward the restroom.

"Do you have a menu?" asked Sam.

"We don't have one," replied the burly man.

"Oh, okay," she replied.

"How about a round of cold beers," asked Troy.

The bartender grunted, then pulled out four chilled mugs.

Troy shifted his gaze to Matt and rolled his eyes.

"What do we owe you for these?" asked Matt, as the bartender slid the drinks across the bar.

"On the house," replied the burly man. "Consider it a parting gift before you get back on the road and head out of town."

The man's blunt manner was startling. He made it perfectly clear he didn't like strangers in his town. But Matt wasn't that easily shaken or scared off. He took a sip from his beer. "We're here to see the Sheriff," he said. "Any idea where he might be?"

The three men at the bar stopped their conversation and stared, their eyes darting nervously from Matt to the large young man sitting at the bar.

"I'm not responsible for monitoring Jorge Ramirez's movements," replied the bartender while shaking his head.

"That's okay," said Matt. "I can get with him later." He leaned against the bar. "I wanted to come here and talk to you as well."

"And why's that?" asked the burly man.

Matt offered his hand. "My name's Matt." He pulled his Texas Ranger badge from his pocket and held it out. "Matt Bennett."

The man squinted at the badge, then peered up at him. "So?"

"I'm looking for information about a girl who came through here a couple of weeks ago," said Matt. He slid a photograph of Ash across the bar.

The older man didn't bother to pick it up, nor did he even cast his eyes down at it. "Doesn't ring a bell," he said.

Matt's patience was wearing thin. He understood that people who lived in places as far out as these tended to be unfriendly, especially to law enforcement, but he hoped this would be different. "Are you sure?" he asked. "You didn't even look at the photo."

The bartender glanced over at the big man at the end of the bar, then back at Matt. "Don't need to."

"Is there anyone else who works here besides you? Maybe they saw her."

"Just me. Now, if you'll excuse me, I've got a keg to see to." Without another word, the man walked away.

"Well," said Troy. "He was both helpful and friendly."

Matt had another sip from his beer and took in his surroundings.

The trio of old curmudgeons didn't appear to be viable prospects to question. Odds were, he would get more of the same treatment from them. He studied the giant man. After another swig of beer, he decided to take his chances with him.

"Good afternoon," he said, offering his hand as he approached. "My name's Matt Bennett."

"I heard," replied the man, neither smiling nor looking up.

"What's your name?" asked Matt. Talking to these people was like trying to pull a conversation out of a rock.

"I don't see how that's necessary," replied the man.

This was going to be a real challenge, thought Matt. Undaunted, he cleared his throat and pressed on. "Well, I suppose I should just get down to business then." He pulled out Ash's photograph and tried to hand it to the man, but he didn't even look at it. His patience wearing thin, Matt placed the image on the bar top and slid it directly under the giant man's nose. "Maybe you could take a look."

The big man glared at him. He glanced down at the image, then, with the bottom of his beer glass, shoved the photo back to Matt. "Ain't seen her," he replied.

"Seems to be a lot of that going on around here," said Matt.

The big man grunted and drank his beer.

"A town like this hardly seems like it would be so busy no one would notice a pretty young visitor," prodded Matt.

Nothing.

There was something deeply disconcerting about the man. Matt had dealt enough with the worst society had to offer, to know when he was face to face with a person who was hiding something.

He scooped up the picture and put it away. "My friends and I are gonna be in town for a couple of days, so if you remember anything, call me." He slid one of his business cards across the bar.

Without even glancing at the card, the big man cocked an eye. "You're staying here? In this town?" His lips twitched with a subtle smirk. "Good luck with that."

"Do you know of any hotels nearby?" asked Matt.

The man chuckled.

"Okay, well then, I guess my friends and I will have to rough it," said Matt. "It's all good, we came ready for anything."

After downing the rest of his beer, the big man rose to his feet. He hovered above Matt, all nearly seven feet of him, and cracked his neck. With a smirk on his face, he stared down with a cunning look in his eyes. "Good luck," he said, then turned and walked out of the bar.

"He was friendly," said Troy.

It was painfully obvious that the locals would not be any help at all. Matt decided he had gotten everything he could from this group, so once everyone finished their complementary drinks, they left the bar.

TWENTY-FIVE

AS SOON AS he stepped out on the sidewalk, the sun hit Matt's face like a thousand-watt light bulb, throwing him into a photic sneezing fit.

Troy, patiently waited with the others, then asked, "You done?"

Matt slid a hand down his face and nodded.

"So, what now?" asked Troy.

"I'm not sure," replied Matt, scanning the tiny town. "There isn't much to see in this place." He turned to Sam. "It looks like we're roughing it tonight. I hope you two are up for camping."

"That's okay," she replied. "I was already planning on it."

Matt squinted up at the late afternoon sky, speculating they had about three more hours of daylight. "Let's go check out the area outside of town. Maybe we can find a place to camp there."

Before getting into the jeep, Matt took one final chance at the Sheriff's office, only to find it was still empty. He scribbled a quick note and stuck it, along with one of his cards, into the crack between the door and frame. After one more scan of the tiny Main Street, he joined his friends in the vehicle and drove out of town.

The surroundings were breathtaking. Vast desert, lined with

rocky mountains and rolling hills, he could see the draw to this place. It was curious that this area had had no sort of growth, considering Texas' expansion, to the point of overcrowding and congestion. Based on what he could see, it appeared as though this area was on a decline, or at least frozen in time. How strange, given that the rest of the state was being swarmed with suburbanites.

Lauren hung her head out the window, allowing her hair to billow in the warm wind. "It's so tranquil out here."

"I bet the night sky is a sight to behold," said Sam. "This is gonna be fun."

They turned down a gravel road, traveling south. Barbed wire fencing lined both sides of the narrow road, hemming in the cattle that grazed here and there among the hills.

"Hey," said Troy, slapping Matt's arm. "Looks like we're comin' up on a couple more of the locals."

Matt slowed and came to a stop alongside two men who were busy stringing barbed wire.

As the jeep rolled up, they paused their work. "Howdy," said a blond-haired man, pushing his baseball cap back on his head. He was young, probably somewhere between eighteen and twenty. He shot a knowing glance at his dark-haired buddy, then flashed a toothy smile. "Y'all lost?"

"Howdy," said Matt. "We're not really lost. Just taking in the gorgeous scenery."

The teen approached the jeep, setting his focus on the backseat where Sam sat with her window open. He pulled off his leather gloves and placed his hands on the door, taking the time to observe all the occupants before meeting Sam's gaze. "Hello," he said, his voice smooth. "My name's Pax. That there is Ezra." The other man gave a curt nod from the other side of the vehicle.

Matt cleared his throat. Yet another couple of locals who set his nerves on fire. Everything and everyone he came across since arriving in this town was strange. He brushed his feelings aside, telling himself it was his own bias against country folk. These men were an opportunity to find Ash. "Hello, Pax. My name's Matt." He handed one of his business cards to the teen. "Do you live around here?"

Pax studied the card. "You could say that."

Ezra snickered.

"I don't understand what's so funny," said Matt.

"It ain't nothin'," replied Pax, with a straight face. "It's just that you drove up on my family's land, then asked me if I live around here."

"Oh," said Sam. "We thought this was just a dirt road."

"It is," he replied. "But it's my dirt road." His face grew serious, then quickly flashed back to his original creepy smile. He handed the card back.

"I'm sorry," said Matt. "We didn't see any signs."

Pax nodded.

"So, your family owns this land?"

"We do," replied the teen. "Along with that." He pointed across the road, then toward a chain of rolling hills. "And those over there." He waved his arms. "Pretty much everything you can see and a lot more you can't." He stared at Matt. "You know, you should take care. People out here don't appreciate it when strangers show up unannounced and uninvited."

"We're sorry," said Matt. "We didn't mean to trespass." The Ranger in him surfaced for a moment. "You should probably post a sign, so people don't inadvertently wander onto your property unannounced."

"In case you didn't notice," said Pax, with a mischievous gleam in his eyes. "That ain't usually an issue around here."

"I suppose you've got a point," said Matt. He glanced around at the hills, recalling the reason for this whole trip. "Well, before we head back the way we came, mind if I ask you a question or two?"

"Depends on the question." Pax winked at Sam, then slowly returned his gaze to Matt. "No harm in asking."

Matt pulled Ash's photo from his pocket and held it up for the teen to see. "Have you seen this girl?" He studied Pax closely.

The teen stared down at the image. A peculiar expression swept across his face; his jaw flexed. He locked eyes with Matt. "Can't say that I have," he said, the smug look back on his face.

"Are you sure?" pressed Matt. "Because the look on your face a second ago says otherwise."

Sam gasped, and Troy shook his head.

In his mind, Matt scolded himself for being so brash. On the outside, he stood his ground, maintaining eye contact with Pax, hoping to shake the kid's confidence.

To his credit, the teen didn't even flinch. He stared back at Matt with an impish smirk. "You know, the dust out here gets in your eyes. Makes 'em twitch." The corners of his lips curled into a creepy snarl-like smirk. He stepped back from the jeep. "It's gettin' late in the day, and as you already noted, we got some work to finish. Best be on your way." he said, then turned to walk away.

"Wait!" shouted Lauren.

Pax stopped and spun around.

"You wouldn't happen to know of any campsites around here. Would you?" she asked.

Matt cringed inside at Lauren's obliviousness. Based on the gasps emitted from both Troy and Sam, they felt the same way.

A strange, almost predatory expression spread across Pax's face. "Well, if y'all want, I can show you a good camping spot. Lots of folks coming through town use it." He gestured toward the hills. "It's nice and private."

The way the teen suddenly changed his tone sent an icy chill down Matt's spine. He studied Pax, wondering if it was just him or was everyone in this dusty town as creepy as he found them to be. Whether his suspicion was because of his own prejudice, or for a good reason, Matt was unwilling to trust the kid and his friend. He flashed the friendliest smile he could muster. "Thanks for the offer," he replied. "But we've got plans already."

Pax nodded. "Suit yourself." He pointed back the way they had come. "The main road's that way." Without another word or moment's hesitation, the teen walked back to the fence and went back to work as though Matt and his friends weren't there.

Matt turned the jeep around, honked the horn twice and waved out the window, then headed back toward the main road.

"Was it just me or was that really weird?" asked Troy, staring back at the duo in the side-view mirror.

Relieved that he wasn't the only one, Matt exhaled. "It was weird alright."

"Think he knows something?" asked Sam.

"I'm not sure," replied Matt. "He is definitely weird."

Sam rubbed her arms. "The way he stared made my skin crawl."

"I thought he was kinda cute," said Lauren.

"Girl," said Troy. "You are just dying to be someone's victim. Have you no sense of self-preservation? How have you survived this long? And don't even get me started on the fact that the kid probably ain't old enough to shave every day."

Lauren shrugged. "I just said he was cute. I didn't say I wanted to sleep with him."

"Well, thank God for that," said Troy. He turned to Matt. "So, what's the plan?"

Matt wasn't sure. He pulled off to the side of the road and put the jeep into park. "Let's see if there's a campsite around here." He took out his phone. "Wow! Talk about a dead zone!"

"What did you expect? Five G?" taunted Troy. "In case you haven't noticed, we're in the middle of nowhere. It doesn't appear as though modern civilization has made it out here yet."

The realization that they had no connection to the outside world sent a shock through Matt's body. He could scarcely recall any time in his life when he was this isolated. A deep sense of foreboding settled upon him. They were out in this wilderness, untethered to civilization, with no safety net and no way to call for help. He fought back the urge to get back on the highway and drive straight to El Paso. This was the last place that he knew for sure his sister had been. He needed to stay here as long as it took to find out where she went and what happened. He clicked open his map app; a sense of ease washed over him when he saw that it worked. Thank God something did. A moment later, his hopes came crashing down when he realized there was nothing by the way of public camping sites for miles.

Troy was busy playing with his own map. "Looks like there's a defunct rest stop along this old highway right here," he said, holding out his phone.

"Where?" asked Matt, trying to zoom into the area that Troy was looking at.

Troy took Matt's phone and pulled up the site, then passed it back. "Right there."

Matt studied the map. Troy was right, there was a rest stop along a narrow highway. The road must have been the main route through the area before the interstate was made. Like it or not, that rest area was their only option if they wanted to stay in town. He glanced around at the others. "What do you think?"

Sam shrugged. "A campsite is a campsite," she said. "It's fine with me."

Troy nodded.

Matt glanced at Lauren, who nodded in agreement. "Okay then, the old rest stop it is."

TWENTY-SIX

PAX WATCHED as the jeep drove away, leaving behind a cloud of dust that hung in the air. This wasn't the first time a family member came around looking for a lost loved one, it wouldn't be the last. It was, however, the first Ranger.

"That was interesting," said Ezra.

"He's law enforcement," said Pax. "I think the other man might be too."

"Who was he looking for?"

"Jewel's friend from a couple weeks ago." Pax stared past the cloud of dust and debris, settling back down to the ground. "We need to tell Caleb." He pulled off his shirt.

"What are you doin'?" asked Ezra. "I thought we needed to tell Caleb."

"I'm gonna follow them and see where they go," replied Pax, taking off his boots and unbuckling his belt.

"Not alone you ain't."

"One of us has to go to the ranch and warn Caleb," explained Pax. "The other needs to see where these folks end up."

"We can use the hand-held."

136

"I didn't bring it," replied Pax.

"Then I'll follow the out-of-towners—"

Pax shook his head. "No!" he boomed.

Ezra sighed. "Now you know damn well Caleb ain't gonna like this." He raked his fingers through his hair. "Times like this, some reliable cell service would be really handy."

"We don't need it," said Pax, letting his jeans drop to the ground. "Besides, reliable cell service would let outsiders call for help." He grinned. "We can't have that now, can we?"

He pulled the trickster forward, savoring the pain as his bones snapped and tendons stretched. His senses were heightened. The world around him was full of vibrant colors, alive with the symphony of chirping birds and the wind rustling the long blades of grass. The air was filled with the earthy scent of dirt and rock, mingling with the delicate fragrance of desert sage and mesquite. He could feel the energy coursing through his body, making every inch tingle with life.

"Just be careful," said Ezra. He walked over to the truck. "I don't wanna be responsible if anything happens to you."

Pax dropped on all fours and completed the change. He glanced at Ezra, and gave a short nod, then took off through the field, taking care to avoid the road. Keeping his head high, he followed the trail of dust the jeep left behind. At the end of the road, he stopped and sniffed. One good thing about older vehicles was all the exhaust they emitted. He followed the scent, keeping his head below the tall grass.

A mile up the road, he found the jeep sitting idle along the shoulder. Lurking in the brush, he moved as close as possible, straining his ears to listen.

The warm breeze rustled the leaves, bringing with it the delicious scent of rabbit. He inhaled, realizing he missed lunch. The occupants of the vehicle were busy complaining about the lack of cell service. His mouth watered—the rabbit was close. He wondered whether he could grab a quick bite without losing sight of the visitors. In the end, he decided it was best to forego eating. There would be plenty of time to satisfy his hunger on the way back to the house. What mattered most right now was gathering as much information as possible for Caleb. He'd want to know where the group was staying and what weapons they had on hand. One thing was obvious, the cop and his friends weren't leaving until they found some answers about the girl. Unfortunately for them, that knowledge would cost them their lives.

The dark man's voice boomed as he suggested they find the old rest stop.

Pax crouched low and crept closer to the jeep, careful not to make a sound. The occupants were so wrapped up in their conversation; they didn't notice much of anything else, let alone the giant coyote lurking nearby. Or so he thought.

"Oh!" shouted one of the women, as she hung out the window, pointing directly at him.

Pax froze in place, every muscle in his body tensed.

The dark man leaned out his window. "It's just a coyote," he said, waving his hand dismissively. "They're probably all over these hills."

"I've never seen one this close before," said the other woman. "That is, aside from the zoo." She stared at Pax with a nervous eye. "He's huge. They don't usually come this close to humans. Do they?"

"They probably don't see many humans out here," said the dark man dismissively.

"Are we done checking out the wildlife?" asked Matt.

A moment later, the jeep pulled out onto the road again.

Pax kept pace, this time taking special care to do a better job at staying hidden. Even though he knew where they were going, he wanted to be sure they made it there before heading home.

The jeep made a sharp turn onto the old highway and came to a halt at the remains of the run-down rest stop.

Under a cluster of mesquite trees, Pax watched as the humans in the jeep climbed out of the vehicle. A waft of desert air rushed past him. The old rest stop held fond memories from his childhood. He and Caleb used to set up snares all along this area. He recalled the night when he and Jewel, angry over being excluded from all the excitement over their older brother's first turning, ran away from home. They set up a ramshackle camp among a cluster of sage brush and stayed there until their food ran out, which wasn't more than twenty-four hours. They returned home defeated, only to find the rest of their family waiting for them with open hearts and arms—and lots of fresh meat.

"Look!" shouted one of the women. "Another one!"

Pax startled from his reverie, only to find the same woman who saw him at the side of the road, staring directly at him. This woman had a keen eye.

Matt walked up alongside her and eyed Pax suspiciously.

"Is it just me or is that the same one we saw back on the road?" asked the woman.

"Not possible," scoffed Matt.

"Why is it just sitting there?" she pressed. "It's almost like it's watching us."

"It's probably just curious from all the noise we're making," said Matt.

The woman locked eyes with Pax. "It's got some creepy eyes."

"It's just a stupid coyote," said Matt. He pulled a handgun from the back of his pants. "Go on!" he shouted, waving the weapon in the air. "Get out of here!"

Pax didn't like being told what to do. His belly burned with a growing anger. He could make short work of these outsiders and end this whole thing right now.

The sudden sound of a gunshot startled him, its piercing noise amplified by his supernatural ears. Hackles up, he leered at Matt and snarled, bearing a mouthful of deadly teeth. He took one step forward, out of the brush.

Another gunshot pierced the air, and Pax could feel the ground shake beneath him as dirt erupted in a cloud around his feet. Tiny particles of dust wafted into his nostrils.

Matt leveled the gun directly at Pax's head.

Unfazed, the trickster stepped closer. Eyes locked with Matt; Pax held his ground. This outsider would not chase him away from his home.

"Don't kill it!" shouted the woman.

"What the hell is he supposed to do?" asked the dark-skinned man. "The damn thing ain't leaving. And now it looks pissed."

"He just shot at it, of course it's pissed," argued the woman. "Maybe he's hungry."

"And maybe he's hoping you're on the menu," jeered the dark man.

The woman's naivete would be the death of her, thought Pax. Some humans really were nothing more than cattle. The pack was going to enjoy hunting this group. All fun aside, it was time to head to the ranch and let Caleb know everything he learned about the visitors. Pax stared at Matt long enough to let him know he wasn't intimidated, then he turned and took off into the hills, running as fast as his supernatural body would take him.

TWENTY-SEVEN

IZZY STUDIED her reflection in the mirror, moving from side to side, gently caressing her belly. "How about Eben," she said. "After your father."

"It's only been a couple of weeks," said Caleb, wrapping his arms around her waist. "We don't even know if it's a boy or girl." He placed his hand on her belly, feeling the warm sensation of her soft skin against his palm. "You ain't even showing yet."

"I feel him in there," replied Izzy. She turned around and wrapped her arms around his neck. "A mama knows." She kissed him. "It's a boy and his name is Eben."

Caleb smiled. Izzy's tenacity was one of the many things he found attractive about her. If she said the baby growing in her belly was a boy, then it was a boy. His baby. The thought of becoming a father both excited and terrified him. What if he sucked at it as bad as he sucked at being an older brother? To her credit, Izzy wasn't apprehensive at all. In fact, her confidence over the whole thing made him believe everything would be fine. He pulled her close for a kiss, feeling her body melt against his.

Downstairs, the front door burst open, then slammed shut. "Yo, Caleb!" shouted Ezra.

Something in his tone set Caleb's hair on end. He moved away from Izzy and gazed into her eyes; the confusion on her face mirrored his own. Eager to hear whatever had his best friend in such a mood, he pulled on a T-shirt and boots. One more quick kiss, then Izzy and Caleb left the coziness of their bedroom.

Ezra stood at the bottom of the stairs, fiddling with his baseball cap, his eyes darting around nervously.

"What the hell is it?" asked Caleb, descending the stairs.

"Remember the woman that Jewel took care of?" asked Ezra.

"Ash?" shouted Jewel from the top of the stairs. She ran down and came to a stop alongside Izzy and Caleb. "What about her?"

Ezra nodded. "Her brother's in town."

"So?" asked Caleb.

"He's lookin' for her."

"And he ain't gonna find her," replied Caleb. "What's your point?"

Ezra shifted his weight from one leg to the other. "He's a Texas Ranger." He stared, waiting for a reply.

"I'm still failing to see what the problem is," replied Caleb. "We've dealt with nosy families before. Law enforcement or not, it makes no difference."

"Is it possible something's changed?" asked Ezra nervously.

"No," said Caleb. "Nothing's changed. All it means is that some dumbass, who also happens to be a Ranger, is in our town, waving his shiny badge around. He's just trying to rile folks up hoping that someone would tell him something."

"Sounds about right," said Izzy.

"What if it's an official investigation?" asked Jewel.

Caleb spun around to face his little sister. "It's not," he stated flatly.

Since the night of her first turning, he had grown closer to Jewel.

While their relationship wasn't quite what it used to be when they were younger, it was improving every day; especially now that she understood and accepted who and what she was. With acceptance came a certain sense of peace—a certain confidence. He smiled. His younger siblings were coming into their own, and it was a sight to behold. Pax. Where the hell was Pax? Caleb turned around to face Ezra.

"Where's Pax?" he asked. "Wasn't he with you working on the fence?"

"He was," replied Ezra. "He took off to follow the Ranger and his friends."

"Come again?" asked Caleb. As if struck by a match, a tiny spark of anger ignited within him. "You're here, and my little brother is out there following some rogue cop and his friends?"

Ezra took a step back. "One of us had to get word back to you."

"He's alone!" shouted Caleb.

Izzy's soft hand landed on his shoulder. "He's a man. He can handle himself."

"He's a kid!" yelled Caleb. In a fit of anger, he shook her off, instantly regretting the force he used, but he was too irritated and worried about his little brother to think about apologizing. He turned to Ezra. "What the hell were you thinking? Why didn't you just call it in on the hand-held?"

"Pax didn't bring one," replied Ezra. "The only way to get word back to you was for one of us to come back and tell you in person."

"Whose brilliant idea was it to have a kid follow the cop?"

"His," replied Ezra. "You know better than any of us how bull-headed that boy can be."

He had a point, Caleb had to agree. When it came to strength of will, Pax was in a league of his own among the men he knew. The boy was also one of the most impulsive. That was a bad mix.

"So where is he now?" asked Caleb.

"Not sure," replied Ezra.

Caleb exhaled and ran his fingers through his hair. "How long ago did y'all see the Ranger?"

"About fifteen minutes now," offered Ezra. "He was gonna follow them and find out where they were staying, then come back and let you know."

"And I'm supposed to what? Stand here with my dick in my hands, waiting to hear from him?"

"I don't see that we have any other option," said Izzy, her tone calm.

Jewel padded over to the front door. "I'll go wait outside for him," she said, as she stepped onto the front porch and slowly closed the door behind her.

Every nerve in Caleb's body was on end. The feeling of helplessness was something he despised with a passion, and unfortunately, that was exactly what he was experiencing now. Questions swirled in his head. How much longer did he have to wait? Where the hell did this cop, and his friends go? Were they armed? Was Pax okay? Was he keeping out of sight? He turned his attention to Ezra. "What's your read on this Ranger?"

"His name's Matt." Ezra shrugged. "Typical law enforcement. Overconfident, blustery, and kind of a dick."

"What about his group?"

"Another guy." Ezra held his hand level with his head. "About this tall, dark skin. Two females. Both pretty."

Izzy scoffed and placed her hands on her hips. "Think with your brain, my dear."

"Well, there you have it," said Caleb, rubbing his chin. "If he came down here with an entourage like that, he ain't here on official business."

Ezra nodded. "I hadn't thought of that. Good point."

The realization that Matt was there on his own improved Caleb's overall mood. All the same, he knew he wouldn't be able to truly relax until he saw his little brother home safe. After all, if there was one thing worse than a cop on a mission, it would be a rogue cop out for revenge.

A loud ring burst forth from the phone hanging on the wall. "Now what?" muttered Caleb as he stalked over and lifted the receiver to his ear.

"Yeah?" he said angrily.

"Good afternoon to you too," replied Sheriff Ramirez.

The old man grated on every nerve in Caleb's body. He had little patience for the man even in normal circumstances, and the current situation only made it worse. "You gonna get to your point? Or are we gonna banter back and forth like idiots?"

Ramirez cleared his throat. "There's a Ranger in town looking for his sister."

"And?"

"And," replied the Sheriff. "He stopped by the bar, waving around his credentials, asking questions."

"What did you tell him?" asked Caleb.

"I didn't tell him anything," replied Ramirez. "I wasn't in town when he came through." A round of throaty coughs erupted through the phone, followed by the sound of swallowing. "I warned you—"

"You what?" demanded Caleb.

"I—I tried to warn you," stammered the old man. "Things are changing. Something like this was bound to happen."

With every word uttered from Ramirez's mouth, Caleb's anger grew. Who the hell did he think he was? He was lucky the conversation was happening over the phone. If they were face to face, Caleb might have already ended the man.

"Stupid asshole," hissed Caleb. "I've got other things going on right now; so, aside from pissing me off, what do you want from me?"

"I want you to clean up your mess!" shouted the Sheriff. He paused and swallowed nervously.

Caleb let Ramirez stew in his own fear while he pondered the old man's fate. Maybe it was time for a new Sheriff. He would take care of that when they finished dealing with Matt and his friends. "We're already on it," he replied calmly, then without another word, he hung up the phone.

The next thirty minutes seemed to crawl. The seconds ticked by slowly; every minute felt like an hour. The only thing barring him from taking off to find Pax was the fact that he had no idea where exactly to run. Again, with the helplessness. If this was what parenthood would be like, maybe he and Izzy should rethink things.

The front door burst open. "He's back!" shouted Jewel.

Caleb was on his feet and out the door a moment later. Relief washed over him at the sight of his little brother loping up the hill toward the house. Izzy walked past him carrying a blanket and met up with Pax on the front lawn. He stopped running and changed back into his human form. Blanket wrapped around his waist; the younger man approached the house.

"You and I are gonna have a talk about what you just did," scolded Caleb.

Pax didn't back down. He stood tall in front of his older brother. "We needed the intel." He shrugged. "I opted to go."

Caleb had to admire the backbone of this young one. His little brother was growing into a man right before his eyes. All the same, if he didn't learn to control his impulses, he wouldn't live very long.

"They're setting up camp at the old rest stop," said Pax.

"Any more of them?" asked Caleb.

Pax shook his head.

"They see you?"

The expression on Pax's face answered the question. A wave of irritation crashed over Caleb. He shook his head. "Boy—"

"They thought I was a regular old coyote," blurted Pax. He snickered. "One of the women would've tried to bring me home with them if it wasn't for the men." The smile melted from his face. "Matt, the Ranger, shot at me a couple times. He's got lousy aim."

Caleb held back the urge to criticize his younger brother, it was clear Pax was enjoying this moment, there was no sense in ruining it for him.

Bass' truck emerged into sight as it slowly made its way up the driveway, leaving behind a trail of dust. He hit the horn twice and waved, then rolled to a stop. The big man sauntered up to the house. "We got some visitors," he said.

"We already know," replied Caleb. "Looks like we're huntin' tonight."

TWENTY-EIGHT

THE COYOTE SLIPPED AWAY from Matt's view, blending effortlessly into the tall, dry grass. There was something off about the creature's behavior, a part of him wondered if it was the same animal from the side of the road. Was it following them? What sort of coyotes were smart and bold enough to follow a vehicle?

"Did you see that thing?" he asked to no one in particular.

Troy raised his shoulders slightly. "It's a coyote. You'd expect to see them in a place like this." He collected a bundle of branches and stacked them beside their makeshift fire ring.

"I'm not saying it's weird that it's out here," said Matt, shaking his head. "I'm talking about its size and the way it behaved."

"What about it?" asked Sam.

"The thing was huge." Matt held out his arms. "It was bigger than a timber wolf."

"So?" asked Troy.

"So, when was the last time you heard of a coyote being that big?"

"We're in a wild place," replied Troy. He scanned the surrounding hillside. "Out here, they're apex predators. It only makes sense they would be bigger. There's no competition." He pulled a small bottle of lighter fluid from a bin.

Troy had a point; it was entirely possible that a predator out here could grow larger than the ones back home. After all, it's not like these hills were teeming with hunters, nor were there any housing subdivisions full of suburbanites to call animal control. Still, there was more to his discomfort about the creature. "Did you see the thing's eyes?" he asked. "The way it stared." Matt glanced at the spot where the coyote stood. "That was no stupid animal."

"It'd have to be smart to survive out here," argued Troy. "I think this place is getting to you. So, we saw a coyote, and it stared at us." He gave a casual shrug. "Big deal. We might be the first humans he ever saw." He doused a piece of paper with lighter fluid. After setting it on fire, he pushed the burning bundle under the carefully stacked kindling.

Matt ran his fingers through his hair. "It wasn't like that. When the thing stared at me, it was almost like it knew me. Like it was studying me."

"Babe," said Sam. "Coyotes are smart animals. Like Troy said, they're apex predators out here. It very well might have been sizing you up, but it took off." She shook her head. "We all saw it run away. It isn't coming back. You made sure of that when you fired your gun."

"Did you see how it didn't even jump when the round went off?" he asked.

Sam sighed and placed her hands on her hips. "You're not gonna let this go, are you?"

"I will if you agree it was an unusually large coyote," said Matt. "And that it was behaving strangely."

"If it'll shut you up about it, I'll agree," said Troy. He crouched over and blew gently on the fire, coaxing the flames to life. "Yeah, that's what I'm talkin' about!" he yelled in celebration.

Lauren turned away from the jeep, carrying pots and utensils. "For what it's worth, Matt," she said. "I agree with you."

Sam scoffed. "Not you too."

"You see?" said Matt. "It wasn't just me."

Troy scoffed. "Yeah, 'cause Lauren's a great source of logic."

She shoved him playfully and stuck out her tongue. "Shut up," she said. "I didn't say it was creepy. All I said was he was right; it was an unusual animal." She gazed out into the distance. "Did you know that it's been documented that coyotes sometimes hunt just for the thrill, rather than out of hunger?"

"Now why the hell would you share that tidbit of information?" asked Troy. "He's already nervous."

"I think it's kinda cool of them," replied Lauren. "It makes them very close to humans. I mean, we hunt for fun all the time."

Troy exhaled and shook his head.

"Besides," said Lauren. "I think he was majestic."

"Majestic, huh?" said Matt. "Remind me to never rely on your survival instinct."

"It was a beautiful animal."

"It was a huge fucking beast!"

"Okay, okay," said Sam. "No need to get so riled up. Majestic or beastly, it doesn't matter," she said, wrapping her arms around him. "The thing is gone. And we're here, with good friends and a warm fire." She tilted her chin up to the sky. "I can't wait for dark, that sky is gonna be amazing."

The sun was low on the horizon, Matt stared up at the orange and red sky, admiring the distinct beauty of the west Texas sunset. His mind wandered back to all the warm summer nights back home in Frisco. He and Ash would sit outside and watch the sunset, competing over who could see more colors.

Ash. He could feel his heart sinking, a heavy weight dragging him down. Deep in his gut, he knew something bad happened. If she was okay, she would've reached out to him by now, knowing full well he would be worried. Alive or dead, he needed to know the truth. Every day that went by without her, a deep hole grew in the center of his heart, threatening to swallow up everything in its wake. He closed his eyes and wondered if he would ever feel happiness or hope again.

"Earth to Matt," said Sam, softly. "Where's your head?"

"Just remembering all the time Ash and I would watch the sunset when we were kids."

Sam placed her head against his shoulder.

"Hear that?" asked Lauren.

"Hear what?" replied Troy.

"Shh, shh," she said with a finger to her lips.

Troy leaned close. "I don't hear anything."

"That's what I mean," she replied. "Hear all the silence?"

Across the fire, Matt perked up his ears and listened. She was right, there was no sound. Surely there would be crickets or frogs or some sort of desert creatures out here making a ruckus. Nature was noisy. Dead silence was unnatural.

"Why is it so quiet?" asked Sam.

"Because we're in the middle of the desert," replied Troy. "What did you expect?"

Matt shook his head. "I think she means there should be some sound, but there is none."

"That's what's so weird," said Lauren. "It's kind of eerie."

"Maybe it's just that time of year," offered Sam. "You know, maybe it's not quite mating season."

"Maybe," agreed Lauren, her tone unconvinced.

"Well," said Troy. "On the bright side, we'll know if something wanders into our camp."

The conversation paused as everyone sat listening to the silence.

"Okay, so," said Lauren. "Creepy factor aside—what did we bring to eat?"

"Yes," said Sam. "I'm starving."

Troy climbed to his feet. "There's food in the cooler in the jeep. While it's still light enough to see without a flashlight, Matt and I will collect some more wood. Would y'all mind figuring out what you wanna eat and get it ready while we do that?"

Sam and Lauren immediately jumped to their feet while Matt followed Troy over to the perimeter of their camp.

The sight of the old picnic tables, their wood tops and benches warped and rotted, added a sense of decay to the surroundings. He tried to imagine what this place must have been like in its heyday, which he assumed was probably sometime during the seventies.

He traced his finger along a set of initials carved into a dried plank of wood. "I bet these would burn good," he said aloud.

"Well, don't just stand there," said Troy. "Get to gatherin' some of it. Dinner ain't gonna cook itself and it sure as hell ain't gonna cook without a fire. I'm starving."

Matt tugged on the plank, to his surprise, it came away in his hands easily. One down. He glanced around, noting all the broken tables. Plenty more to go. As he stepped toward the next table, something crunched under his boot. He glanced down to find a cell phone. That wasn't something he expected to come across in such a dilapidated place. He bent down and picked it up, then gasped, recognizing the pink, jewel encrusted case. It was Ash's phone.

Troy reacted to the strange sound Matt just made by asking, "What's up? Is that a phone?"

Matt swallowed, feeling his throat tighten as if a vice were squeezing it. He rolled the device around in his hand. "It's Ash's," he choked.

"What?" blurted Troy. "Are you sure?"

Matt nodded. He hit the home button and the tiny screen lit up, then swiped his finger across the cracked glass and input the passcode. The phone came to life in his hand. "She was here," he said incredulously. A profound feeling of despair took hold of him as tears pooled in his eyes. He spun around, searching. "She was here!"

"Who was?" asked Sam as she and Lauren ran up to Matt's side.

"Ash," replied Troy in a subdued voice.

Sam took a sharp breath. "Oh, my god! Is that her phone?"

Matt's thoughts twisted and churned; his emotions raged. She was here. His little sister was here, right in this spot. Panic filled his chest. Where did she go from here? What the hell happened to her? His heart was racing, making it difficult for him to catch his breath. He crumpled to his knees and pressed the phone against his chest. She was here! She was here!

TWENTY-NINE

THE SKY WAS ABLAZE with yellow, orange, and deep red. It won't be long now, thought Caleb. According to Pax, the outsiders had set up their camp at the old rest stop. How convenient, they set themselves up directly at his back door. This was going to be a tricky hunt with at least one member of law enforcement among the group, possibly two. He knew Matt was armed with a handgun; he didn't know if any of the others were carrying, so they would have to proceed with caution until they knew for sure. Not that a basic handgun was a hazard to any of them in their trickster form, firearms were only perilous when they were in human form.

He gazed up at the sky, noting the slight purple hue overtaking the deep red. Caleb propped his feet up on the porch rail and relaxed against the chair, watching Pax, Ezra, and Bass by the fire pit. He didn't want to say it aloud, for fear his praise would encourage more of the behavior, but his little brother impressed the hell out of him. It was probably time that Caleb came to terms with the fact that Pax was no longer a little boy. The screen door behind him creaked open.

"I want to come tonight," said Jewel as she settled into the chair next to him.

"We talked about this."

"No, we didn't," she blurted. "You talked about it; as usual, I could only listen."

Caleb's patience for younglings was wearing thin, and he refused to put up with this any longer. As much as Pax had matured, Jewel was still very much a child. Having only recently turned for the first time, she wasn't ready for a full-scale hunt. "No," he stated flatly.

"Why not?" asked Jewel. "Pax is going."

"Pax is different."

"Because he's a boy?"

Caleb stared at his sister, trying to see anything other than a little girl. "You're not ready," he said.

"Yes, I am," she argued. "Need I remind you, I'm the one who took out that Ranger's sister."

The prideful tone in his little sister's voice made him smile. It was good to see her finally accepting who and what she was. That aside, it was far too early for her to go on a hunt. She just wasn't ready. There was a considerable risk involved if she were to come along, as she could put herself and the hunt in jeopardy. He shook his head.

"Give me one good reason, why not!"

"You're inexperienced."

Jewel huffed. "How the hell am I supposed to get experience if you won't let me get experience?"

"This one is different," he said. "At least one of 'em is law enforcement, which means he's had training. He's also probably full of emotions over his sister's disappearance."

"So? You and I both know guns aren't a threat to us."

Caleb sighed; strong-headedness ran in the family. "So, anything could go wrong at any moment. If it does, I don't want you getting caught in the way."

She folded her arms. "I can handle my own."

The screen door swung open again and Izzy walked outside carrying a cold beer. She smiled at him. "What are we talkin' about?" she asked as she handed over the bottle.

"Caleb's being an asshole," said Jewel.

Izzy smirked. "Yes, he does have a tendency to be that way from time to time."

"He's being a jerk," said Jewel, pouting. "He acts like I'm a little kid."

"That pouty face of yours doesn't exactly scream adult," said Caleb.

"I'm sure he's coming from a place of love," replied Izzy. She flashed him a warning glare.

Caleb scoffed and Jewel scowled.

"I've already explained it to you," said Caleb.

"Bullshit!"

"How about a compromise?" asked Izzy.

"Like what?" asked Jewel suspiciously.

Izzy studied Caleb. "She can stay with me. I'll keep an eye on her."

He shook his head. "If she's not experienced enough to be with me, then being with you is even worse."

With an angry huff, Jewel jumped to her feet and paced in a circle.

Izzy stared at him in confusion. She wasn't quite grasping his point. It was time to be blunt. He sighed and resigned himself for the coming barrage of anger. He locked eyes with her. "I've been thinkin' about it. You two are gonna stay home tonight."

"Now he's telling you what to do!" shouted Jewel.

Irritation swept across Izzy's face.

Before his eyes, Caleb watched as the flicker of irritation gave way to tightly controlled anger.

"Let me be clear," said Izzy, with an icy tone. "When I go out for the hunt tonight, Jewel will run with me." She glared at him in defiance. "I'll keep her safe."

Caleb shook his head. "Neither of you are going out on this one." He glared at Jewel. "You both are staying right here. And that's the final word on this." He stared at Izzy, but the way she glared back told him that wasn't the final word.

"Jewel, sweetie," said Izzy with a soft voice. "Would you give your brother and I a minute alone?"

Jewel smirked. "Yes." She stood up and stuck her tongue out at Caleb.

"You're only making my point here," he taunted.

As the door shut, Izzy spun around to face him, her face contorted in a mask of rage.

"We need to get something straight," she said, poking a slender finger into his chest. "I make my own decisions. You do not do that for me. Are we clear?" Her eyes glowed as a little of the trickster came out.

Caleb could hardly recall a time when she looked so pissed. "I just want you safe—"

"Not your job."

"The hell it ain't!" he yelled. His anger swelled inside, threatening to bubble over into a confrontation he didn't want to have. He pressed it down. "Look, Izzy, I realize your people do things a little different from mine, I'm trying to do my job and make sure you two are safe." He pointed to her belly.

"Then you know that we're safest when I've changed," she replied. "Nothing can harm us when we're in our trickster form. It's more dangerous to walk around like this." She gestured with her hand.

He could think of no counter argument.

Her posture eased up. She climbed onto his lap and wrapped her soft arms around his neck. "I have just as much interest in keeping both of us safe." She kissed his neck. "Maybe more."

"You're not gonna take no for an answer. Are you?" he asked, pulling back to peer directly into her eyes.

She shook her head.

Caleb sighed. "One of 'em's a cop. That might add an extra level of difficulty."

"We'll hang back," she replied. "She'll be safe with me."

"And who's gonna keep you safe?"

Without another word, Izzy climbed off his lap and gave him a sly wink before disappearing inside the house.

Once again, he was alone with his thoughts. The vibrant colors of sunset had disappeared, and in their place was a cool blue that was rapidly turning dark. He mulled over the conversation with Izzy, her strength was one of the many reasons he found her so attractive. She had a feral streak that was both terrifying and fascinating.

A slight smile spread across his face as he recalled the first time he laid eyes on her.

The October sky was clear and dark, a vast expanse of darkness adorned with a dazzling array of stars. Standing alone at the edge of the highway, Caleb inhaled deeply, filling his lungs with the calm and quiet of the desert. The air was crisp, carrying a hint of earthy fragrance that mingled with the faint scent of distant wildflowers.

He took a long swig from his flask, then wiped his mouth with the back of his sleeve and shoved the slim bottle into his pocket. This was where he was meant to be; surrounded by the west Texas mountains and rolling hills. He wasn't meant to be a rancher, let alone a father figure, for two young kids who clearly didn't want that from him.

From the moment of his first turning, his mind was consumed with the desire to live a life completely devoid of responsibilities. A life filled with hunting and traveling; just him, the open road, and an endless parade of prey. But here he was, barely a full-fledged adult and burdened with responsibilities he never asked for.

It wasn't as though there were no other options for the care of his siblings. Their uncle Weston should have been the one to step up, but for some reason, he hadn't come around in almost a year. In fact, the last time Caleb had laid eyes on the man was during the funeral. As soon as the boxes went into the ground, the older man strolled over to his truck and drove away.

Caleb didn't mind that much, if he were to be completely honest, he cared little for his uncle Weston. Something about the man made his skin crawl. He reeked of lies and manipulation.

The pulsating beat of music reached his ears long before the vehicle appeared. Caleb lifted his gaze out on the horizon, his body vibrating with excitement as he saw the headlights come into view. Eyes locked on his target, he stuck his thumb out and waited.

It was a large camper van, one of the newer, fancy models, not the old type from the nineteen seventies. The vehicle rolled closer, coming to a stop two yards in front of him. From where he was standing, Caleb could see the driver was a young man, who looked about his age. A pretty young woman sat next to him in the passenger seat. The license plate told him they were from California.

He pulled the trickster forward, peering into the darkness in the back of the van. Gradually, he discerned the unmistakable silhouettes of another man and woman, accompanied by a mysterious shadowy figure.

The shadow shifted in the back, then a beautiful woman leaned forward, positioning herself between the driver and passenger. She met his gaze with a cunning grin and a pair of shimmering amber eyes.

Well, this was new. Not once in all his months of hunting alone did he encounter one of his own. Curiosity piqued, he casually walked over to the vehicle and peered inside. With a calculating eye, his gaze shifted from the two in the front seat to the mesmerizing creature in the back.

"Need a ride?" asked the driver.

Caleb shifted his body and locked eyes with the driver. "I most certainly do," he replied.

"I guess you're lucky we came along," said the man. He peered around at the vast, open space that surrounded them. "I'd suck to be left out here all night." He moved his gaze up and down Caleb's body, then smiled and said, "Well, hop on in."

The side door to the van slid open, revealing a shiny, modern interior. On the sofa, a woman with short, dark hair sat next to another man. With welcoming smiles, they motioned for Caleb to enter. Needing no prompting, he climbed inside, taking a seat on the bed alongside the dark-haired beauty.

"Alright, that's it," said the man on the sofa. "There's no more room in here. First Izzy, and now him; we're all out of room. If we come across another hitchhiker, they're going to have to fend for themselves." He glanced around. "Is it just me, or is it weird that we keep running into random hitchhikers out here?"

"Excuse my boyfriend," said the driver over his shoulder. "He doesn't like cramped spaces."

"I've also seen far too many horror movies," added the man on the sofa.

"I'm Margot," said the woman in the passenger seat. She pointed to the driver. "This is Ty." She gestured toward the other woman on the sofa. "That's his sister Claire, and the one doing all the whining is Michael."

Caleb nodded in greeting to everyone, then turned his attention to the beautiful creature beside him. "And you are?" he asked.

"Izzy," she replied.

"What's your name?" asked Margot.

"Caleb," he responded, keeping his gaze fixed on Izzy.

As the van pulled onto the highway, Izzy and Caleb bumped into each other. A flash of heat to exploded in his belly, spreading rapidly throughout his body.

"So, Caleb," asked Margot. "Where're you heading?"

Eyes still locked on Izzy, he replied smoothly, "Wherever you want to take me."

"That's a little weird," said Michael. "Did you mean that literally, or were you just hitting on her?"

"A little of both," replied Caleb, smoothly. "I don't live far from here. I went for a short walk, and it ended up getting dark. When y'all came along, I figured it couldn't hurt to hitch a quick ride."

"Ah, a local," said Izzy.

"Where'd they gather you from?" he asked, truly intrigued as to how such a beauty could have gone unnoticed by him. Caleb was sure he knew every trickster family in the valley.

She flashed a sweet smile. "I grew up in Oklahoma."

He nodded in understanding. He had heard of families of tricksters who lived in Oklahoma, but he never met any. The only thing he knew about them was that they clung to the old ways, preferring to live independently from humans. They were feral. They had no desire to mingle, instead preferring to live on their own as if there were no such thing as modern conveniences. No one knew exactly how many clans lived up there; as far as Caleb knew, no one cared to find out.

"Tell you what," said Caleb. "It's getting kind of late, and the nearest hotel is at least two hours' drive from here. I can set y'all up at the edge of our ranch to camp for the night."

"Two hours?" asked Michael.

"At least," replied Caleb.

"I'm in," said Margot, followed by Ty and Claire.

Michael remained silent; he studied Caleb with a wary eye. "I don't know," he said. "I kinda had my heart set on relaxing poolside with a margarita. It's been a long day riding back here."

"I'll make you a margarita," said Ty. "We have all we need to spend the night off grid. Besides, since we got this thing, we've yet to do that, we're always staying in hotels. I wanna camp for once."

"Okay Caleb," said Margot. "Looks like you're the co-pilot." She moved out of the passenger seat and worked her way back to the bed where she settled her body between Caleb and Izzy.

There was a moment where he imagined ripping the stupid woman's throat out for being so intrusive, but that would ruin the fun. With a wink of encouragement from Izzy, Caleb took his new spot in

the passenger seat up front. From there, he calmly guided the blissfully ignorant occupants of the van to their death.

"Stop here," he said. "I gotta open the gate." Without another
word, he jumped out of the vehicle. The air, tranquil and refreshing,
held a gentle breeze that brushed against his skin. It was the perfect
temperature for a fire. He inhaled, filling his lungs with the scent of
desert sage and mesquite.

"Come on, don't dawdle," called Margot from the van. "I gotta go
pee."

"Is there ever a time when you don't have to pee?" asked Ty
jokingly. "Seriously, you must have a bladder the size of a walnut."

Caleb unwrapped the chain and swung the gate wide, then he
waved the van through. As soon as it passed, he quickly swung the
gate closed and re-wrapped the chain. "Just drive straight up this
road," he said through the window. "You can park anywhere."

"Aren't you getting in?" asked Ty.

"Nah," he replied, shaking his head. "I'll meet y'all up there." He
flashed a smile and winked. "Margot's not the only one who has a
small bladder."

A round of laughter erupted from inside the van as it rolled past
him, following the narrow road.

Alone with his thoughts, Caleb pondered the events of the
evening so far. Izzy was a pleasant surprise, an intriguing addition to
what was setting up to be an interesting night. As her face occupied
his thoughts, his body instinctively reacted, manifesting a myriad of
physical sensations. He could hardly wait to see her in her trickster
form.

When he sauntered into the campsite, the others were in full setup mode.

Michael was insistent on setting up his hammock, but the
absence of large trees made it difficult to find a suitable location. Ty
struggled to explain this to him, but Michael remained unwilling to
listen.

A few yards away, Claire and Margot, with the help of Izzy, were busy building the fire ring.

"Just in time," said Izzy. She stood up and brushed her hands off on her jeans, then reached out and took hold of Caleb's hand and said, "You and I are gonna go collect some wood for the fire."

She didn't have to do much coaxing because Caleb was more than happy to go wherever she wanted. In fact, he would have walked away from his prey completely, if it meant he could spend the rest of the night in Izzy's arms.

"So, how are we gonna do this?" she asked as soon as they were out of earshot of the others.

He hadn't really thought through that part. His first inclination was always to just play it by ear, when things heated up, they took their own route, anyway. "I suppose we could just dive right in." he said, half fooling around and half not. If he were being honest, ever since laying eyes on Izzy, she was all he could think about. Every inhale was filled with her scent; every thought was about her. His desire for hunting had almost dissipated, replaced with a desire for something else.

Izzy stopped abruptly, spun around to face Caleb, and pressed her lips firmly against his.

His initial surprise quickly gave way to a rush of heat that consumed his entire body. The trickster in him had awakened in a way he had never experienced before, and he was more than ready to surrender.

She pulled away; her eyes glowing as she stared up at him. "Now that we got that out of the way, we can focus on what we came here to do."

"You mean this ain't it?" he replied. He faked confusion. "Oh, you're talkin' about the people over there," he said as he pointed. He snaked his arms around her waist and pulled her body close. "I kinda like what's goin' on here."

Izzy shook her head and sighed playfully. "As tempting as that is, I didn't put up with their stupid banter for the past two hours just so I can let them go on their way. I intend to get what I came here for." She leaned close and kissed Caleb on the lips. "After that, we can do whatever we want."

A piercing whistle cut through the air, and Ty's voice echoed, "Are you guys alright out there?"

The sound of laughter could be heard, followed by playful chatter. Caleb didn't bother to hear what they were saying, the only thing he cared about was standing right in front of him. Resigned to doing whatever Izzy wanted, he quickly gathered some logs in his arms, then followed her back to the others.

"We thought you two got eaten by a bear or something," said Margot.

"That's ridiculous," scoffed Michael. "There're no bears out here. This is the desert." He glanced into the darkness that surrounded them. "There might be mountain lions, though."

"Nah," said Caleb. "There ain't any of those around. They've all been hunted or chased away."

"Really?" asked Claire. "Interesting. So, there are no predators left out here?"

"Oh, there're predators," replied Caleb. "They're just really good at hiding in places you'd least expect. They like to stalk their prey, taking their time to choose the right one, then, when the moment is right, they attack."

"Okay," said Michael. "It doesn't sound like we're talking about animals anymore." He glanced around at his friends nervously.

Ty kissed the side of Michael's head and laughed. "Don't worry, I'll protect you," he said. "I wouldn't let anything happen to you."

Caleb watched as Izzy's face lit up with a wicked smile, her eyes sparkling mischievously. Unnoticed by the others, her nails grew long and deadly. She wrapped her arm around Michael's shoulder and pulled him close. "Challenge accepted," she said calmly, then with one swift motion, she swiped her claw across Michael's throat. Thick, hot blood exploded into the air, showering down upon the group, and splashing into the flames.

A scream erupted, Caleb wasn't entirely sure which woman had let it loose, as he was far too enthralled with Izzy's transformation. The scent of fear in the air was intoxicating.

Both Margot and Claire jumped to their feet and bolted into the darkness, all the while screaming and crying. Ty leaped to his feet and bolted for the safety of the van, only to find himself face to face with Caleb.

"Now where do you think you're going?" he asked through a mouthful of sharp teeth.

Trembling, the terrified man took a step back, only to bump right into Izzy.

She wrapped her arms tightly around him, pinning his arms at his side. "Fast or slow?" she asked in a playful tone.

Ordinarily, slow, and painful would have been Caleb's answer. But on this night, he wanted to dispatch these humans and get on with the real fun of the evening. "I yield to whatever the lady desires," he said with a low bow.

Izzy ran her tongue along Ty's neck, causing the man to recoil in fear. She peered up at Caleb with glowing eyes, then opened her mouth and bit deep into Ty's neck. With a sharp jerk, she pulled back, tearing his throat wide open. She released the man, letting him drop to the ground, all the while gasping and clutching uselessly at his neck.

Her face covered in fresh blood, she stepped over the dying man's body and kissed Caleb deeply.

Unable to control the trickster, and unwilling to try, Caleb let himself transform completely. His senses on high alert, his entire body was on fire. With Izzy by his side, he took off after the two women. With all the screaming and crashing about in the dark, it was an easy task to take care of them.

When all was done, the young couple spent the rest of the night together, under the stars, surrounded by the bodies of their prey. From that night, forward, she was a permanent fixture in his life.

Resigned to having no control over the situation, Caleb finished what remained of his beer and joined the others by the fire pit.

"Looked like you were getting worked over pretty hard back there," teased Bass, grinning from ear to ear.

"I see you came to help," said Caleb.

Bass put his hands in the air. "I ain't goin' up against Izzy." He shook his head. "Not even for you. I like my head right where it is. Besides, I'm the good-looking twin."

Caleb had to agree, Izzy was a force to be reckoned with. She certainly didn't need anyone keeping her safe. He snickered at himself for being so stupid. She didn't need him—he needed her.

"So, is Jewel coming with us tonight?" asked Pax.

Caleb nodded. "Looks like it." He watched the smile spread across his little brother's face. At least he was happy with the idea.

Bass howled.

"Looks like it's time," said Pax, his eyes glowing with excitement.

Caleb pulled off his T-shirt, reveling in the surge of energy coursing throughout his body. He popped his jaw to make room for his growing teeth, then stripped down the rest of the way.

The door to the house swung open, then Izzy and Jewel spilled out and joined the others by the fire.

With eyes glowing in the moonlight, the pack stood in a circle and patiently waited for his signal.

Caleb inhaled, filling his lungs with clean night air. He released a long howl; the others responded, then the pack took off into the hills.

The earth was soft between his claws, tall blades of grass tickled his nose, each leap releasing a bouquet of desert scents. In trickster form, every sense was heightened. He was more alive in this form than the human one. He thought back to a time when he dreamed of staying in coyote form forever. The elders warned him against that. There were tales of tricksters who failed to return to their human form, opting instead to remain animal. They eventually became feral and disappeared into the mountains, never to be seen again. At the time, he struggled to understand why that was a bad thing.

Caleb stopped at the crest of a hill, down below, the rest stop was plainly visible. He called out. One by one, the others responded, their calls echoing in the darkness. He crept closer, breathing in the scent of his prey. City people had a distinct stench to them—a sickly sweet odor. Given how much perfume and floral scented laundry soap they used, he supposed they must know this.

He hovered in the darkness, studying the campers. It wasn't smart to jump right in, particularly since both Jewel and Izzy were by his side. Caution was the way to proceed.

The group of campers were in a heated discussion. He focused his ears to listen, picking up most of their conversation. Apparently, they had found something that belonged to Ash. He inched closer, the anticipation building as he observed the campers, unseen, and patient, waiting for the right moment to strike.

THIRTY

SEATED ON THE DUSTY GROUND, Matt slowly flipped the phone around in his hand.

Ash was here.

From the first day of her disappearance, he knew instinctively that something terrible had happened to her. On some level, he hoped he was wrong, but holding her phone, brought the painful reality crashing down on him—he would never see his sister again. Profound sadness and absolute rage stirred in his heart. He would find whoever or whatever was behind this, and he would stop at nothing to ensure that they paid the price in the most painful way possible.

Matt rose to his feet and studied the area, his eyes falling on an object suspended in a cluster of prickly pear cactus. He reached down to retrieve a small, stuffed rabbit. Dried droplets of blood were splattered like freckles all over its brown fur. Its soft ears had patches of baldness.

A mournful smile spread across his face as he recalled a stuffed bear in similar condition. B.B. the bear. Ash didn't go anywhere without him. Whenever she grew tired, she would rub one of the ears between her tiny fingers until she fell asleep. Over time, this created small areas of patchy baldness, exactly like the ears of this rabbit.

Sorrow threatened to overwhelm him. He laid the toy reverently on the ground and wiped his hands on his jeans. As far as he could tell, there was nothing more to find here.

"What do we do now?" asked Sam, with a gentle tone. "Should we go back to town and get the sheriff?"

"Did you see a sheriff when we were there?" asked Troy.

"He's right," said Matt. "We're on our own out here."

"Well then," said Sam. "What do we do?"

Matt launched the map app on Ash's phone and searched the history. Based on what he could gather, she was making her way to the highway. It was highly unlikely she ever made it. He went a little farther back in her history and found a search for a random spot on one of the many back roads around the area. He switched to the satellite view, and zoomed in. As far as he could see, there was nothing there. The location wasn't far from where they stood.

An eerie feeling crept up on him as he recalled the encounter with the local named Pax. He said something about owning a large amount of land in the area. In this area.

Matt moved the map over to the road, where they met up with the two men. It could very well be all the same plot of land. But out in the middle of nowhere, with no internet, there was no way of accessing county records to view plot maps.

"I think we should go to this area," he said, showing the map to Troy. This was the last place she searched for before looking for the highway."

Troy stared down at the screen. "You think we'll find anything there?"

"Your guess is as good as mine," replied Matt. "But it's all we got to go on right now."

"It's a start, at least," said Troy.

"Hey guys," called out Lauren. "Looks like he's back."

"Who is?" asked Troy.

Lauren pointed and took a step forward, only to be halted when Sam seized her arm.

Matt glanced across the road and found himself eye to eye with a large coyote. The creature stared at him with glowing eyes. This time, he was sure it wasn't a simple animal; this one was smart—scary smart.

"Uh, Matt?" said Troy, cautiously. "We got a problem."

Several yards away stood a second coyote, this one was easily double the size of the first one. The beast stared in that same cunning way, sending an icy chill down Matt's spine. There was nothing natural about this encounter.

A third emerged like a phantom from the thicket.

Lauren gasped, "There's another one!"

Matt turned around to see yet another coyote staring directly at him. This one wasn't hiding in the grass. It made no effort to protect itself, instead it sat calmly in the center of the road a few yards away from the jeep. Two smaller coyotes flanked him on either side. As Matt watched the animal, he got the clear impression the beast was studying him.

"Maybe they want food," said Lauren.

"Something tells me they ain't lookin' for chips and beer," said Troy.

Matt stood spellbound, staring into the eyes of what he suspected was the alpha coyote. He couldn't help but wonder if this pack had anything to do with his sister's disappearance.

"That makes six," said Troy.

"What are we going to do?" asked Sam.

Matt locked eyes with Troy just as his friend pulled his gun from the back of his belt. Remembering his own, he reached behind, all the while keeping his eyes locked on the coyote in the middle of the road.

Troy fired a warning shot into the sky.

His ears ringing in protest, Matt flinched, but the beast didn't move at all. As far as he could tell, the creature was completely unfazed. He knew little about coyotes, but he was damn sure the sound of a gunshot would be enough to make any animal flee for cover. Not only did this one show no fear, but it also even seemed to mock them with a wide yawn. Matt could swear it was smirking at him.

"We need to get into the jeep," he called over his shoulder. "Now!" He pointed his gun directly at the coyote and stared down the site, aiming for the center of the animal's chest.

"Matt!" shouted Sam. "Come on!"

He cast a quick glance behind him, taking note that the others were already climbing into the vehicle. When he looked back at the beast, he was surprised to see the animal was now standing. The creature lowered its head, revealing a menacing snarl and a mouth full of long, deadly teeth as it approached.

Another shot rang out. This one hit the ground inches from the feet of the coyote.

As though nothing had happened, the beast prowled forward, its muscles tense and ready to strike.

Matt stared in astonishment, spellbound by the whole spectacle of such a powerful and fearless predator.

"Get over here!" shouted Sam.

"Matt!" yelled Troy. "Step aside so I can get a clear shot!"

The beast was close enough that if it desired, it could pounce on him and tear his throat out before anyone could do anything.

With his heart racing in his chest, Matt stood his ground. He needed to get to the jeep, but he would not show any fear.

From the chest of the beast came a menacing growl, resonating with an eerie intensity. Its eyes glinted pale blue in the moonlight. Hackles up, it crouched, then launched into the air, flying directly for Matt.

A gunshot rang out. Thick red blood exploded from the side of the animal, raining down all over Matt. The coyote landed on its feet and cast a quick glance at its side. Blood stained its mottled brown fur, yet the beast showed no sign of pain or distress.

"Matt!" screamed Sam.

With a sneer, the coyote crouched down, its muscles tensing as it prepared for another leap.

Behind him, the horn blasted. Matt pivoted and ran for the jeep while Troy, leaning out the driver's window, provided cover, buying just enough time for Matt to jump into the vehicle. He slammed the door closed right before one of the beasts crashed into the side.

Lauren screamed.

"Drive!" shouted Matt.

Troy hit the gas pedal and pulled a U-turn, only to come to an abrupt stop, throwing Matt against the windshield.

The alpha coyote stood firm in the middle of the road, its teeth bared in a vicious snarl, its eyes glimmering in the headlights. How could this be? How was that thing not injured? Matt watched the bullet strike the creature. Droplets of the beast's blood were splattered all over his body. It should be dead or mortally wounded, not standing alert in front of them, ready to attack again.

The small hairs on Matt's arms stood on end, hot rage building up in his stomach. In his gut, he knew these creatures were the reason his sister disappeared.

"Hold on!" shouted Troy.

Matt clutched the bar above his head as the jeep sped straight toward the animal.

The coyote crouched low, waiting until the very last moment, then sprang into the air as the jeep passed over the exact spot it had occupied. A heavy bump on the roof told Matt that the beast had landed on top of their vehicle.

Troy swerved. Nails gently tapped on the metal above their heads, followed by a long, deafening scrape all the way down the roof, then silence.

As he watched in amazement through the rearview window, the alpha landed smoothly on his feet and receded behind them.

It wasn't until they had driven nearly three miles before Troy allowed himself to slow down. He pulled over to the side of the road, leaving the engine running.

"What the fuck was that?!" he yelled, still holding onto the steering wheel with a tight grip.

"Why are we stopped?" cried Lauren.

"She's right," said Sam. "We need to keep driving. Those things could be right behind us."

"We need to head back to town," said Lauren.

"And do what there?" asked Troy.

"I don't know," she said. "Get some help or something."

"There is no help!" shouted Matt. He pressed his finger to his lips and held up his other hand, and said, "Listen."

There was no sign of the pack.

"I think we left them back there," he said, unsure if he honestly believed his own words or not.

Troy shook his head. "Those were not normal coyotes."

"No, they weren't," agreed Matt. "I think that's what happened to Ash and her friends."

Sam gasped. "So, if they weren't normal coyotes," she said. "What the hell were they?"

"I don't know," replied Matt. He stared at Troy. 'You shot that thing. I saw the bullet hit it in its side." He wiped his hand across his forehead and pulled it away to show blood. "But it never even flinched. Something isn't right about them. It's almost like they have some sort of supernatural strength."

Troy scoffed. "Now you're sounding like Lauren."

"Hear me out," said Matt. "What if those things are tied to the creepy kid we met earlier?"

"Like how?" asked Sam.

Matt didn't know. He realized how crazy this sounded. He wasn't sure he understood what he was saying himself. A few hours ago, the mere mention of supernatural coyotes would have made him burst into laughter.

A lone howl erupted in the night, followed by another and then another.

"We need to get out of here now!" shouted Lauren, her voice

hysterical.

Something heavy landed on the roof. The distinct sound of careful footsteps could be heard overhead. With a soft thump, a coyote landed on the hood of the jeep. The beast pivoted to glare into the window.

The bloodstain on its side told Matt that this was the alpha again. This creature was fearless. It leered at him through the windshield, baring its teeth, its eyes glowing with intelligence. He was more convinced than ever that these were not simple coyotes.

Troy hit the gas, peeling out onto the road, spewing a cloud of gravel and dust in their wake.

The monster stood firmly on the hood, digging its claws into the metal to maintain its grip.

"You think you can hold on, motherfucker?" shouted Troy. "Hold this!" He slammed the brakes.

The abrupt stop tore the beast away from the hood and flung it toward a tree on the side of the road. Its body slammed against the trunk, then slumped to the ground in a heap.

"Ha, ha!" shouted Troy. "Take that! You mangey motherfucker!"

Matt watched in horror as the creature gradually regained its strength and pulled itself up onto its feet. It gazed back at him and fired off a volley of yips. How could this be? Animals don't laugh, but this one clearly was.

"Go, go, go!" he shouted.

Once again, Troy hit the gas, sending the jeep barreling down the dark country road at warp speed. Matt kept his eyes on the road behind them until he couldn't see any sign of the pack.

"Slow down," he warned Troy.

The vehicle didn't slow down.

"Troy!" shouted Matt. "You're going way too fast for out here."

The road curved abruptly to the left. Troy spun the steering wheel trying to keep control of the vehicle, but the turn was too tight, and they were going too fast. The jeep swerved, then veered off the road, rolling over twice, finally slamming to a stop amid a cluster of mesquite trees.

Matt crashed into the windshield so hard it cracked. Blood flooded his vision. His head was swimming. All around him were the muffled sounds of his friends. He shook his head and wiped the blood from his eyes. Beside him, Troy was barely conscious, his head bleeding. In the back seat, Lauren and Sam were okay.

"Come on, brother," said Matt, gently tapping his friend.

Troy blinked his eyes and lifted his head. "Is everyone okay?"

"Yeah, I think so," replied Sam.

"Shit!" shouted Troy. "Now what?"

"We're stuck!" cried Lauren.

"Everyone stay calm!" shouted Matt. "We're okay."

"No!" shouted Lauren. "We're not!"

Sam slapped her across the face, leaving Lauren to sag against her door, whimpering.

Unable to open his door, Matt resorted to climbing through his window. Once outside, he carefully examined the punctured holes in the jeep's hood, where the alpha had perched. A solitary claw was firmly lodged in the cold, metal surface. With a determined grip, he wrenched it free, feeling the weight and texture of the deadly weapon in his hand. Puzzled, he couldn't help but wonder, "What in the hell are these things?"

The left front tire was bent at an unnatural angle, pressing against the fender. Its rubber was shredded and tattered, a visual testament to the damage. The rear tire fared no better. His once sturdy jeep now stood as a lifeless hunk of metal, its engine silent and useless. Matt took a deep breath, then exhaled, steeling himself for the reaction when he told the others the bad news.

"The jeep's out of commission," he said. "We have to walk."

Lauren shook her head frantically. "I'm not stepping a foot out there."

"Honey," said Sam, softly. "We don't have a choice "

"No!"

Coyote calls exploded all around them, followed by gleeful yipping.

Matt's spine tingled with a deep, primal sense of danger. "We don't have time for debate." He pulled open Sam's door. "Let's go!"

Sam clasped onto Lauren, who screamed and twisted her arm free. "Lauren, please," she begged. "I know you're scared, but we have to go right now."

Matt was losing patience. They needed to get going. Leaving Sam to work this out with Lauren, he rushed around the back of the jeep, where he met up with Troy. As quickly as possible, they collected supplies. Who knew what they were going to run into or need out there in the hills? It was best to make sure they had as many bases covered as possible.

When they were done, Matt went up to Sam's door again. "Come on!" he shouted.

Lauren shook her head just as her door burst open. Without another word, Troy wrapped his arms around her and pulled her out of the vehicle.

That was good enough for Matt. He seized Sam's hand and shouted, "This way!"

They sprinted through the long grass and up the steep hill. Somewhere in the dark shadows behind them, Matt could hear the yipping sounds of the pack. More haunting laughter. The words Lauren said earlier came to mind. Sometimes coyotes hunt just for the thrill of it.

THIRTY-ONE

MATT HELD Sam's hand with such force, he wondered if he was hurting her. She didn't pull away, so either he wasn't gripping as tightly as he thought, or she wasn't able to feel anything.

Behind them, Troy dragged Lauren along.

Over the years, Matt had become so accustomed to Lauren's unconventional opinions that he enjoyed hearing her perspective from time to time. As much as he teased her, the woman's intuition was rarely off, which was probably the reason her current reaction to their situation was so disturbing.

The landscape was harsh. It was hard to decide what was worse between the loose, rocky soil, tall grass, steep inclines, and limited visibility. More than once, Matt lost his footing and almost tumbled down the hillside, dragging Sam along with him. He longed for the ease of strolling along a paved sidewalk.

The lack of cover was probably the worst thing about their whole predicament. There was nowhere to hide that offered camouflage or protection. They needed to find a safe place to hunker down and get their bearings. They were running blind in the desert. For all he knew, the pack was leading them straight into a trap.

Behind him, Troy cursed, followed by the sound of Lauren whimpering.

Matt halted and spun around to find Lauren sitting on the ground, her head was the only thing visible above the tall grass.

"Come on," said Troy. "We gotta keep going."

"I can't!" she shouted. "I think my ankle's broken!"

"What the hell happened?" demanded Matt as he approached.

Sam crouched beside Lauren to examine her injury. "I can't see a damn thing." She cursed under her breath, then clicked on a flashlight.

"Turn that shit off!" shouted Troy. "It'll guide them right to us."

Sam didn't argue, she quickly turned off the light and put it away. "Can you stand up?"

Lauren allowed Sam to help her to her feet. Once upright, she attempted to shift her body weight onto her damaged ankle, causing her to cry out in pain.

"Dammit!" shouted Sam furiously, brushing herself off.

"What's wrong?" asked Matt.

"Ant mound!" she replied. "As if things weren't bad enough." She glanced over at Lauren, who was busy brushing herself off, one hand holding on to Troy's shoulder for support. "Can you walk?" she asked.

"I'm not sure," replied Lauren.

"We don't have time for this," said Troy. He crouched down in front of Lauren. "Climb on my back, I'll carry you."

"You can't carry her the whole way," said Sam.

"I'll take her when he needs a break," said Matt.

The pack's cries pierced the air, bouncing off the valley walls and making it impossible to figure out their location or how far away they were.

As soon as Lauren was secure on Troy's back, the group quickened their pace. They needed to put as much distance between themselves and the pack as possible.

At the top of the hill, Matt carefully examined the landscape, taking in every detail. From his perch, he could see the vast expanse of the area stretching out before him. Behind them lay a spacious meadow. Going back that way was not an option as that would lead them directly into the path of the coyotes. From the vantage point atop the hill, he could make out a narrow river cutting through the countryside below. If nothing else, the trees would provide cover long enough for him to figure out where to go. The short break would also allow Troy a much-needed break after carrying Lauren for so long.

"Let's get to those trees." He pointed.

Once more, he took hold of Sam's hand and slowly worked his way down the slope of the hill, taking care to make sure each foothold was solid. The last thing he wanted to do was trip and tumble uncontrollably to the bottom. They already had one injured member; they didn't need two.

Plodding along slowly, they made it to the tree line with no more injuries, this was a small triumph that provided a much-needed boost of confidence.

Matt turned to the others. "Let's pause here for a second."

Troy let Lauren down. Wincing, she hobbled over to a tree stump and, after making sure there were no ants nearby, she sat down.

Sam quickly took advantage of the downtime, and tore strips from the bottom of her t-shirt, using them to wrap Lauren's ankle. "Any support would be a good thing," she explained.

Meanwhile, Matt pulled his phone out and opened the map. It took a hot minute, but eventually their location appeared on the tiny screen.

"Where we at?" asked Troy, peering over his shoulder.

"The middle of nowhere," replied Matt. He pinched his screen, hoping to get a wider view. This was taking forever. He glanced around anxiously, fully expecting to see a set of glowing eyes staring at him through the trees, but there was nothing.

"What's that?" asked Troy, pointing to the phone screen.

Matt zoomed in. There definitely was something there. He zoomed in closer. A large metal building came into view, with what appeared to be vehicles scattered around. "This has to be some sort of scrap yard."

"Out here?" asked Troy.

"Why not?" replied Matt with a shrug. "It's not like spare parts are easily available in a place like this. I imagine a scrap yard would be necessary."

"Well, if there's a scrap yard," said Troy. "There's a tow truck, which means there's a way out of here. Is there a road anywhere near there?"

The map wouldn't zoom in any closer, leaving Matt at the mercy of his eyes and a lot of squinting. He found what appeared to be a driveway and followed it by dragging the map with his finger. "There!" He pointed. "That's a road." He showed the screen to Troy, who squinted and nodded in agreement.

"How far do you think it is from here?"

Matt stared down at the screen. "Looks like it's a couple miles."

"We can make it," said Troy.

"You wanna lead?" asked Matt. "If so, I can carry Lauren."

Troy shook his head. "You're doin' just fine taking the lead. I've got the rear."

The pack howled; their call sounded different this time. Something had changed. Matt wasn't sure exactly what that might mean, but he was sure it wasn't a good thing for him and his friends.

He scanned the hilltop, noting six distinct silhouettes. To his surprise, the beasts weren't moving. They appeared to be lounging atop the hill. What the hell were they waiting for? Why hadn't they come down into the trees? He watched them pace around, then one by one, they turned and disappeared down the other side of the hill. His mind reeled with explanations. Maybe the pack lost their scent. Maybe they lost interest. Could they be so lucky? A tiny ember of hope sparked in his chest. For the first time since this nightmare began, Matt felt as though they might get through this. His mood lighter, he led the group along the river toward the scrapyard.

As they slowly picked their way through the barren landscape, images of an entire convoy of hunters in camouflage descending upon this barren wasteland, played out in his mind. An army of men with weapons would hunt those monsters to oblivion.

"Where the hell did all this come from?" asked Sam, as she weaved her way through several rusted cars.

"Be careful," warned Matt. "You don't want to cut yourself on anything out here. God knows, the last thing we need is tetanus or an infection."

A rusty van sat among the tall grass, the side door gone, exposing the nineteen seventies interior complete with carpeted walls and ceiling. Matt peeked inside where all manner of desert plant life had taken up residence. He spied a bag tucked away in the far corner and pulled it out. After blowing off the dust, he inspected the contents. A wallet, a birth control pill case, an old paper map and moldy snacks. Who would leave this behind? Something was off. A sense of dread crept over him.

"Check this out!" called Troy, standing beside another vehicle.

"What is it?" asked Matt as he walked over.

"Found this wallet in here," said Troy. He flipped the billfold open. "There's a bunch of photos, but no ID."

Matt went back over to the van and pulled the wallet from the bag. Sure enough, the ID was gone. His instinct was right, something was off.

"So, who the hell would leave the wallet and take the IDs?" asked Sam. "And no woman would ever just leave her birth control like that."

Matt shook his head slowly. He locked eyes with Troy. "If this is just a scrap yard, then all these vehicles would be empty—there would be no bags left behind. For sure, no one would leave their wallets."

"What are you saying?" asked Sam.

"That this isn't a scrap yard at all," said Lauren. "It's a graveyard."

"Who the hell would do this?" asked Sam.

Troy moved to another vehicle, after several moments of rifling around, he stood up, holding yet another wallet in the air.

Fear came back with a vengeance. Matt didn't believe in coincidences, he suddenly realized why the pack hadn't pursued them.

"There's so many," whispered Lauren.

"This one's fairly recent," said Troy. "Jesus!"

Matt joined him by a newer van. An obvious set of grooves were cut through the grass from the tires. The side door was completely gone. Whatever tore it off had immense strength. Upon closer inspection, he found large claw marks along the edge of the door frame, right about where the seam would be. A twinge of deep, primal fear surged through his body. Inside the van, dark red blood covered virtually every surface. A touch of his finger told him it was dry, but relatively new. His heart raced in his chest. Camping gear, backpacks and various odds and ends lay littered all over the place. He moved some of it aside, exposing a blue hoodie. He pulled it out and held it high.

His mouth went dry. His mind whipped back to a concert years ago—a concert his little sister wanted so badly to attend, but she wasn't old enough. He remembered her face through the window as he and his friends pulled out of the driveway. Her expression embedded itself so deeply in his mind, that he stood in line for almost thirty minutes, missing the opening of his favorite band. It didn't matter, all he could think of was how sad Ash was that she missed out. Matt held the hoodie, remembering the way her eyes lit up when he gave it to her. She wore it every day for almost a month before their mom made her take it off and wash it.

A moan of anguish escaped his lips as he stared at the bloodstained garment. He clutched the soft hoodie tight against his chest. Whoever did this was going to pay.

A lone coyote called out in the darkness, followed by a cacophony of yips. The pack had found them.

Was found the proper word?

Matt's ears picked up a low growl, sending a shiver down his spine; he whipped his head around just as the alpha wandered into view. As it snarled, he couldn't help but notice the mouth full of sharp, deadly teeth and the eerie glow in its eyes.

"Get to the building!" shouted Troy.

Sam's grip tightened around Matt's hand, trying to drag him away, but he stood defiantly, refusing to divert his gaze from the menacing beast.

"Matt, please," she begged as she tugged.

With unwavering focus, the creature stood still—its piercing gaze fixed on its target.

"Matt!" screamed Sam. "We need to go!"

With a shake of his head, he snapped back to reality and let Sam guide him away.

As they ran, the jungle of twisted metal closed in around them, creating a maze-like path. How many people had met their end in this godforsaken place? Some of those vehicles were old. How long had this been going on? What exactly did they stumble into?

The walls of the building echoed with the sharp sound of metal banging against metal as Matt and Sam joined the others. Clang, clang, clang. Troy hammered away at the padlock with a tire iron, while Matt scanned the surrounding area for any sign of the creatures.

The largest beast prowled around the corner emitting a menacing growl.

Matt aimed and fired his handgun. The round hit the creature square in the chest, that alone would have killed another animal, but this one—it hardly even twitched. Red blood spread out from the wound. He watched in horror as the bullet tumbled to the ground.

"Get inside!" shouted Troy, then he pushed Sam inside the building.

Lauren screamed. One of the beasts was closing in on her. Its body a deadly barrier between her and the others.

Matt fired off several more rounds, this time aiming for the head of the animal. The bullets merely bounced off.

Two more creatures appeared, surrounding Lauren. They made no move to lunge, instead, taking slow, deliberate steps as though they were herding her farther away from the safety of her friends.

Their guns were useless. Whatever the hell these things were, a handgun had little to no effect. Matt had to divert the creature's attention long enough for Lauren to get to safety. He ran up to the nearest one and kicked. The animal yelped, then spun around to face him.

"That's right," he said. "Come and get me." He stepped backward, trying to lure the creature away. But the beast turned its focus back to Lauren. Working in tandem with the others, the pack slowly pushed her farther into the metal graveyard.

With a sudden burst of speed, a coyote lunged forward, latching onto her shoulder, dragging her away in the debris field. Lauren's screams pierced the night, bouncing off the sea of rusted metal all around them.

Matt and Troy traced the sound of her voice. They found her in a clearing, metal rod held high, ready to swing at the creatures that surrounded her.

The pack closed in, their heads low and teeth bared.

She swung for the nearest one, missing as it jumped back too quickly. A round of yips erupted—the beasts were laughing.

Troy signaled for Matt to go around one way, while he went the other.

Staying low, Matt crept around to the other side of the circle, hoping that he could get close enough to Lauren to pull her to safety. An eerie silence descended upon the area. He poked his head out from behind a rusty car door to see the pack standing still. All but one beast was facing Lauren.

The alpha locked eyes with him, sending an icy chill down his spine.

Troy charged out from between two sedans, with his gun aimed at the circle of coyotes; he fired off several rounds. The largest beast of the pack leaped into the air and slammed all four paws against

Troy's chest, knocking him to the ground. Rusted metal toppled from precarious perches, burying him.

All the while, the alpha stared at Matt with cunning eyes—smirking.

Lauren screamed as one of the other beasts leaped forward and knocked her to the ground.

Matt needed to do something now. He searched the area for a weapon, settling on a long piece of rebar.

Metal rod held high; he charged out from behind the car. Drawing on his high school javelin tossing days, he cast the metal rod, sending it hurtling toward the alpha in a straight path.

The creature let out a sharp yelp, then turned and leered at Matt, the piece of rebar lodged deep in its side. This would have ended a normal animal, but the alpha merely lifted its head to the sky and howled. With one smooth motion, it took the metal rod between its teeth and pulled it free. Blood gushed from the wound momentarily, then stopped, leaving behind no sign it was ever there. After one last glance at Matt, the beast huffed, then turned and trotted off, disappearing among the debris, with the rest of the pack in tow.

The sound of Troy's moan emerged from beneath the heavy pile of rusty vehicle parts. It took several nerve-wracking minutes before Matt and Lauren were able to dig him out from beneath the rubble.

With no sign of the pack, they quickly made their way back to the safety of the metal building where Sam was waiting.

THIRTY-TWO

THE METAL DOOR slammed shut behind Matt, causing the entire building to shake. The smell of grease, rust, and something else that was curiously familiar, yet just out of reach, permeated the air. With great care, they placed Lauren on a metal chest, blood trickling down her upper body from her wounded shoulder.

While Matt remained behind to lend a hand with Lauren, Troy ventured off to explore the mysterious building.

"What happened?" asked Sam, as she examined the wound. "I need bandages," she yelled. "Or something that can be used as one, just as long as it's clean."

While she consoled Lauren, Matt rummaged through drawers and bins, until he finally discovered a red case adorned with a white cross on the side.

"This isn't happening," cried Lauren, shaking her head. Her whole body trembled with each breath.

"We need you to stay calm," said Sam. "Can you do that?"

Lauren quieted but continued to sob. "What are those things?"

That was a good question. Matt mulled over everything he knew so far. On the surface, they appeared to be coyotes, but one glimpse into their eyes said they were something more—something terrifying. With his own eyes, he witnessed Troy empty his clip on the giant one, and it had no effect whatsoever. He may as well have been shooting rubber bands at the thing for all the damage the bullets did. Matt himself impaled the alpha with the metal rod, but the creature pulled it out like it was nothing more than a bothersome splinter.

The eyes. Matt's blood ran icy cold as he recalled the look in those eyes. Cunning and cruel, they were the eyes of a predator with the intelligence of a human.

Troy returned from his inspection of the building, the expression on his face told Matt that bad news was coming.

"You should come with me," he said stepping back as he stared directly into Matt's eyes for emphasis.

"Is the building secure?" asked Matt.

"For the most part," replied Troy. "It is."

"You two stay here," Matt said to Sam. "We'll be right back."

"No!" shouted Sam, wiping her face. "I'm going with you."

"Me too," said Lauren.

"Besides," said Sam. "Whatever he has to show you, it's best if we all know about it."

He knew better than to argue; she had a good point. He had Lauren lean against him, then they followed Troy to the back of the building.

What met his eyes was like a scene from every gory horror movie he had ever seen in his life; except this wasn't a movie set. This was real. A stack of what seemed to be bleached human bones was arranged neatly atop the stained workbench. The strangely familiar scent was overpowering in this area, he took in a lungful of air then gagged upon realizing exactly what it was—blood. It stained every surface.

He moved closer to inspect the bones on the workbench, noting how impeccably clean they were. What the hell are these people up to? Some bones had deep scratches and teeth marks, while others were pristine. The sizes ranged from full-grown adult to small child.

Troy handed a thin shard to Matt. "This is one of the things they made out of these," he said.

Rolling the item over in his hand, Matt observed the intricate carvings of a snake's head and scales. Whoever did this was a gifted craftsman. "What the hell is this?"

"I've seen these before!" said Sam as she took the item from his hand. "It's a hair stick."

"A what?"

"A hair stick," she replied. "They're used to put your hair up instead of using clips or hair ties."

"So, why would they make so many?" asked Troy. He held up a box full of carved snake sticks.

Sam studied the item in her hand. "They're selling them." She glanced back and forth between Matt and Troy. "I've seen these sold online. I almost bought one." With a shudder, she handed the stick to Lauren. "The listing said it was carved from bone. You told me not to buy it because it didn't say where the bone came from."

This time it was Matt who gasped in horror over the thought of how many unsuspecting women were out there wearing human bones in their hair.

Lauren examined the delicately sculpted snake. "I thought it came from an endangered animal. I never once thought it could be human bone." She placed the stick down on the table.

"There's a lot of shit in here," said Troy as he rifled through various bins. "Hair clips, knife handles, buttons and even pens." He pointed to a lathe with a bone shard mounted on the spinners.

Matt picked up a small button. The back was smooth; the front had four paw prints surrounded by a circle of intricately carved runes. A memory nagged at the edge of his mind, this symbol was familiar, but he didn't know how. He handed it to Troy. "You ever see anything like this before?"

Troy shrugged and shook his head. "I don't know. I mean, it seems familiar, but I don't know how."

"I've seen it before too," said Matt. "I just can't seem to remember where." He stuffed the talisman in his pocket so he could research it later.

"So, what," said Troy. "Those things out there murder people and some human freaks gather the bodies to make trinkets out of the bones and sell online? Whose guard dogs are they? What the hell kind of person would train animals to do this sort of thing? What kind of monster would do this?" He waved his hands around at the collection of bone carvings. "What the hell have we stumbled into?"

A thought came to Matt's mind, he told himself it was impossible, that there was no way something like that could exist. But there was no other viable explanation. "What if," he said, "those things out there aren't really animals?"

"What are you talking about?" asked Troy. "If those things aren't animals, what are they?"

"We all saw them," said Sam. "What else would they be?"

Matt struggled to formulate the right sentence to explain his thoughts. There was no way his friends were going to accept what he had to say—he wasn't even sure if he could accept it himself.

It was Lauren who got to the chase before he could. "What if they're shapeshifters," she said, letting the last word linger on her lips.

"Like werewolves?" asked Sam, incredulously.

Troy scoffed. "All y'all have lost your damn minds."

"Lauren's right!" blurted Matt. "We all saw those things. They're huge—much larger than any coyote I've ever seen. I'm gonna bet that neither of you have ever seen or heard of one that big, either. They look like animals, but they act with the intelligence of a human."

"There're a lot of explanations for that," said Troy.

"Name one."

Troy blinked and stammered, but he couldn't provide any examples.

Sam shook her head. "They're not werewolves," she said. "There's no such thing. Besides, if there was, they would be wolves, not coyotes."

"That's why I called them shapeshifters," replied Lauren. "They could be humans who can turn into coyotes."

The tension in the room was like a heavy cloud, casting a shadow over everyone present. Matt watched his friends' faces reflect his own turbulent emotions as they tried to come to terms with this revelation.

"Nah, nah, nah," said Troy, shaking his head. "That's insane. I am not following you down that rabbit hole. There's another explanation."

"Just think about it," implored Matt. He locked eyes with Troy. "It's the only thing that makes sense."

"No!" boomed Troy. "It isn't."

Matt's patience was gone. "Then why don't you give me another explanation that makes sense!"

"Everyone, calm down!" shouted Sam. "The last thing we need to do is fight among ourselves right now." She pointed. "Those things are still out there, and we need to figure out a way out of here."

She was right, the last thing they needed to do was argue. Matt sighed and turned to Troy. "I realize how insane this sounds."

Troy nodded and folded his arms. "It's always the simplest answer."

"So, can you come up with a simpler explanation?"

"Yeah," replied Troy. "Some serial killer, bred and trained a pack of giant coyotes to hunt people down in the desert so he can make trinkets from their bones and sell them online to unsuspecting housewives."

An explosion of laughter followed. Even Troy himself couldn't hold back.

"Alright," said Troy, nodding his head. "I get your point."

"But the moon isn't full," said Sam.

"Why is that relevant?" asked Troy.

"Because all the lore says that werewolves need a full moon to transition."

"These aren't werewolves," said Lauren.

Sam released a deep breath and let her shoulders sag.

"Okay," said Troy. "Let's go with your assumption. How do we fight them?"

"We have to find out what makes them tick," said Matt.

"Any ideas how we go about that?"

Matt rubbed his chin. "We have to catch one of them."

"And do what with it?" asked Troy. He stepped back. "In case you haven't noticed, we don't exactly have the means to take the damn thing to a lab for testing."

"Then we do it here."

Both Sam and Troy stared at him in shock.

"I'm saying," he said. "That we catch one of them and do a few experiments on it right here."

His friends remained silent.

"We have all the tools we need." He gestured to the bench. "And we have no other choice. If we're gonna get out of this alive, we need to know exactly what we're up against."

"Torture," said Troy. "You're talking about torture.'"

"Is it really torture if the subject isn't human?"

Troy nodded. "Yes. Yes, it is."

"We have to level the playing field," explained Matt. "Right now, they know more about us than we know about them. Until we fix that deficit, we're on the losing end." He paused for emphasis. "I just want to get us all out of this alive. If I have to abandon some ethical standards along the way, then so be it."

"You saw what I saw out there," said Troy, rubbing his chin. "Bullets have no effect. How the hell are we supposed to catch one of those giant things?"

"We go for one of the smaller ones," said Sam.

Matt nodded. "That's exactly what I was thinking."

"Do you seriously think the bigger ones are gonna let us saunter up to one of the smaller ones and catch it?" asked Troy. "The minute they realize we snagged one of theirs, they'll rip this place apart like a tin box."

Matt scoured his mind for an idea. He snapped his fingers, recalling something he had seen when they first turned on the lights inside the building. "Follow me," he said over his shoulder as he ran toward the door. He led them over to a series of large metal cages stacked against the wall. "One of these might work."

"What are those?" asked Sam.

"Giant hog cages," replied Matt.

"Why would they want to trap hogs?" asked Sam. "Wouldn't they just hunt them down and eat them?"

Matt raked his fingers through his hair, honestly, he had no good explanation for why the cages were there; he was just thankful they were.

"The cages are big enough to house an adult," whispered Lauren.

"An adult what?" asked Sam.

Lauren swallowed, then said, "Human."

Matt scrutinized the cages, realizing that she was probably right.

"Remember," said Lauren. "Sometimes coyotes hunt for fun." She strolled over to the stack of cages. "In England, if there are no wild foxes for the hunt, they bring one to the woods and release it." She turned to face the others. "Then they hunt it down and kill it."

"That's enough!" boomed Troy. "Can we just table the creepy talk for a little while?" He walked around and inspected the cages. "Hmm," he said. "This might work."

"How are we supposed to get the thing inside the cage?" asked Sam.

"That's the tricky part," replied Matt. "It's also the most danger-ous." He glanced around at the others. "We have to lure it in."

"How?"

Matt swallowed; he could hardly believe what he was about to say. "I'll be a lure."

Troy and Sam gasped. Lauren simply shook her head.

"The hell you will!" shouted Sam.

"She's right," said Troy. "That is the dumbest idea you've ever come up with."

Sam placed her hands on her hips. "If you go out there, the entire pack will be on top of you before you would even have a chance. It's suicide."

"I'm all ears if either of you have another idea," said Matt. He stood, waiting.

"We both go," said Troy. "Matt and I will set up a trap, then create a distraction," he explained. "We'll get the pack to separate, then lure one of the smaller ones inside one of these cages."

"And what am I supposed to be doing while all this is going on?" asked Sam.

"You're gonna wait inside here with the cage," replied Troy. "Once we get the thing inside, it'll be your job to lock it up."

"I'm in," said Sam with a nod of her head.

Matt's stomach sank. It was one thing to offer his own life for a bad idea; it was another to risk the lives of the three people he was closest to. He struggled to come up with an alternative, but in the end, he had to admit, Troy was right. The plan had a better chance if they all worked together. Doing nothing wasn't an option, it was a guarantee that they would be dead by morning.

THIRTY-THREE

ALTHOUGH HE MASKED IT WELL, Pax still carried a lingering resentment over Caleb's earlier reaction. He was tiring of his brother's constant need to be in control. When would Caleb stop treating him like some child under his supervision and finally start showing Pax the respect he deserved?

He was no longer the novice, the one who needed supervision; Jewel had stepped into that role in the pack. A position he was more than willing to hand over. He hated it when Caleb treated him like a child. Pax was a man and when he was in full trickster form; he was invincible. He didn't need his big brother or his friends watching over him, treating him like a weakling.

He was more than capable of taking care of himself.

The last confrontation with Matt and his friends was merely a teaser—a way for the pack to gauge the strength of their prey. By now, the interlopers had figured out that their weapons were useless. They were probably scared stiff in the workshop. The thought of the arrogant cop trembling with fear made Pax smile.

He watched Caleb pace back and forth among the trees. No doubt, his mind buzzing with ideas as he considered all the ramifications of every move they made. Even though he got angry at times, Pax had a deep admiration for his older brother. For as long as he could remember, he wanted to be just like him. More than anything, he wanted his brother's respect.

Caleb's presence was a perfect balance of strength and cunning, enabling him to exist in both the human and trickster realms. He knew when to turn on the charms in order to manipulate humans to bend to his will, he also knew when to use brutal force. Pax was well-versed in brutal force, but his teenage years still clung to him with their trademark awkwardness. Hence, he lacked the ability to charm people to do his bidding.

The pack lounged on the rocky ground, waiting for the next phase to begin. The plan was to take things slow, let their prey marinade in their own terror, then pick them off, one by one. This was Caleb's preferred way. Truth be told, in this instance, Pax would prefer to dive in and get it over with.

Jewel hovered close to Izzy. The two had developed a strong bond over the past several months. Of course, not close enough to keep Jewel from running away. Pax was happy that they moved beyond all of that. It was good to see his little sister embrace her true self. Every day she showed signs of maturing, but she still had a long way to go before she could be allowed out on her own.

Although he kept it to himself, Pax was deeply bothered by Jewel's inclusion in the hunt. When Caleb told him she was coming along, he was stunned. He felt slighted by the decision. There was no doubt that Izzy played a role in it. It certainly wasn't Caleb's idea, after all, he didn't allow Pax to take part in a hunt until at least a year after his first turning.

Of course, Pax didn't blame Jewel, if someone would have offered him the chance when he was her age, he would have jumped at it. To her credit, she was holding her own and keeping up with the pack, which was a good thing.

Ezra returned from checking the workshop where the humans

had barricaded themselves. The stupid fools thought they were safe inside that building.

A moment later, Caleb stretched and gave a long, slow howl. The hunt was back on.

Excited and more than ready to get on with the fun part of the evening, Pax paced anxiously in a small circle. After a round of yips, they were off.

Long blades of grass brushed against his fur, tickling his nose. Pax loped along, though at a slightly slower pace than he preferred. He was the fastest runner in the pack, easily able to outpace any of the others—including Caleb. But he was not the alpha, so he had no other choice than to hang back and stay to the rear of the pack.

They slowed as the workshop came into view. Pax sniffed the air; the scent of the humans was strong. He hunkered down among the rusty debris, close enough to detect their fear but far enough away to remain hidden.

Izzy and Jewel stood farther away, waiting for Caleb's signal, while the others spread out, forming a perimeter around the building.

Pax's heart raced with anticipation. Adrenaline surged through his veins, causing every muscle in his body to be on high alert.

The door swung open. Matt and the dark man stepped out.

The intoxicating aroma of fear hung heavy in the night air. Pax inhaled deeply. His pulse quickened as he waited, hidden among the debris. As soon as Matt and his friend stepped away from the safety of the workshop, the pack would separate them, and the hunt would be on.

The two men nodded at one another, then signaled to the women inside. One of them sported clean bandages that covered the wound Pax inflicted on her shoulder when he attacked her earlier. He licked his muzzle, still able to taste her blood on his tongue.

The men glanced at one another nervously, then stepped forward.

With a swift leap, Ezra placed himself behind the men, his body serving as a physical barrier between them and the safety of the building. Next entered Bass leering and snarling.

From the workshop door, one of the women screamed, startling the men.

Unfortunately, it was too late for them to be any help because Ezra and Bass already closed in.

Matt and his friend stepped to the side, keeping their eyes on Ezra and Bass while peering over their shoulders. "Get back inside!" barked the dark-skinned man. Without debate, the two women shrank back inside the building, slamming the door closed behind them. That left Matt and his friend outside to fend for themselves.

Still hidden, Pax studied them as he waited for the signal. Both men were in peak physical shape. This was going to be an interesting chase.

Caleb crept out of the dark with both Izzy and Jewel close behind, teeth bared, he emitted a low growl.

The two men stole a quick glance at one another then sprinted off, weaving, and darting between the vehicles. Their agility was impressive.

A series of playful yips erupted, then Pax took off.

The chase was always the fun part. The pack would give their prey just enough lead to believe they had a chance, this kept them running. The harder they ran, the more tired they grew, while the trickster's bloodlust increased. Like the others, Pax enjoyed a good chase, but deep down, he preferred the final kill. That last moment when the prey realized their fight was all for nothing. When they surrendered to death with their heart pounding and their blood saturated in adrenaline and fear—was pure perfection.

Matt and his friend ran around an old van, then split off in two different directions.

What's this? Some sort of counter measure? It was almost cute how they were implementing this plan of theirs. It hadn't even dawned on them yet that half the pack was missing.

Ezra and Bass went after Matt, while Pax turned his focus on the dark-skinned man. He seemed less adept at navigating through the debris field in the dark. Pax sniffed the air, taking in the full scent of the man, then launched after him.

Much to his delight, his prey proved faster than he thought. It didn't matter—nothing the man did would matter in the end. Tricksters could outrun any human. Pax slowed his pace a little, it wasn't often he encountered worthy opponents.

He stayed close on the man's heels, fully aware that, at any moment, he could overtake him, opting instead to play a little while longer.

The man ran past an old RV, looking as though he was going to cut right, then quickly cut left. Pax snickered, nice fake out. He stopped and studied the direction where his prey had gone. Two vehicles sat a few feet apart, creating a narrow passage.

Pax sniffed the air; the man's scent was strong. He moved slowly, taking care to monitor all directions, in case the dark-skinned man jumped out. Not that it would make any difference, this man's life was ending and there was nothing he could do to prevent that from happening.

He edged nearer, his hackles on end.

The man sprang out from behind a vehicle and doubled back toward the building.

Running at full speed, Pax followed him, determined to stop him from escaping. He could practically taste the blood on his tongue. He was so close.

The door to the warehouse swung open, and the man bolted inside.

His bloodlust had taken control of his senses. There was no way Pax would allow this man to get away. He picked up his speed and charged into the building. Before he could prevent it, he smashed headfirst into the rear wall of a cage. Behind him, the metal grate closed with a loud bang, followed by the door to the building.

"Gotcha, you son of a bitch!" shouted the man, triumphantly.

Pax growled and thrashed against the walls of his prison. The iron bars held firm. He inhaled, filling his lungs with air, preparing to release a howl of rage.

A shock coursed throughout his body; his muscles tensed. Pax struggled to make sense of what was happening. He looked up at the man, who was standing close, his hand holding a metal clamp over a large battery. Another surge of electricity burst through his body, his muscles spasmed, then locked in a state of paralysis. Unable to move, Pax was vaguely aware of the scent of burned fur emanating from his own body. Heart pounding in his chest, he struggled to breathe, but his lungs refused to do his bidding. Hovering outside the cage, the man cursed something under his breath, then the world went dark.

THIRTY-FOUR

CALEB WATCHED AS EZRA, Bass and Pax drove the men farther into the debris field, away from the women. Once they were out of sight, he turned his focus to the workshop. Their plan to separate their quarry was working as expected. Stupid humans. They never seem to realize that tricksters aren't simple animals. Everything they do is calculated, especially during a hunt. The men were never really the target of this raid.

The metallic scent of blood hung heavy in the air from the woman's wounds; he breathed it in, making his mouth water in anticipation. His powerful ears picked up the sound of the women's fearful sobs inside the building.

Izzy sauntered past him, sniffing along the gaps of the door frame.

Enough fooling around, it was time to get what they came for. Caleb moved stealthily around the back of the building, stopping in front of a short metal door suspended by brand new hinges. He installed them three days ago. He pushed against the corrugated surface, making sure it moved easily. Another sign of simple human stupidity. You would think that they would have searched the entire building to make sure there were no hidden entrances. Crouching low, he crawled through the door.

The scent of fresh blood was much stronger inside. The trio split up, creeping around the equipment and various items scattered all about the vast workshop. Over by the main door, the women comforted one another, their voices bouncing off the metal walls.

"Do you think they'll be okay?" asked the one with the injured shoulder.

"They know what to do," replied the other.

"What if something goes wrong?"

"I really need you to be calm, Lauren. It's gonna be okay."

"Sam?"

"Lauren, now is not the time!" shouted Sam. She got to her feet and went over to the door, leaving the wounded one alone.

Teeth bared, Caleb crept out from the shadows, emitting an ominous growl. The injured woman pointed, her entire body trembling in fear, but her friend was busy by the door.

Izzy materialized on one side of him and Jewel on the other.

The one named Lauren screamed in terror, but some sort of ruckus had erupted at the door, drowning her out.

He lunged, taking hold of her leg; his powerful teeth piercing the soft flesh, warm blood rushed into his mouth, igniting his senses. Stepping backward, he pulled the woman away from the false safety of her friend.

The woman's screams went unheeded as Caleb bit down, using enough pressure to shatter her femur. The bone snapped like a flimsy rubber band in his powerful jaws. Hot blood, tinted with the intoxicating flavor of fear, exploded into his mouth, pouring down his throat. He released her leg and took hold of her by the shoulder. The woman cried out in agony, swinging her arms wildly to stave off his attack. To her credit, she fought furiously, unfortunately she never had a chance.

Kicking and screaming, he hauled her away into the night, carrying her far away from the warehouse and into the hills. When they reached a small clearing, he stopped and released the woman from his grip. Terrified and bleeding profusely from her wounds, she scurried backward, bracing herself against a tree as she trembled and sobbed in fear.

Her warm, flavorful blood ignited Caleb's bloodlust. He wanted to jump in and tear her apart, but he had to wait for the others. Restless and driven by his desires, he paced around in circles, terrifying the woman even more. The scent of her fear driving him further into madness.

The others finally arrived. It was about time. Caleb turned his focus on Lauren. She seemed to understand it was all over for her. She released an ear-piercing scream. In response, the pack yipped and howled. They pounced upon her in a volley of sharp claws and piercing teeth, ripping the soft flesh from her bones.

When it was all over, the sounds of nature settled in the area once again. Bloodlust sated, Caleb sat propped up against a tree, while Izzy and Jewel rinsed their bodies off in a narrow stream. He watched them laugh and splash water at one another playfully.

Noticing his gaze, Izzy turned away from Jewel and sauntered over, taking a seat beside him.

The feeling of her warm body against his set off another reaction, but now was not the time. From what he could tell, they had six hours before daylight, and there were three more things that needed taken care of.

"Who's ready for round two," he asked.

A round of chuckles were the only response.

Caleb quickly scanned the members of the pack. Jewel had taken a seat beside what remained of the woman, poking at the gory bits like a curious cat. Ezra sat propped up against a large rock, his body covered in blood and gore; his eyes were closed, and his head was tilted toward the sky. Bass sat nearby, gnawing the marrow from a large bone. There was no sign of Pax.

"Where's Pax?" asked Caleb.

Both Ezra and Bass glanced around, confused.

"I thought he made it back before we did," replied Ezra.

Anxiety swelled inside Caleb's chest. "When was the last time you saw him?"

"The two men split off from one another in the middle of the chase," replied Bass. "He must have gone after the other one."

"No one's seen him since?" asked Caleb.

The others glanced at one another uncomfortably.

"Goddammit!" cursed Caleb. He jumped to his feet and quickly changed.

A moment later, he was sprinting through the hills, back into the debris field, where he picked up his little brother's scent. Following the trail, he realized that Pax's scent was mixed with that of the humans. That made sense, considering that Pax was chasing the man. Or did it?

Something wasn't right. Caleb's heart raced in his chest as deep fear clawed its way to the surface. He bolted, following the trail that led him all the way back to the door of the workshop. His little brother was inside.

With a savage cry, he frantically slammed his entire body against the door.

THIRTY-FIVE

MATT'S HEART was beating furiously in his chest, pounding so hard against his rib cage, he was sure that it would break free at any moment. Primal fear triggered the rush of adrenaline that coursed through his body, propelling him forward. He weaved and dodged between the vehicles and hopped over rusty debris. More than once, he barely avoided falling atop a sharp metal object laying askew on the ground. This place was worse than a minefield.

Behind him, the two large beasts kept pace with his every move. Much to his amazement, they never caught up to him. Given that he was pretty sure it was impossible for a human to outrun a wild animal, he found this odd. As much as he wanted to believe they hadn't caught him yet because he was outrunning them, he knew, deep inside, there was something far more sinister at play. It was almost as though they were toying with him. If they were as cunning as they seemed, it would only make sense that they had something planned. He said a silent prayer that Troy was okay.

Back in the workshop, when they drafted their plan, Matt knew exactly how he would go about getting the information they needed.

He didn't want to go another round over the morality of torture, so he kept those details to himself.

He told himself it would be okay, that when the time arrived, they would all be on board with his plan. After all, this was a matter of survival. Despite this, he knew the odds were high that one of the others would attempt to change his mind—to convince him it was wrong. For that reason alone, he decided that for the time being, all they needed to know was the most straightforward part of the plan. They didn't need to be aware of the rest of it until it was too late to back out.

Matt believed the creatures were indeed shapeshifters. He would have a hard time accepting this, had he not witnessed the alpha recover several times from what should have been a deadly blow.

Yes, the creatures had supernatural strength and healing abilities, but everything that lived and breathed had to die somehow. As far as he was concerned, he had never heard of an animal or man, that could withstand electrical shock. Bare minimum, it would allow them to incapacitate one of those things long enough to get the answers they needed.

The trap was set; confidence was high. So far, the plan was working. After splitting off from Troy, Matt peered back over his shoulder, dismayed to only see two of the beasts loping behind him. Maybe the rest of the pack was slower and thus lagging. He hoped that was it. The alternative wasn't something he wanted to consider.

The sound of a woman's blood-curdling scream stopped him in his tracks. He spun around to find the two beasts who were chasing him had stopped, as well. They didn't attack—something was wrong.

More screams. It sounded like Lauren. Matt looked around, paralyzed by the shock of realization, as he finally understood why the rest of the pack wasn't behind him. The tricksters had their own plan all along, and both he and Troy walked right into it.

The two beasts huffed to one another, then turned and ran off through the debris, leaving Matt alone to listen to their laughter.

The screams stopped; Matt stood alone in the darkness. His mind told him to run back to the workshop now, but fear had taken hold. He was terrified over what he might find. What if Sam was dead? What if he was the only one left? Either way, he had to find out, standing in the middle of a junkyard was not an option.

Fearing the worst, he took off, making his way back toward the building, not sure what he would find.

The metal workshop loomed large up ahead. Matt crept closer, listening for any sign of danger. It was dead silent. That didn't help allay his fears.

Suddenly, the door to the workshop swung open with a bang.

"Come on!" shouted Troy. "Get inside!" He waved his arms furiously, gesturing for Matt to hurry.

As soon as he was close to the door, Sam burst out of the warehouse, her face soaked with tears. She ran to Matt and wrapped her arms around him. Her entire body trembled as she sobbed uncontrollably.

"What happened?" he asked.

"They came in from a door in the back of the shop," she said. "A trapdoor. We were too busy with the one in the cage. We didn't notice it until it was too late." Tears streamed down her cheeks. "They took Lauren. We didn't even know until we heard her screaming outside."

"It's okay," said Matt, holding her close.

"We need to get inside," said Troy. "There's no telling when they're gonna come back. They're gonna be pissed as soon as they find out we caught one of theirs. Wait till you see what we got."

Matt pulled away from Sam and kissed her forehead, then followed Troy into the workshop. He peered inside the cage, ready to see, for the first time, who this person really was.

Rage swept over him as he realized the man they had captured was none other than Pax, the same kid they met earlier. He knew there was something strange about the kid, but he never would have imagined anything like this.

A tiny part of his mind still refused to accept the whole shapeshifter aspect. "Are you sure he was one of those beasts?"

"Do you seriously think I would've zapped a naked kid running around in the dark?" Troy peered down at Pax. "This motherfucker chased me, intending to rip my throat out." He ran a hand down his face. "After we knocked him out, I watched him, with my own eyes, turn from the coyote I zapped to who you see right now."

"They really are shapeshifters," said Sam. She locked eyes with Matt. "I always thought those sorts of things were fantasies."

Matt crouched down and studied Pax. For all intents and purposes, the kid looked like every other kid he had ever seen. Nothing noteworthy at all. It was hard to believe that this unconscious teenager was some sort of supernatural beast that could survive gunshots and impaling.

His anger grew. This creep and his friends killed his sister, he was sure of it.

Troy cleared his throat, then said, "He's out, but we don't know for how long. Whatever we're gonna do, we need to get to it."

Inside the cage, Pax moaned and shifted his body. His eyes fluttered open as he rubbed his head, then suddenly, he bolted upright, grabbing hold of the bars of the cage and shaking them furiously.

"You're not getting out," said Matt, holding back a smirk.

"Fuck you!" shouted Pax.

"You're awfully mouthy for a naked son of a bitch locked up in a cage," replied Matt, this time he allowed himself to chuckle.

Pax raged, then glared at Matt. "Let me out!" he roared.

Matt shook his head and sighed. "Ain't gonna happen."

The teen snarled and began to shift right there in front of him and the others. His teeth grew long and sharp, hair covered his body, his eyes glowed.

Sam gasped and stepped back, but Matt was ready for this. He picked up the connectors for the battery and waited.

"What are you doing, man?" asked Troy. "Knock him out!"

Matt didn't respond, he was too busy watching in fascination, as

Pax's entire body transformed. He needed to see this with his own eyes. The sickening sound of bones snapping and popping echoed throughout the warehouse.

"Matt!" shouted Troy. "Knock that thing the fuck out!" Instead of waiting any longer, Troy lunged forward, ripped the connectors from Matt's hands and touched them to the battery.

The beast in the cage cried out in pain. His muscles tensed, and his body stiffened then suddenly, he was unconscious. A moment later, he was just an ordinary teen.

"Why did you do that?" asked Matt, barely able to mask his anger.

"Because you were fucking around," replied Troy. "What the hell were you waiting for?"

"I wanted to see what we're up against," replied Matt. "I needed to see one of them change with my own eyes. Now there's no more doubt. We know what they are."

"How the hell are we gonna interrogate him?" asked Troy. "You saw how he acted. Something tells me he ain't gonna sit down and tell us all about himself and the others."

"I got a plan for that," replied Matt.

"What sort of plan?"

"We need to know what these things are," said Matt. "What makes them tick. How many of them there are. And how can we kill them?" He studied Troy's reaction to his words and waited for a response.

"He was changing," said Sam. "He was changing into one of those creatures." She peered up at Matt with tears in her eyes. "He was changing into one of those things that took Lauren." She stepped closer to the cage and stared down at Pax. "How can that be?" She shook her head. "We talked to him. He's just a kid. How is this even possible?"

"We can't deny what we've just seen with our own eyes," said Matt.

"So, what's this plan of yours?" asked Troy.

Matt stared down at the unconscious body in the cage. "Well, we're gonna use him to find out everything we can about his kind. So we can use it to destroy them all."

"Destroy them?" asked Troy. "With what? A couple of old car batteries? We need help. We need to contact the office and get some Rangers down here." He paused. "Maybe even some Troopers. Hell, we need the National Guard or the Marines."

"What are we gonna tell them?" asked Matt. "That a bunch of shapeshifting coyotes are out here in west of nowhere, Texas, killing off hikers and tourists?" He paused, letting his words sink in. "Do you realize how crazy that sounds?"

He left Troy to mull over their conversation and wandered around the warehouse, searching for something sharp.

"What the hell are you looking for now?" asked Troy.

"A knife, an ax or something like that," replied Matt as he shifted tools around on a bench.

"What are you gonna do with it when you find one?"

"I'm gonna see exactly how regenerative he is," replied Matt. He pulled out a drawer and found what he was searching for. With a smile on his face, he held up a hatchet.

"Matt," said Troy. "I'm not so sure—"

"Not so sure about what?" he asked. "Would you rather wait here for the rest of his group to come and pick us off one by one? Do you want to suffer the same fate as Lauren? The same fate as my sister and her friends." He stalked over to the cage. "The whole time we thought we were creating a plan to capture one of them, they made their own plan to take away one of us. What are they planning now? Who's it gonna be next? Me? You? Sam?" The thought of those beasts coming for Sam sent a shock of adrenaline throughout his body. The realization that they had already murdered his little sister Ash ignited his rage.

He opened the cage.

"What the hell are you doing?" demanded Troy. "Don't open that!"

Matt shrugged him off. He fed Pax's arm between the bars of the cage, then closed and locked the door again, then he raised the hatchet over his head.

"No, no, no, no. Matt!" shouted Troy.

With one swift motion, he brought the ax down atop Pax's arm, right at the elbow. As the metal sliced through the young man's flesh, he awoke, screaming. Blood sprayed everywhere. The teen scooted back against the cage, holding what was left of his arm, while the rest lay on the floor.

Troy continued to yell something, so did Sam, but Matt was too enthralled with what was happening in the cage. Before his eyes, Pax began to turn again, this time, however, his arm grew anew while the change was happening. He had grown a whole new arm!

The beast growled and lunged at the cage, causing the whole thing to shake and rattle. Matt wondered whether the rusty metal would hold.

So captured by the spectacle before him, Matt didn't see it when Troy grabbed the clamps and applied them to the battery. The electrical current coursed through the metal into the beast's body. The creature tensed, then, once again, collapsed on the floor and became Pax. His arm was fully intact. The only sign of it ever having been cut off was the discarded limb still laying on the floor outside of the cage.

"Did you see that?" asked Matt excitedly.

"Yeah, I saw it," replied Troy, his tone was much quieter now. He seemed to be coming around to the reality of their situation.

Matt poked the discarded arm with the toe of his boot. "The fucker grew a whole new arm!" He peered up at Troy, then Sam. "Can you believe that?"

"If I hadn't seen it," replied Sam. "I wouldn't believe it was possible."

Matt reached into the cage.

"Don't," exclaimed Sam, nervously.

"I need to see," replied Matt. He touched Pax's new arm; it was warm with a healthy pulse. Aside from blood splatter, there was no scarring, no sign whatsoever that any damage had occurred. He could hardly believe what he was seeing.

"Alright," said Troy. "We know those things ain't human, and we now know they can regenerate."

"Only after they change," said Matt.

"How do you know that?" asked Sam.

"If he could regenerate without changing, he would have," replied Matt.

Troy nodded. "So, where does that leave us?"

"We need to find out where the rest of the bastards are, and how many," said Matt. "Then we figure out how to kill them."

"What if we can't?" asked Sam.

"Everything dies," he replied flatly.

They needed to gather all the facts they could before the rest of the pack noticed that one of theirs was missing. Before they returned for another one of his friends.

Matt scavenged a section of thick wire and a small propane torch from one of the tool chests.

He pulled Pax's new arm through the bars, then, using the wire, tied his hand tightly to the cage. He filled a bucket with water from the sink, then walked back to the cage and splashed it all over the kid.

Pax awakened with a moan and moved to touch his head. As soon as he realized his arm wouldn't move, he panicked and thrashed around, pulling against the wire. Upon realizing what was holding him in place, he reached over with his other hand to untwist the wire, but Matt was having none of that. He ignited the blow torch and held the flame against Pax's hand.

The boy howled in pain. The noxious stench of burned hair filled the air. Pax tried to shift, but Troy let just enough current of the battery through to bring him to the edge of unconsciousness. It was working.

"Keep the power on like that," said Matt. "I don't think he can change when it's on." He set his focus to the task at hand.

"Now Pax," said Matt. "I'm gonna ask a few questions, and you're gonna answer."

"Fuck you!" shouted Pax. His eyes glowed icy blue, while tiny hairs sprung from his skin.

Troy upped the voltage just enough to coax a scream of pain from the teen.

"We can make it hurt even more, if you insist," said Matt. "I'm only gonna warn you once, don't try to change. Every time you do, my friend here will up the voltage. Are we clear?"

Pax glared at him with hate-filled eyes.

Matt inspected the teen's hand, the skin was red and blistered from the flame, there was no sign of healing. A vicious smirk spread across his face. "Looks like you can't heal unless you change," he said.

Silence.

Matt ignited the torch again. "Let's start over," he said. "How many of you are there?"

Nothing.

"Where are the others?"

Pax continued to glare.

"What did you do with my sister, Ash?"

The teen sneered; his lips curled into a malevolent smile. He said nothing.

The sight of that wicked grin sparked white hot rage inside Matt. He positioned the flame against Pax's hand, and this time, let it sit there long enough for the skin to blister, then blacken. Blood and clear liquid oozed from the charred member. He waited for the kid to stop screaming, then he spoke once again.

"Answer my questions, damnit!" he shouted. "If you tell us what we want to know, I promise, we'll make your end as quick and as painless as possible."

Pax stared at Matt with cold, cunning eyes. "None of you are leaving this valley." He sneered and stared directly at Sam. "Caleb's gonna rip the skin from your bodies while you scream in pain and beg to die."

"Who's Caleb?" asked Matt. "Is that the alpha?"

The teen's only response was to laugh maniacally.

"Light him up, Troy," he said, climbing to his feet. "Knock the fucker out."

Pax seized and collapsed in a heap, once again unconscious.

Matt sighed. The kid was much stronger than he imagined. He had to admire his will. Unfortunately, they didn't have the time to continue playing this game. He was sure the rest of the pack would be returning soon. What mattered most at this point, was getting Sam to safety, then he could worry about revenge.

"Now what?" asked Troy.

"He's not gonna crack," replied Matt as he opened the cage.

"You're not letting him go?" asked Sam.

Matt shook his head. "No, I'm ending this so we can get out of here." Grabbing a hand full of blond hair, he pulled Pax halfway out of the cage, then lifted the hatchet and brought it down onto the boy's neck. With a sickening crack, the blade sliced through, but not all the way. He lifted the ax and brought it down again and again until Pax's head rolled free, onto the floor.

"Gather what you can find as far as weapons go," ordered Matt. "I'm sure the others will be here soon and we gotta be long gone before they get here."

While he stayed with the body, Sam and Troy collected supplies. He lifted the head and stared into the boy's dead eyes. The kid was certainly not coming back after this. At least he knows of one way to kill the damn bastards. He placed the head atop the cage as a message. They took his sister; he'll kill them all.

Hurrying through the debris, the trio ran away from the work-shop of horror. The map had shown that there was a farmhouse just over the rise. Matt had a deep suspicion who the house belonged to; he didn't care anymore. If there was a phone, they could use it to call for help. Or, even better, maybe there were weapons, the kind he could use to destroy the monsters, and then he would call for support.

So many questions rolled over in his mind. Who was Caleb? He was sure that was the name of the alpha. Was he also Pax's blood? Were they all one family?

With no breaks, he ran for miles on pure adrenaline, and even though his entire body ached, he pushed on. The climb up the hill almost did him in. His heart pounded as his tired body fought to keep moving. They arrived at the top of the rise just as a howl erupted from the valley below.

The sound hurt Matt's ears. There was an undertone to it that hadn't been there before. He smiled, feeling proud of himself. The pack had found his little message.

THIRTY-SIX

THE SCENT OF BLOOD, burned flesh, and ozone filled the air. The silence was suffocating. Something was horribly wrong.

Caleb slammed into the door, but it refused to budge. He ran around the side of the building and crashed his body against the side door of the workshop. The humans had put something heavy in the way. No matter how hard he rammed into it, the door wouldn't budge. Driven by blind rage, he rammed his body into the door again and again—it made no difference.

He moved backward, ready to charge one more time, when Izzy leaped between him and the building.

She brushed her body up against him, gently pushing him aside.

Struggling to contain his anger, Caleb braced himself against her prodding, but as soon as he saw Bass, he understood her intent. He moved aside and let the giant beast do his thing.

With a single forceful blow, Bass smashed through the door, shoving aside the heavy crates that the humans had stacked as a barrier.

Caleb stood at entrance to the dark cavern of the warehouse. The icy fingers of fear clenched tightly around his heart. His instincts warned him about what he might find, but his mind refused to accept it without proof.

Inside, the building was silent. He sniffed the air; the scent of fresh blood was strong. The subtlety of the human's scent told him they were no longer there. That was no surprise, he expected that. They would be fools to have stayed. He breathed deeply, filling his lungs with Pax's scent, but it was weak, almost not there, buried by the metallic scent of blood. Caleb's heart sank, knowing what that meant, but still unwilling to admit it to himself.

He prowled through the building, slowly—cautiously. Not because he was concerned about his safety, but because he dreaded what he was sure he was about to see.

Unable to contain her emotions, Jewel ran past, disappearing around a row of tool chests. Her pained cry told Caleb everything he needed to know.

He traced her path and halted in front of the gruesome display the humans had left behind. The floor was covered in thick red blood, pooling around his feet. Inside a rusty metal cage, the lifeless body of his little brother lay on the floor, his head perched on top as if on display. Caleb's heart shattered into a million tiny shards of glass. A profound emptiness threatened to overwhelm him.

The sound of Jewel's heart-wrenching whimpers bounced off the metal walls as she lay on the floor beside Pax's lifeless body.

Caleb's mind went blank. Pax—What have they done to you? He wanted to collapse in a heap of despair. Driven by an intense thirst for revenge, he inspected his brother's body, noting the small burn marks. They smelled of ozone. It appeared as though they used electric shock to incapacitate him. He circled the cage, coming to a stop by Pax's hand. Crudely tied to the bars, the metal wire dug deep into blackened and blistered skin. They tortured him with fire; Caleb would be sure to pay that back tenfold.

The hatchet they used to decapitate his brother lay in a pool of blood on the concrete floor. He took in the scent on the handle, the wielder of this weapon would experience the greatest suffering. He studied his brother's head resting atop the cage. This was a message—one he received loud and clear.

Caleb lay on the floor next to Jewel, the weight of his deep sorrow pressing down on him, leaving him unable to take any further action. Pax was gone. His little brother was tortured, then murdered by the humans. Memories of their childhood played out in his mind like an old family movie. His soul broken over the loss of yet another family member. He failed. He was supposed to keep his siblings safe, to help them grow into the full adults they were meant to be. Pax would never realize his full potential; his life was snuffed out too soon.

Lying on the cold concrete floor of the shop, Caleb's despair transformed into a smoldering rage deep in his gut. A malevolent calm settled over him. His mind clear, he vowed that this group of humans were going to pay. By the time he was finished with them, they would beg for an end to it all.

He strolled outside, the scent of his prey was strong. It will be easy to track them, there was no need to rush. He drew in a lungful of cool night air and let loose a chilling howl that echoed throughout the valley. All around him, the pack called out in response, the force of their collective cries shook the metal building on its foundation.

Filled with hate and ready to exact his revenge, Caleb took off, following the trail of his prey. His mind reeling with all the different ways he intended to torture the humans. There would be pain—lots of it.

Stopping atop a hill, Caleb searched the valley. The fools were heading straight for his family's ranch. How convenient. The ranch was roughly five miles away—an easy run for the pack, but most humans would struggle. He slowed his pace; it didn't serve his plan to catch up with them too soon. He wanted them to feel as though they had a chance of surviving. His thoughts returned to Pax, to the condition they left his little brother in. This group was smarter than most—but not smart enough. Pax underestimated the humans; Caleb wouldn't repeat the same mistake.

THIRTY-SEVEN

TROY LED THE WAY, leaving Matt to bring up the rear. With little more than an image on the map, they trekked through the valley toward the ranch. If Matt's suspicions were correct, it wasn't just any ranch—it belonged to the shapeshifters. Much to his surprise, the going was relatively easy. There was little need for concern regarding wildlife, all thanks to the feral pack of monsters.

"Up ahead!" called Troy, pointing.

An old farmhouse stood silent against the steep, rocky hillside, a detached garage barely visible not far behind. On its right was a large barn; on its left, a long, winding driveway that disappeared around a cluster of trees.

"It looks quiet," said Sam.

Matt scanned the area, as far as he could discern, they were alone. He strained his ears, listening to the sound of the wind, and nothing more.

They passed a large, stone rimmed firepit, surrounded by a circle of rustic wood chairs. The ground was littered with jeans, T-shirts, boots, and empty beer bottles. The scent of fire hung like a cloud over the area.

Several yards away, a soft light emanated from the welcoming front porch. Up close, the house was quaint and obviously well maintained. The home stood three stories tall, with a cozy, wrap-around porch. Ornate shrubs surrounded the structure, bathing the area in a light floral scent. A giant oak tree, its leaves rustling in the breeze, stood sentinel beside the home, its mighty branches reaching out toward the roof.

Matt's nerves were on edge as he crept closer, the sound of gravel crunching under his boots was painfully loud. He found this unnerving. Even though it seemed there was no one home, it was uncertain. If, by chance, there was somebody around, all the noise they were making would alert them.

The railing was sturdy in his hand as he slowly climbed the stairs. Not a single step creaked under foot. To his right, a wood swing swayed gently on its chain; to his left stood a pair of white, rocking chairs with a small table in between.

He continued around to the back of the house. At the bottom of the staircase stood a massive smoker, a dark cloud of thick smoke billowed from its chimney. As he stood there, he could feel the intense heat and smell the mouthwatering scent of meat being slow-cooked. His stomach churned in disgust, as he thought about what sort of meat might be cooking inside the giant black grill.

Several yards away stood the garage with its four bay doors tightly shut. Matt stepped off the porch and stormed over to the building. He tugged on one of the rolling doors, not surprisingly, it didn't move. Just to be sure, he tried the second, third and fourth; none of the doors budged. He walked around the building in search of a man door to enter, noting the peculiar cave-like opening in the rock wall behind the building. Determined to keep on track, he continued around the garage until he finally found what he was looking for. A slight turn of the knob and it opened. Confidence washed over him as he flipped on the lights inside the garage and entered.

Two pickup trucks sat idle, a lone motorcycle in between them. He recognized one truck as the one Pax and Ezra were working out of earlier when they ran into them, working on the fence. Anger welled up inside his gut. To think he was so close to the bastard earlier—close enough that he could have wiped that smirk off the punk's face forever. That skinny little liar looked him right in the eyes. A sense of satisfaction swept over him as he reminded himself that Pax was dead —along with his creepy smirk. Matt peered inside the trucks, unfortunately there were no keys visible. He didn't expect it to be that easy, nevertheless; it was worth a try.

Across the room, Troy and Sam scoured the walls and shelves, both in search of the missing keys or some kind of weapon for defense.

Matt leaned into the first truck and pulled open the glove box, where he found a switchblade resting atop papers and a care manual. He pocketed the knife and opened the manual. Paxton Riggs was the name on the insurance card. A tiny glimmer of guilt sparked in his heart as he recalled the events back in the warehouse. Pax was just a kid. He shook his head. No, he wasn't, that kid was a feral monster who only resembled a normal young adult. He and his friends murdered Ash. Who knows how many other poor souls had the misfortune of wandering into this area unprepared over the years. He thought of the field of broken-down vehicles, some from decades ago, all of whom belonged to innocent victims of these monsters. How many children were in those vehicles? The discarded toy rabbit, covered in blood, came to mind. A sense of righteous anger swept aside his guilt. Matt was right in doing what he did, the kid deserved it, in fact, he deserved so much more.

"There's nothing here," said Troy. "Maybe they keep the keys in the house."

"This is Pax's truck," said Matt, holding the papers in the air. In a fit of disgust and rage he flung the papers inside the truck where they scattered across the seat and onto the floor. "I guess we know who owns this house." He turned on his heels. "The keys are probably inside somewhere. But before we go in, I got one more thing I wanna check out."

He walked around the back of the garage, coming to a halt in front of the cave's entrance. Something about the place triggered a deep primal fear. He glanced over his shoulder to find both Sam and Troy standing nearby.

After clicking on his flashlight, Matt took his first tentative steps inside. The air was cool and heavy with the scent of earth, along with something else. Torches rested in iron holders that were hung along the rocky walls. The sound of dripping water echoed all around. With slow determination, he followed the narrow passageway, not sure what he might find at the end. Dark stains marred the walls. He raised his light to get a better look. Dried blood was everywhere. Behind him, Troy shined his light along the walls and ceiling, illuminating everything. He, too, seemed unable to voice what they were all thinking.

Matt led the group further into the cave, the stains became more pronounced, sometimes coloring the sandy floor. The hair on the back of his neck stood on end.

The scent of kerosene assaulted his senses, a lone torch, rested in a holder on the wall. The cloth wrapped around the tip was sticky to the touch. Using his lighter, he lit the torch on fire and held it aloft, bathing the cave in flickering light. The walls came to life with dancing shadows. A long, narrow tunnel disappeared into the unknown on one side of the room. In the pitch-black he could only make out a few feet in front of him, but he could feel a cool breeze rustling through the air.

On the opposite side of the cavern, a wall of rusty iron bars closed off what appeared to be a small room. Matt wandered up to the bars and peered through at the worn cot resting along the far wall. Every inch of the walls was stained with blood—even the sandy floor was deep crimson. He pulled open the rusty gate and stepped inside the cell. What the hell was this place? How many people have died down here?

Something glinted in the light.

He picked up the item, studying the shiny necklace in the warm glow of the torchlight.

As he stared down at the tiny silver fairy holding an ice blue gemstone, a vivid memory surged forward from the recesses of his mind. A wave of heartache crashed over him, unleashing an overwhelming fury as he recalled the first time he ever laid eyes on the trinket.

Christmas morning, when he was fourteen years old. He and Ash had spent over an hour opening all the gifts under the tree, but one present had her attention. A tiny, red velvet box.

"Can I open it now?" she begged.

"Open what?" replied Wyatt, their father. He flashed a playful smile at Mel, their mom, and winked.

"Please, Dad."

"How do you know it's yours?" asked Mel.

Matt, sensing the game they were playing, joined in, even though he had no idea what might be in the tiny box. "Yeah Ash, that could be for me."

She scoffed and poked her tongue out at him then without a word, turned her attention back to her parents.

"Come on," she whined. "This is killing me."

Wyatt nodded at Matt, signaling for him to pull the box down. Tiny box in hand, he held it out to Ash, who reached for it enthusiastically. Matt pulled it just out of reach.

"I don't know," said Wyatt. "Maybe she's not ready for something like this."

"Hmm, good point," replied Mel.

Matt could barely contain a giggle.

"I am, I am," shouted Ash, practically bouncing up and down. "Please."

"Alright," said Wyatt. "But you have to promise to take good care of it and not lose it."

"I will, I will, I will," she shouted.

"Okay then," said Wyatt. "Go on Matt, give your sister the little box."

Her delicate hands trembled as she pulled the ribbon free and flipped open the lid. Ash gasped as she lifted the shiny little fairy from the silk pillow and held it high for all to see. "It's so pretty!" she exclaimed. She shoved the necklace into Matt's hand, and spun around, saying, "Help me put it on!"

As soon as he closed the clasp, she bolted across the room to the closest mirror and stared at her reflection. With the brightest smile on her face, she stated, "I'm never taking this off." She ran her finger across the tiny gemstone and said, "I'm gonna wear it forever."

Matt gazed down at the necklace in his hand. His eyes filled with tears, breathing in the scent of blood mixed with sand and rock all around him. He glanced around the cell, at the walls and ceiling covered in blood. His sister's blood mingled with that of countless others. Ash's life ended in this room.

Sorrow gave way to rage as he shoved the necklace into his pocket, then quickly made his way back out of the cave. More determined than ever, he stalked his way over to the back door of the house. On his way, he stopped by the smoker and kicked the giant black beast over on its side. Smoke billowed into the air as partially cooked meat toppled to the ground.

The back door was unlocked, of course it was, who would need to lock things up in such a desolate place. He stormed inside, taking in the tidy country kitchen. He didn't really know what to expect, but he found himself completely unprepared to find such an average scene.

Cast-iron pans hung from a pot rack above the large stove. A set of dishes sat drying in the rack at the edge of the sink where an unusual wooden spoon caught his eye. Upon closer inspection, he noticed it was hand carved like the items they found in the workshop. He moved it around in his hand, feeling the smooth, polished surface between his fingers. This wasn't wood at all, it was bone—human bone. How dare these animals pretend to be normal people? He threw the spoon across the room, then shoved the drying rack from the counter. Dishes shattered into pieces as they crashed to the floor.

Troy and Sam stood silently as Matt rampaged. He tossed canisters filled with coffee, sugar, and flour, sending the fine white powder spewing into the air like a fluffy cloud. He knocked over shelves and ripped open cupboards, only to throw the contents to the floor. He wanted to tear the entire place down with his bare hands. Once he eliminated the entire pack, he would be sure to light the biggest fire this area had ever seen, burning everything down in its wake.

Heart pounding in his chest, Matt stopped and surveyed the damage. He glanced over to Troy and Sam and said, "Let's check out the rest of the house."

A narrow hallway connected the kitchen to the rest of the old house. Halfway down, Sam gasped and ran over to an old phone suspended on the wall. She lifted the handset and held it to her ear. "It's working!" she exclaimed. With shaky hands, she dialed nine one-one. "H-Hello?" she stammered into the phone. "We need help! Please send the police!" She paused. "I-I don't know where we are!" she shouted to the invisible operator at the other end, her voice sounding hysterical.

Troy took the phone from her hand and spoke calmly. He pulled out his phone and opened the map, zooming in on their location, then he slowly relayed that information to the operator. He cast a swift glance toward Matt. "They're calling in the State Police," he said. Relief washed over his face. "Help is on the way."

Matt scoffed. "They won't get here in time," he said flatly. "We're too far out."

"That's not true," said Sam, shaking her head back and forth as she sobbed.

"Look at me," said Matt. "Look at me!"

Sam wiped her face as she stared back at him.

"We're in the middle of nowhere. By the time help gets here, it'll be too late." He paused, waiting for her to acknowledge his words. "Our only chance is to find out what we can and fight back as though our lives depend on it." He held her by her shoulders and stared into her eyes. "Do you understand?"

Sam nodded.

Matt locked eyes with Troy, who nodded in acceptance. He didn't say it aloud, but deep inside, he didn't want help—at least not yet. He wanted revenge.

He turned his attention to the rest of the house. If he was going to make these monsters pay, he needed to learn everything possible about these creatures. The hall dumped into a large, but cozy living room with walls made of stained wood. A giant metal windmill wheel hung suspended from the tall ceiling. Across the room was a grand, rustic fireplace, complete with a roughhewn wood mantle. A library of photos adorned the walls—a vast, multi-generational history, in what appeared to be chronological order. He followed the progression of images from antique daguerreotypes to black and white, to vintage color and finally to contemporary images. He studied the pictures. A typical smiling family stared back at him; it was almost hard to believe they were really monsters. These people could be anyone. He could have stood beside them anywhere and not had a clue. A pretty, blonde-haired woman smiled lovingly, holding a toddler, her hair up in pigtails. Beside her stood a small boy, and another who was a few years older. Positioned behind them all, his muscular arm resting protectively on the woman's shoulder, stood a rugged-looking man.

Next to that was another photo of a very young Fax beaming at the camera with a mouth of missing teeth. Such an innocent face. Matt shook his head and moved on, pausing before an image of a young boy. There was a strong resemblance to Pax, but this wasn't him. This one had a cunning glare in his eyes—those eyes.

Farther down the wall were even more photos of the same family, just slightly older. The young toddler was a pretty pre-teen, with a strong resemblance to her mother. Pax was a young adolescent and the older one, he had become a fine-looking young man. His face more masculine, his eyes more cunning. Matt had seen those eyes before. He remembered the alpha. The way the beast stared at him when it pulled the rod from its side was identical to the stare of the young man in the photo.

Matt took the picture down from the wall, studying every detail of the young man's face.

"What is it?" asked Sam, peering over his shoulder.

"This is him," replied Matt.

"Who?"

"The alpha," he said. "This was the one I impaled with the rod." He tapped the glass. "This is Caleb."

Troy took the photo and studied the face of the teen. "This is a kid," he said.

"These are older pictures," replied Sam as she studied the wall of photographs. "Their whole life is on this wall. They seem to stop around the time the oldest son was about nineteen or twenty." She scanned the wall. "I think something happened to the parents around that time."

"Why do you say that?" asked Matt.

Sam turned to face him. "Because this is the work of a mom who loves her family. If the images suddenly stopped, as they seem to have, it could only be because something happened to her."

He'd heard enough. Matt flung the photograph across the room where it shattered against the wood mantle. With rage in his heart, he swept his arms along the wall, sending every picture hurtling to the floor in pieces.

"I don't give a shit about their family trauma!" He stormed out of the living room and up the stairs, taking them two at a time.

He peered into the first bedroom. A simple bed with a rumpled, dark blue comforter stood between two windows with billowy curtains. Dirty t-shirts and jeans littered the floor, while posters of pretty women stared down provocatively from the walls. A typical teen boy's bedroom. Matt was in no mood to foster fond thoughts or even sympathy for Pax. He turned and walked away from the bedroom, closing the door behind him.

The next door was nothing more than a linen closet. The floral scent of fresh laundry accosted his senses. He moved to the next door; it was another bedroom. This one was fancier with floral curtains and matching quilt. A light coat of dust lay atop every surface, this room was hardly used.

He stalked past a bathroom door and another linen closet, coming to a stop in the threshold of what appeared to be the master bedroom. A large bed made of rough-hewn wood was the focal point of the room. The white sheets were rumpled, pillows and quilt lay on the floor, right next to a woman's bra. He walked over to the dresser, examining the items laid out neatly across the top. A long knife with an intricately carved handle made of bone sat beside an ornately carved wooden box. Matt stuffed the knife in his belt, then lifted the lid of the box and inspected the contents. After finding nothing noteworthy, he slammed the lid closed and hurled the box across the room.

Inside the top drawer, he found necklaces, earrings, keychains and even some pocketknives resting atop a pile of driver's licenses from every state. Matt thumbed through the cards, wondering how many people these monsters murdered over the years. Up until this moment, he had given little thought to all the others that came before. Sure, the sea of rusted vehicles gave him an idea. But standing there, looking at the actual faces, reading the names, the sheer magnitude of this family's crimes came to light. They were evil.

His eyes fell on a familiar face peering up at him from the corner of the drawer. With a trembling hand, he lifted Ash's driver's license from the pile. White hot rage exploded in his gut. Matt roared and pulled the dresser over, spilling the contents of the drawer all over the floor. He stormed across the room and pulled out the knife, then stabbed the mattress, cutting a foot long gash into the top layer. Stabbing and slashing repeatedly, he didn't stop until the mattress was destroyed. He stormed into the bathroom where he kicked the sink off the wall, shattered the mirror and smashed the clawfoot tub.

"There's something up these stairs," Troy called out from the hall.

Matt joined him at the base of a set of stairs. "Must be the attic," he said. Without another word, he stomped up the steps, coming to a halt at the top.

The room was massive, with its vaulted ceiling. A small desk sat quietly in the corner, adorned with a delicate string of twinkling Christmas lights that painted the room with a vibrant spectrum of colors. Matt wandered over and studied the pictures on the mirror and pinned to the board. More images of happy, smiling faces. Yep, just another typical all-American family. He had seen enough of this charade. He was ready to bring this all to an end—a slow, painful end.

As he prepared to descend the stairs, a lone howl echoed through the hills, followed by a chorus of calls. The pack had arrived.

THIRTY-EIGHT

CALEB CROUCHED LOW; his eyes focused on the shadows slithering around the outside of the house. He watched them enter the cave, gradually fading from his gaze. He crept along the ground on his belly to avoid being seen, he didn't want to alert the humans until he was ready to strike.

He watched as Matt and his friends emerged from the cave, their slumped shoulders and rapid steps depicted an air of resolve. They stormed over to the house, pausing by the smoker just long enough for Matt to kick it to the ground.

Well, shit, thought Caleb, there goes a perfectly good brisket. He wondered if the intruders thought he was smoking human meat. He supposed he could, but when it came to human flesh, the real flavor was fresh from the kill. When the blood, full of adrenaline and fear, was still infused in every fiber—in every bite.

The humans entered the house. Caleb wasn't worried, he knew every inch of that building. There wasn't much they could do in there, so he hung back and waited. Let them get an eye full, then spring the trap.

Outside, standing in the darkness, he listened to the sound of glass breaking; of items being tossed about. A tiny spark of anger ignited in his belly over the clean-up work he would have to do after this.

Jewel sauntered close, her steps slow and heavy, her body language reflecting her deep sadness. In a display of empathy, Caleb lowered his head and tenderly brushed against her, letting her know he understood. She leaned against him, emitting a small whimper.

A sharp pang of grief stabbed his heart as he thought about Pax. He was going to make sure the humans paid dearly for what they did to his little brother—to his family.

Inside the house, footsteps pounded up the stairs. A primal scream exploded from the lungs of one of the men, followed by the sound of even more destruction.

Caleb crept over to the front of the house, stopping roughly six feet from the bottom step. The rest of the pack took their places, surrounding the building. He inhaled, filling his lungs with cool night air, then let out a long howl. A chorus of howls mimicked his own, their cries echoing all around the valley. The game was on. The humans inside the house knew the pack had arrived to claim their prize.

The front door burst open, and the one called Matt stepped out onto the porch. He locked eyes with Caleb. "I know who you are! You don't scare me!" he shouted, his voice thick with rage.

The scent in the air told Caleb a different story. He huffed in response but didn't move.

Matt took a step forward, only to have the woman behind him reach out and grab him by the shoulder. A silent conversation took place between the two, in a show of shaking heads and mouthed words.

In the corner of his eye, Caleb could see Bass slink away, toward the back of the house. On his other side, Ezra did the same. The two humans were so busy with their private disagreement, they didn't even notice the shift in dynamics.

The deafening roar of a truck engine suddenly erupted from the garage, its powerful rumble resonating through the air. Matt and the woman ceased their back and forth and quickly backed up into the house, closing the door behind them.

Caleb picked up his jeans off the dusty ground, then leisurely strolled around the back, joining Izzy and Jewel as they eagerly observed the spectacle.

The door to the garage rolled up, exposing Pax's truck with the engine running. Anger flashed in Caleb's gut at the audacity of these humans to take his brother's truck—after what they did to him. The darker skinned human sat in the driver's seat, gunning the gas pedal, revving the engine. His fingers clenched around the steering wheel as he stared directly at Caleb. The fool didn't even see Bass slink closer.

A flurry of activity erupted from the house as the back door flung open, spilling Matt and the woman onto the porch. The woman lifted her hand to her throat—terror washed over her face, as she watched Bass melt into the shadows in the garage.

"Troy!" shouted Matt, waving his arms furiously.

The one named Troy didn't hear, his gaze locked onto Caleb. He revved the engine, his face twisted in a scowl of rage.

"Troy! No! Get out of there!" shouted Matt, his voice thick with fear.

The woman by his side mirrored his warning, but their friend could hear nothing over the loud engine.

Troy let out a loud yell then threw the truck into gear; the vehicle lurched forward. In a fit of confidence, he flipped off Caleb, oblivious to the enormous beast lurking behind him in the truck bed.

From the porch, the woman screamed and pointed a trembling finger.

The sound of breaking glass erupted over the roar of the engine. In a flash of glistening white teeth and glowing eyes, Bass attacked. Troy screamed as blood exploded against the windshield from the inside. Slowly, the truck rolled forward. That was when Ezra jumped through the passenger side window. The life-or-death battle reverberated through the vehicle, causing it to sway back and forth.

Thick red blood obscured the view of the carnage. The sound of anguished cries mixed with menacing snarls. The truck engine roared as the vehicle veered out of control, heading directly for the giant oak tree, where it crashed with a loud bang.

Caleb turned his gaze to Matt and stared until the man finally glanced over in his direction. Eyes locked on one another; he turned into his human form. He wanted Matt to see the transformation—wanted him to know for once and for all that he was up against something he could never defeat. Wearing nothing more than a mile-wide smirk, Caleb slowly pulled on his jeans. As he buttoned up his pants, he couldn't help but chuckle with glee at the shocked and horrified expressions on the humans' faces. All the while, visions of the many ways he would make them suffer played out in his mind.

Maybe he would murder the woman and leave her body to decompose in the cell with Matt. Or maybe, he would keep them both alive long enough to feed them tiny morsels of one another until they begged for death.

The driver's side door burst open. Troy toppled to the ground, covered in blood from head to toe. He faced his friends and opened his mouth to speak, but the only thing that came out was a crimson waterfall.

Once again, the pathetic woman screamed, then buried her head against Matt's chest.

Caleb studied the couple on the porch, reveling in their sorrow, knowing their pain had only just begun. He turned back to the one named Troy, excited to see what came next.

Izzy and Jewel joined Ezra and Bass as they closed in for the final kill. Step by step, they inched closer to the man, the longer it took, the more terrified he became. He fell to his knees and begged for his life. But there would be no mercy. The pack paused a mere three feet away from Troy and yipped gleefully.

Caleb smiled at how deliciously cruel this was.

Bass snarled, exposing a mouth full of long, white fangs. He leaped forward, crashing down atop the man, knocking him to the ground where Ezra took hold of one arm and Jewel took the other. Izzy and Bass clamped their mighty jaws down onto the man's legs. The four beasts pulled back in a brutal game of tug of war. With each step backward, Troy's screams grew louder and more desperate. The sound of tearing muscles and tendons played out as a soft undertone.

Caleb glanced over to the couple on the porch once again, locking eyes with Matt. He wondered if they could hear their friend's body being torn apart. Probably not. Human ears were notoriously weak compared to every other creature on the planet. He turned his gaze back to the spectacle before him.

Troy screamed as his tendons were pulled to their limit. There was a loud pop, followed by a wet, tearing sound, then suddenly his arms and legs were no longer connected to his body. What remained of the man lay flat on his back, blood pumping out of his wounds in time with his heartbeat. His head rocked back and forth in the sand.

Bass climbed atop the man's chest and stared him in the eyes. He snarled, then opened his powerful jaws and bit down on Troy's face. With one mighty shake, he dislodged the head and flung it toward the house, where it rolled to a stop at the bottom of the stairs.

With one final scream, the couple disappeared inside the house, slamming the door closed behind them as if that could keep them safe.

The pack descended on their kill, celebrating as they tore flesh from bone.

Caleb had other things in mind. He turned and strolled toward the back door, whistling. "Come out, come out, wherever you are," he taunted as he took the steps slowly, one at a time. There was no need to hurry, time was on his side.

THIRTY-NINE

"OH MY GOD! OH MY GOD!" cried Sam, repeatedly, collapsing in a heap on the kitchen floor.

Matt wanted to comfort her, but he didn't know where to begin. The horror of what they just witnessed was still too raw in his mind. They ripped Troy apart. Matt closed his eyes, trying to purge the image of his best friend's body on the ground, limbs strewn around like a broken toy. And the alpha—his eyes, the malicious, jester-like smile plastered on his face as he watched the carnage. He changed right in front of them. Matt struggled to make sense of everything his eyes had witnessed, but his mind was refusing to cooperate. He leaned against a kitchen cabinet, ready to let his body slip to the floor.

The sound of whistling, followed by Caleb's jeering, broke his spiral. The doorknob turned slowly.

Fear gripped Matt's heart like a vise. Sam was still on the floor, rocking back and forth in a trance-like way. They needed to run. Death was on the other side of that door and any moment, he would enter.

Matt reached down. "Come on," he said softly.

Sam didn't move.

"Come on," he said, more forcefully this time. When she still didn't move, he took hold of her arm.

She pulled away and shook her head, still making no effort to go anywhere.

Matt was done playing games. If they didn't go now, they would end up exactly like Troy, Lauren, and Ash. The thought of his little sister living through this horror alone broke his heart. He took a deep breath and calmed his nerves, then he grabbed hold of Sam and lifted her off the floor. "Come on." he said calmly.

Luckily, Sam snapped out of it, she locked eyes with him, then slowly turned her gaze to the back door, watching the handle turn. Her expression reflected his own emotions.

"This way!" he shouted, pulling her through the house, toward the front door.

The kitchen door burst open, and Caleb stepped inside. He glanced around at the destruction, then said with a sneer, "Somebody has been sitting in my chair, and it's all broken."

Pressed against the wall in the hallway, Matt held Sam close, listening as Caleb moved about the kitchen, kicking the shattered debris around.

"Now this ain't no way to treat other people's things," said Caleb. "I should make y'all clean it up." He stood in the kitchen's threshold and stared down the hallway at Matt with glowing eyes. "That is right before I eat your hearts," he said with a low, growling voice.

Matt pushed Sam out the front door. He knew there was no way they could outrun the pack; their only hope was to find a place to hold up until help arrived. He forced himself to believe they had a chance; that help was on its way. The alternative would be to accept that neither he nor Sam would ever leave this place.

Outside, standing on the front porch, he scanned the area. The tree line was far away, but they had to make a run for it.

Behind them, Caleb clucked his tongue. "Now, where do you

think you can run off to?" He leaned his head back and laughed maniacally.

A sudden jolt of realization struck Matt; this was all a game to Caleb—he was enjoying this, and he had no intention of hiding it. They weren't defying the pack; they were playing right into their hands. How could he have been so stupid? By allowing his rage to take control of his thoughts, he dragged his friends with him right into the monster's lair.

Heart racing in his chest, Matt held tight to Sam's hand as they launched off the porch onto the gravel driveway. Dragging her behind him, he ran faster than he thought possible. The edge of the trees was almost within reach, they could make it—just a little farther.

"That's right," hollered Caleb from the front porch. "Keep it interesting. I love a good hunt."

As they ran for the cover of the tree line, Matt's mind reeled. Was this another instance of him playing into Caleb's hands? The pack! Where was the pack? He hadn't seen or heard any of them since Troy. He glanced around his shoulders, fearful that he might lay eyes on one of the giant beasts, lunging for them. Nothing. As far as he could tell, the only pack member in pursuit of them was Caleb. If only that was all they had to deal with, they might make it out of this mess alive.

The thorny branches of mesquite trees scratched his skin and tore at his clothes as he led them deeper into the woods. Sam cried out. Matt stopped running and turned to face her.

"You okay?" he asked, struggling to maintain some sense of calm.

Sam nodded and pulled her hand away from her face, exposing a thin, red gash along her cheek, below her eye. She studied the blood in her hand, then wiped it off on her jeans. "Yeah," she replied, nodding.

Caleb stood halfway between the house and the trees; his thumbs shoved into the waist of his jeans. Eyes glowing in the darkness, he made no move to run after them, instead he stood there, calmly watching them through the trees.

"We have to keep going," said Matt. "Can you keep running?"

Sam nodded.

Once again, they took off, this time heading toward the hills that lay just beyond the cluster of trees. Branches and twigs lashed out at them as they moved purposefully through the thicket.

The sound of a coyote howling to their right startled them both. They stopped suddenly, scanning the darkness.

Another howl, followed by yet another. The monsters were close. Matt stared back toward the house. A shock of adrenaline coursed through his body upon realizing that Caleb was nowhere in sight. Where the hell did he go? The noise intensified; the pack had surrounded them.

Matt frantically searched the ground for a branch or something large enough to use as a weapon. After everything he had seen so far about these monsters, he had little hope that he could kill any of them without serious weaponry. The best he could hope for would be to inflict enough damage, to buy him time to get Sam to safety.

A low growl erupted close by—too close. He spun around to find himself staring into the eyes of one of the smaller coyotes. It leered at him and snarled, showing off a mouth full of long, white teeth dripping with saliva.

The creature crept forward; its luminescent green eyes locked on Sam.

"Stay there," shouted Matt. He pulled a thorny branch backward, feeling the tension mount. Never taking his eyes off the creature, he yelled, "Take a couple steps back."

Sam did as she was told.

The coyote reared back, then launched into the air, heading straight for Sam.

Matt released the branch. It connected with the beast's body with a hollow thud. The coyote yelped as it flew toward a larger tree, slamming against the trunk and falling to the ground. The once fierce creature let out a feeble whine. A triumphant smile spread across Matt's face. He may not be able to kill them right now, but he could inflict pain.

With the rest of the pack working their way closer, it was time for a new plan. He set his focus on the only other structure in sight. With no other options, he guided Sam toward the safety of the barn, praying that he could find a weapon.

As soon as they got inside, Matt ushered her over to the back door. "You have to run," he said.

Tears streamed down her cheeks. "No, I won't leave you."

"Sam, stop," he said. "If you don't run, we're both dead."

She leaned her head against his chest and sobbed.

He lifted her chin and stared into her eyes. "I want you to run. Don't stop. Just keep going until you're safe. Can you do that for me?"

Sam sniffled, then wiped her face, and nodded.

He kissed her on the forehead. "Don't look back and don't stop running," he said, then he stepped back. "Go!" he prodded.

With tears in her eyes, Sam turned around and took off running.

Matt watched until her silhouette was no longer visible, then he set his focus on finding a weapon. His eyes settled upon a pitchfork. As he held it ready, he stood guard in the shadows of the entry.

Outside, Caleb's laughter boomed, followed by the sound of his singsong whistling as he moved closer to the barn.

Palms sweaty, heart pounding in his chest, Matt stood ready.

The whistling stopped.

"If you come out now," said Caleb. "I won't hurt you." He snickered. "Nah, nah, nah, I'm just foolin'." He laughed. "If you come out now, I promise I'll make it quick for your girl. But you, you're gonna suffer." He took a step closer. "You gotta know by now that you ain't leaving this valley."

The seriousness of Caleb's tone sent a cold chill down Matt's spine. No matter how this played out, he needed to figure out a way to buy time for Sam to get as far away as possible. This wasn't her fight. At this point, he didn't really care how it went for himself. If he went out fighting the monsters who murdered his sister, then so be it. Thinking about Ash sent a surge of anger through his body, giving him a much-needed jolt of courage.

"You talk a lot of trash for someone who is too chicken shit to come and say that to my face," taunted Matt.

Caleb chuckled and sniffed the air. "You reek of fear."

Matt stepped into the doorway, holding the pitchfork protectively in front of him. "Do I look scared to you?"

"Yes," replied Caleb, smirking. "Yes, you do." The smirk melted away from his face. "You murdered my little brother."

Seeing an opening, Matt decided to poke at it, hoping he could shake Caleb's confidence enough to get the upper hand. "Murder?" He shook his head. "You can't murder a dumb animal."

Caleb sneered, all the while glaring at him with hateful eyes.

"Truth be told," said Matt. "He wasn't the sharpest tool in the shed. If you ask me, you failed with that one."

"Enough!" bellowed Caleb.

"I guess that means I'm right," said Matt, trying his best to sound confident. "And you know it."

Caleb's eyes ignited with ice blue fire. "When I'm done with you, you'll have wished for death a hundred times over."

Sensing now was the right moment, Matt let out a battle cry and charged, but Caleb was ready. He dodged to the right just in time to avoid the prongs of the pitchfork. Matt staggered and nearly fell to the ground. He spun around, kicking up a plume of dust at his feet. Realizing he may never get another shot; he understood it was now or never. He raised the pitchfork and charged. This time, as Caleb moved to the side, Matt moved also, his forward momentum halted when the teeth of the pitchfork pierced Caleb's flesh.

A surge of hope coursed through Matt's heart. This could be the one and only chance he had to take this son of a bitch out. He pushed forward, feeling the pressure release as the prongs burst through

Caleb's backside. He let go of the handle and stepped back, surveying the damage, hoping for what he already knew was impossible.

Caleb staggered backward, gripping the wooden handle with bloody hands. Dark red blood oozed from the corner of his lips. He peered up at Matt with electric blue eyes, then slowly stood up straight. His lips curled into a sinister snarl, exposing a mouthful of wicked, sharp teeth, stained red with his own blood. The muscles in his arms and chest rippled and grew. His fingers became long, sharp claws. "Didn't we already do this tonight?"

Caleb shifted his gaze down to the pitchfork protruding from his body, then with a low, humorless laugh, he gripped the handle and pulled it free.

Matt watched the spectacle unfold. He didn't expect the wound to be life threatening, thanks to Pax, he understood there was only one way to kill these shapeshifters. He allowed a small smile to spread across his lips, at least he bought enough time for Sam to get away.

FORTY

AS IF IT were nothing more than a useless twig, Caleb dropped the bloody pitchfork onto the ground. The peculiar expression on Matt's face made him chuckle. The scent of fear hung heavy in the air. He inhaled, relishing the flavor, then lunged forward, not to make contact but to provoke Matt into a full assault. He wanted to drag out the game a bit more.

To his surprise, Matt stood firm, with his chest out and shoulders back holding fists high, ready for a fight.

"Come on, motherfucker!" he shouted.

Caleb sneered, far be it for him to pass up an invitation. He charged, slamming into Matt so hard it knocked them both to the ground. Dust plumed into the air, creating a cloud around them as he sat atop the pathetic human, repeatedly punching him in the face. As the cloud settled, Caleb climbed to his feet. He could have ended it all right at that moment, but he wanted to take his time. After what this asshole did to Pax, there would be no kindness offered. The man would suffer. He would only be granted a release from his misery when Caleb decided he was done.

Matt scooted back in the dirt, raising himself up on his elbows.

He wiped the blood from his nose and staggered to his feet. Fists raised, he sneered and said, "That all you got?"

Caleb swung, only to be blocked, but he expected that, so he brought his other fist around to land a blow. He could feel the snap of bone under his knuckles when his fist connected with Matt's face.

Blood sprung forth from a new gash on Matt's cheek. He hollered and charged only for Caleb to send him careening forward with a swift leg sweep. With arms outstretched, his hands clawing uselessly at the air, he toppled to the ground.

Once again, the pathetic human pushed himself up on his feet and turned to stare at Caleb through swollen eyes.

"You've got balls," jeered Caleb. "Too bad it won't do you any good." He pushed Matt backward, causing him to fall on his backside.

"Let's see you fight like a man," taunted Matt. "If you think you're so strong, come and fight me on equal footing."

Caleb pulled his inner beast back, his strength subsided, his teeth melted back into basic human teeth. He grinned and asked, "You mean like this?"

Without a word, Matt charged.

Caleb pulled the trickster forward. He grabbed Matt by the shirt and lifted him in the air, then tossed him several yards like a rag doll. As though he were in no hurry, he sauntered over to Matt and placed a foot on his back, pinning him to the ground.

"Something you need to understand about us tricksters," said Caleb. He leaned close. "We're liars." He stepped away from Matt. "And we like to play with our food."

Inside the barn, a woman screamed. Matt jerked his head, and shouted, "Sam!" He scurried to his feet and shambled over to the barn with Caleb trailing close behind.

Izzy came out of the shadows, wearing nothing more than Caleb's T-shirt from the fire pit. She stared at Matt with a feral glare. At her side, Matt's female companion struggled against her grip. Behind them stood Jewel, wearing the bloody shirt of the man named Troy.

"We found a little something in the field," said Izzy.

"Let her go!" commanded Matt as though his demands would hold any leverage. He spun around and locked eyes with Caleb. "Please," he begged. His voice breaking with each word "Let her go. She had nothing to do with what happened to Pax, that was all me."

The sound of his little brother's name rolling off the lips of the man who tortured and murdered him made Caleb's blood boil. "Shut the fuck up!" he bellowed. "Never say his name again!"

Startled and fearful, Matt closed his mouth. To his credit, he didn't say another word.

Caleb stepped close enough the touch noses with him if he wanted to. He glared directly into his eyes. "Did you really think this was gonna end with you?" He took hold of Matt by the shirt and dragged him over to the barn, dropping him on the ground at the women's feet. "Did you really think we would let anyone you cared about go free?"

An unusual scent wafted on the air. Caleb sniffed; a sinister smile spread across his face. "So," he said. "When's the blessed date?" The confusion that swept across Matt's face, made Caleb laugh out loud. He crouched down on one knee. "You mean to tell me you don't know?" With a mischievous chuckle, he stood up, walked over to Sam and inhaled, breathing in the scent. "I can smell it all over her." He peered down at Matt. "I'm surprised you don't already know."

Caleb stared directly into Sam's eyes as he flashed a sharp toothed grin and said, "Motherhood has a particular scent."

On the ground, Matt gasped.

A single tear ran down Sam's cheek.

Caleb wiped it away with his thumb. He placed his hand against her belly, feeling her entire body recoil at his touch. "What do you say?" He spun around to face Matt. "Should we keep her alive until the baby is born?" He folded his arms and tapped his chin with a long, clawed finger.

"Fuck you!" shouted Matt.

"Not a bad idea," taunted Caleb. "But you're not really my type." He jerked his head toward Sam. "However, she is."

The explosion of fury that erupted from Matt was spectacular. Under different circumstances, Caleb would have tremendous respect for the man's bravery. All the same, it was time to put the pathetic man in his place.

He placed a firm hand on Matt's shoulder. "Ah, ah, ah," he said, wiggling a finger. "If you move again, Izzy's gonna rip her throat out before you can take a single step."

Matt's countenance melted, gone was the robust man struggling to protect his woman, leaving in its place, a small, broken substitute. "Please, please," he begged, tears spilling out of his eyes. "Just let her go."

"And what?" asked Caleb. "Let her continue your blood line? How fair would that be when you so viciously ended a member of mine?"

A malevolent growl erupted from the barn. Teeth bared and eyes aglow, Jewel took a step forward. Before Caleb could say or do anything, she plunged her clawed hand deep inside Sam's belly and ripped out her uterus. Eyes glimmering with savage rage, she held the organ up for inspection in the moonlight. With a vicious sneer, she crushed it in her hand, letting the blood ooze out between her fingers.

At the same time, Izzy released her grip on Sam, who toppled to the ground, gripping the open wound in her belly.

Watching his little sister act on her rage was an impressive sight. Caleb wouldn't have done it so quickly, but he had to admire the savagery of his little sister's actions. "Well," he quipped, spinning around to face Matt. "Looks like that matter's been settled."

FORTY-ONE

MATT SCREAMED and crawled over to Sam, cradling her in his arms as she trembled in shock, unable to speak. He wiped away a thin rivulet of blood from the corner of her mouth. This was all on him; this was all his fault. Many people, Sam included, tried to warn him away from this senseless mission, but he insisted on going. Had he gone alone like he originally planned, his best friend would still be alive—the woman he loved wouldn't be bleeding out in his arms.

He swept a lock of her long, brown hair behind her ear while she peered up at him. Tears streamed from her glassy eyes.

"I'm so sorry," he whispered.

Sam reached up with a soft hand and wiped away his tears. "I love you," she sighed. The light in her eyes faded, her hand dropped limply, and she stopped breathing.

Clutching her lifeless body against his, Matt broke down, weeping uncontrollably as he rocked back and forth on the ground.

His mourning was interrupted by the sound of slow clapping. He peered up at Caleb, who stood towering over him, wearing a malicious smirk. He leaned down and stared directly into Matt's eyes. "It hurts to lose someone you love. Doesn't it?" A hateful shimmer reflected in his eyes. "Too bad you didn't care enough about her or your friends to stay the fuck home."

Matt screamed and using every ounce of energy left in his body. He launched at Caleb, knocking him down to the ground, leveling one punch, then another, hitting the bastard directly in the center of his face.

He raised his fist to level another barrage of blows, but Caleb was ready this time. His eyes ignited, staring back at him with an icy blue glow. His lips curled into a wicked grin as he caught Matt's hand, mid-swing, gripping it in his powerful hand; claws digging into Matt's flesh as they grew longer.

The wounds on Caleb's face healed, the only sign of injury left was the blood splattered around his nose. Caleb squeezed Matt's hand. Bones shattered and crunched in his grip.

Matt cried out in pain and tried to pull his hand away, only to have Caleb apply more pressure.

The bones in his wrist screamed in agony as Caleb bucked his entire body, tossing Matt off him. He twisted and wrenched the arm behind Matt's back and pulled him up to his feet.

"Nice try," seethed Caleb.

Pain shot throughout Matt's entire body; he could feel Caleb's hot breath against his neck. "Just do it!" he shouted.

"Do what?" asked Caleb, feigning confusion.

Matt inhaled, filling his chest with air, he stood tall with shoulders squared and his chest out. "I'm not afraid of you," he said. "I'm not afraid of dying. Just kill me."

Caleb released his grip and stepped back. He studied Matt. "I imagine you aren't," he replied. "I'd be beggin' for it too if I just brought about the death of everyone I ever loved." He jumped back, chuckling as Matt lunged toward him.

Matt shook his head and forced a smile. "I guess that's one thing we have in common. Isn't it?"

Anger swept across Caleb's face; eyes glowing with rage, he sneered, then slammed his forehead against Matt's face.

Tiny sparks flew in the corners of Matt's eyes as he staggered back, struggling to keep himself upright. His face hurt and he was pretty sure his nose was broken, but it was worth it. He had struck a nail; he intended to keep hammering away at it. He no longer had any hope of surviving this ordeal, even if he could, he didn't really want to. His best course of action was to provoke Caleb into ending it quickly.

Matt wiped the blood from his nose. "Nice wall of photos in there," he said, jerking his head toward the house. "You almost look like a normal, all-American family. Too bad there's only two of you left. Were you responsible for mom and dad's deaths also?"

Caleb stood in place, glaring at Matt, seething as he clenched his fists.

"Just think," said Matt. "Pax—"

"Stop!" shouted Caleb. He leveled a punch to Matt's jaw. "Don't you ever say his name again!"

The force of the blow sent Matt staggering backward on unstable feet. He rubbed his jaw and laughed. "What are you gonna do?" he taunted. "Kill me?" He let loose a torrent of maniacal laughter. "I believe that's how this is gonna end, anyway." He stepped forward, preparing his body for another blow. "I will say this," he said. "Pax was probably the better of you two." He spat at Caleb's feet. "Even if he was a pathetic psycho like the rest of your god damn family."

In a fit of rage, Caleb flew to Matt, knocking him so hard it sent him careening several yards. Before the dirt could settle, he stormed over and took a handful of Matt's hair, then raised him to his feet.

The sound of a helicopter erupted in the night sky, a beam of light exploded, illuminating the entire area. A sandstorm whipped up a cloud of tiny pebbles that swirled around like shrapnel.

"Let him go," boomed a disembodied male voice over the loudspeaker.

To Matt's surprise, Caleb let him drop to the ground. He held his hand to his forehead, attempting to shield his eyes from the sand that was swirling all around him. The phone call. He doubted that any help would come, but here he was, watching it hover above. Hysterical laughter erupted from his chest as tears flowed from his eyes.

FORTY-TWO

CALEB MOVED AWAY from Matt and turned around slowly to face the helicopter. He was not in the mood for any of this. The door to the house opened and Ezra emerged onto the front porch, still buttoning his jeans. Bass was right behind him. They made their way to stand alert, several yards away from Caleb and wait for their guests to land.

Two official vehicles glided along the driveway, their blue and red lights casting an eerie glow. One boasted the emblem of the state troopers, the other belonged to Sheriff Ramirez. Caleb smirked; this should be interesting.

With a powerful gust, the helicopter settled onto the ground, scattering sand and small rocks in every direction. As the blades slowed, the door slid open. Three men stepped out followed by a small army of large men wearing dark suits and ties. While impressive, not a single man came close to Bass' height and size. Caleb stood firmly in place, shoulders back, holding his ground. "What can I do for you gentlemen?" he asked.

"I think we can dispense with the small talk. Don't you?" said one of the men. As soon as the wind subsided, he placed a cowboy hat atop his bald head. His silver Texas Ranger badge glimmered in the glow of the artificial light.

"Well, well, well," said Caleb. "If it ain't Levi. What brings you all the way out here?"

The older man stared back at him with a stern glare. If his aim was to frighten Caleb, he'd have to step up his game.

"Mr. Deputy Director," he said with a tone of derision. "How generous of you to grace us with your presence. I haven't seen you in these parts since your father died. It's a shame he left the ranch to your brother. Must suck to know that even your own parents didn't think much of you." He turned to the other man and sneered, "I don't know you. Are you one of his lap dogs?"

Levi cleared his throat and turned to the other man. "Go check him out," he ordered, pointing a finger at Matt.

There was no way Caleb was going to allow anyone to get close to Matt. The human was his. He slid sideways, creating a barrier in front of the lap dog. "He's mine," he said, holding up a hand. "Step off."

The man paused, unsure of what to do next. He glanced nervously over his shoulder for help from his superior.

"Alright," said Caleb. "I'll bite. To what do we owe this little visit?"

A third man stepped forward, brushing dust from his expensive suit. "Now son," he said. "I think you already know the answer to that question." He gestured toward Matt, who was kneeling on the ground with his head down, muttering gibberish under his breath.

"I ain't your son," sneered Caleb. "You're another one we haven't seen around here in a long time." He scoffed. "Nowadays, you can't be bothered to spend time among the rabble." He glared with cold eyes. "So why don't you tell me what brought you all the way down here from the Governor's office."

"Caleb—"

"Weston," he jeered back. "You might be kin, but you gave up the right to any preferential family treatment when you deserted us."

Weston stepped forward, halting a foot away from Caleb. "I didn't desert you, if that's what you're on about." His eyes glowed with anger. "I'm still a member of this clan—and your uncle. We're all doing our part to keep the pack safe."

From the corner of his eye, Caleb watched as Sheriff Ramirez and the State Trooper approached.

"Please, allow me to talk to him," said Levi's man.

"Why?"

"It's my fault he's here," replied the man.

Caleb shot a quick glance at Weston, who responded with a curt nod and pleading eyes. He scoffed and stepped aside, allowing the man to pass.

"Captain?" said Matt. He glanced around at the men in confusion. Tears streaming down his cheeks, he pulled himself up on his feet. "Troy." He swallowed. "They killed Troy. His body's around the back of the house. In pieces." He sobbed. "There's a cave there. There's no telling how many people they've killed."

Caleb shook his head and snickered. The poor fool actually thinks help has arrived. He wondered whether he should burst the simpleton's bubble right now or wait for the big reveal.

The older man sighed. "Why did you have to come down here? I told you to leave it alone."

Surprise swept across Matt's face as realization settled in. He blinked and staggered back as though he'd been struck. He glanced around at all the men gathered. "No," he said, shaking his head, then he collapsed to his knees.

The man leaned down and offered his hand.

Matt slapped it away and scurried backward along the ground.

"Leave him alone," ordered Caleb. "Your time with him is done. He's mine."

"Now son," said Weston.

Caleb snapped his head around and glared. "Why the hell are you here?"

"You need to let him go," said Levi.

"The hell I do!"

Weston reached out to place a hand on Caleb's shoulder, but the younger man stepped out of reach. "Son," he said, calmly. "We're here to ask you to let him go." He took a deep breath and exhaled. "I'm asking you—as family."

"As family!" shouted Caleb. "You know I can't do that."

"Why not?" asked Weston.

"Look around!" shouted Caleb, waving his arms. "Do you notice someone missing? Or has it been so long you don't remember your nephew, Pax?" Tears flowed from Caleb's eyes at the mention of his little brother.

Weston scanned the surrounding faces. "Where is he?"

Waiting for realization to descend upon his uncle, Caleb merely stared.

The older man's face turned red with rage. His eyes lit up with blue fire as he stormed over to Matt and kicked him in the face.

"Woah, woah, woah!" shouted Levi. He placed his body between Matt and Weston. "Remember, we came here to save a few lives."

"Ain't no lives being saved here tonight," said Caleb, flatly.

The older man paused and studied Caleb. "Why don't you let us handle this," he said. "Let us take him."

Caleb growled, there was no way he would allow these people to deny him his revenge.

The State Trooper stepped forward and said, "If you let us take him, we could arrest him." He shrugged. "Prosecute him for murder."

"What?" said Matt in shock. He stared at the Rangers in the group. "They murdered my sister, her friends, my best friend, and—," He swallowed. "Sam." He glared at Caleb. "He's a monster—they all are."

Levi moved closer to Caleb. "Sometimes it's best to step back and let justice do its job."

"Are you fucking kidding me?" hollered Matt.

Levi spun around and leaned down to stare directly into Matt's eyes. "You don't seem to realize the situation you've caused here," he said. He turned to the captain. "Set him right!"

"Matt," said the captain. "I need you to listen to me."

A mix of anger and confusion swept across Matt's face. "I don't want to hear about it," he said, shaking his head.

"Well, you're gonna listen to me!" boomed the captain. "There are things at play here that are older than the state of Texas. More powerful too." He locked eyes with Matt. "I warned you to stay away."

"You knew!" shouted Matt. "You fucking knew this whole time! Yet you did nothing to stop any of it!" In a move that startled even Caleb, Matt bolted to his feet and lunged. "You knew who killed Ash! You could have warned us! You could have warned everyone! Sam would be alive right now if you hadn't been such a coward! Did they pay you enough? Were the rewards worth selling your soul?"

In a fit of rage, the man knocked Matt to the ground. Not a very difficult thing to do under the circumstances.

"He didn't have a choice," said Levi. He flipped his lapel over, exposing the clan's brooch, so Matt could see. He parted his lips, exposing his sharp white teeth.

Matt gasped but held his ground. He turned his focus to his senior. "How long?" he asked. "How long have you been turning a blind eye to what's going on out here?"

"Longer than you've been alive," said Caleb. "And we'll be doing it long after you're gone."

Matt's shoulders slumped. "All fucking monsters," he muttered, shaking his head slowly, tears streaming down his cheeks.

Levi turned away from Matt, setting his focus on Caleb. "You stand at a fork in the road, son," he said. "The ability to show restraint is a display of strength and maturity. It would go a long way to further your elevation within the pack."

Caleb growled; he couldn't care less about elevation within the pack. As far as he was concerned, these old men sold out long ago for trinkets, fancy dinners, and political power. He didn't need politics to be powerful—he was born with all he needed.

"There's a bright future ahead of you," said Levi. He nodded toward Weston. "You could work side by side with your uncle here in the Governor's office." He paused. "Who knows, maybe you could even be Governor someday."

Weston turned to Caleb. "A famous man once said, an eye for an eye and sooner or later everyone is blind."

He moved to place a hand on his shoulder, but Caleb shrugged him off and glared at his uncle. He sauntered over to Matt. "Well, then," he said calmly, stretching his hands, allowing his long claws to grow. With one swift movement, he slashed a sharp claw across Matt's throat. "I guess everybody's goin' blind."

A thin red line appeared as Matt reached up, eyes wide in disbelief. Crimson blood poured through his fingers, gushing down his arms, pooling on the ground in front of him. As his life bled out in his hands, he stared up at Caleb with a mix of horror and relief. He collapsed to the ground.

Caleb kneeled beside him and stared directly into his eyes. "I told you; you weren't leavin' this place." He waited until the last ember of life left Matt's eyes, then he rose to his feet and locked eyes with Weston. He allowed the trickster to push forward, transforming him into a partial beast. "Leave!" he bellowed.

A sudden shock of pain erupted in his chest. Stunned, he stared into his uncle's eyes, who stared back at him, his face a mask of cunning disdain. Caleb glanced down to find Weston's hand buried deep within his chest. He could feel the grip of his uncle's fingers wrapped around his pulsating heart.

Howls of pain erupted nearby. Caleb turned his focus in the direction of the cries just in time to see Ezra fall to his knees. Two large tricksters stood over him, one holding his still beating heart in his bloody hand.

Bass was nowhere to be seen.

"I tried to warn you," Weston hissed in Caleb's ear. "You

wouldn't listen." He flexed his fingers, sending a shock of pain throughout Caleb's body.

His uncle flashed an empty smile. "You know, in a lot of ways, you're just like your old man. He didn't want to make way for progress either. He wanted to stay out here in the middle of nowhere, squatting on this piece of land—living off scraps." He paused and glared at Caleb. "Well, I want more and I'm gonna have it." He shook his head slowly. "You and your siblings could have joined me. But you chose otherwise."

The sound of Bass crying out in pain pierced the night. Caleb's thoughts went to Izzy and Jewel, realizing he hadn't heard or seen them since the helicopter landed.

Somewhere off to the side, Levi barked orders, "What are you standing around waiting for? Make sure you got them all!"

Weston's hand tightened around Caleb's heart; the pain was unlike anything he ever experienced before. He sneered at his uncle as he called the trickster forward.

But the older man was ready for this. Weston pulled his hand free, sending an explosion of pain throughout Caleb's body. With an evil glint in his eyes, his uncle held up his bloody, pulsating prize.

Watching his heart take its final beat, Caleb collapsed to the ground. As the world went black and fuzzy around the edges, his mind filled with images of his life. His parents, Pax, Jewel, and Izzy. He thought about his unborn son, deciding that Izzy was right, Eben would have been a perfect name.

The End.

AFTERWORD

Thank you for giving my little nightmare a read. I hope you enjoyed it.

Please take a moment and leave a review or rating, these are the lifeblood for us authors and it helps other readers find great works. So please, share your opinion.

Also, feel free to drop me an email if you so desire. I love hearing from my readers.

www.nancylmclaughlin.com

SIDE QUEST
A TRICKSTERS/CROSSROADS CROSSOVER SHORT STORY

Vibrations from the old truck's tires on the asphalt coursed through his body. Colter kept his eyes on the dark road, breathing in the refreshing west Texas desert air.

He'd been driving for almost thirteen hours since leaving Twenty Nine Palms, California, stopping only occasionally to grab a bite to eat, refuel and stretch his legs. With seven or eight hours remaining, his arms were weary, and his rear end had long since gone numb, making him question his decision to skip an overnight stop in Las Cruces or El Paso.

Four years. That's how long it had been since he had seen his childhood home. It was hard to believe it had been that long. Time flew by. He couldn't help but wonder how many things had changed while he was away. Was the old man still angry? Would he still get the side eye from the old folks in town? Do places like that ever forget? He wanted to believe they do, but deep down inside, he knew; small towns kept their bad memories close, like the lingering smell of a dead rodent trapped beneath the floorboards of an old house.

Anxious thoughts swirled in his mind. Should he have stayed away? Why the hell did he even want to step foot in that town again?

He recalled the night he told his father that, rather than work the family ranch, he chose to join the Marines. The look on his father's face said it all. He was relieved. There was no argument—no pleas to reconsider. Just quiet acceptance. The fact that his son—his only son, was leaving to join the military was a source of relief for the old man.

To this day, Colter wasn't entirely sure how he felt about that.

On one hand, he could understand—after all, he wasn't exactly a model son. On the other, it hurt tremendously to think that his old man didn't really care about him. The thought of that being the case hurt him deeply.

Did he deserve to be punished for what he did to Lori? Maybe. But he never forced her to do anything with him. She could have said no at any time. Okay, so maybe posting the video was in poor taste, he could accept that. But after her father came and beat up both Colter and his dad, putting Colter into a coma for three months, things should have calmed. Folks should have moved on about the whole thing. Chalk it up to youthful stupidity and move on.

But they didn't.

Lots of the older folks in town treated Colter like a pariah. Going to church on Sundays was a particularly uncomfortable experience, so he simply stayed home. For the most part, his friends at school were cool, though there was a definite change in the way they interacted with him.

Home wasn't much better. The look in his mother's eyes every time she looked at him broke his heart. His sister Kayleigh never brought it up. Despite her attempts to act like everything was normal, her refusal to go anywhere with him in town made it clear that their relationship had changed.

As for his father, that was worse than any of the others.

The old man raised Colter to be his heir—the man who would one day inherit the ranch and keep it alive in his name. They had always shared a special bond. But after the shit hit the fan, a vast emptiness opened up between them. Gone was the casual closeness of a father and his only son, in its place were words unspoken and a massive wall of separation.

His first reaction to his newfound notoriety as the town asshole was shock. That quickly became sadness for what he lost reputation-wise, and eventually anger over the fact that no one seemed to let the past go. No matter how hard he tried to prove he wasn't that stupid kid anymore, no one listened. No one cared. Was he supposed to pay for one little mistake for the rest of his life?

The day the recruiter came to the school was a blessing. Joining the Marines would allow him to escape his past for once and for all. He could start over—create a new Colter, one who was worthy of praise. His family could finally put the image of him in the video aside and replace it with him in his dress blues. He would be considered an honorable man once again.

From day one, Colter threw himself into being the best Marine possible. For a country boy like himself, it wasn't all that difficult. In fact, he rather enjoyed the routine of it all—the camaraderie. Thanks to his childhood on the ranch, hard work and long days were no issue for him. This earned him the respect of his peers. In no time at all, he was surrounded by a loyal group of close friends. Friends who knew nothing of his greatest mistake—he preferred it that way. As for leadership, he respected the hell out of his senior NCOs; he would have followed his Gunny straight into hell. His one Achilles heel was the rest of the chain of command. No matter how hard he tried, he simply couldn't bring himself to respect most of the officers he came into contact with.

For a while, he seriously considered staying in and making a career of it. But in the end, he decided he wasn't capable of playing the game of stroking the fragile ego of some officer. It didn't help when he found himself demoted to Lance Corporal from Corporal, all because he told the new butter bar lieutenant to go fuck himself.

His lips curled into a wistful smile. That pasty little dough boy deserved so much more than an insult.

He downed the remnants of his last energy drink, then crushed the can and tossed it behind his seat, where it landed with a hollow clang atop the small mountain of empties. He would need to stop soon, if for no other reason than to empty his bladder.

Bright lights up ahead signaled a rest stop. Just in time, he thought. His back was numb and his legs were in dire need of a good stretch. Old trucks were cool and all, but they had a long way to go on the comfort side. He hit the blinker and turned off the road.

Two large eighteen wheelers sat idle on the truck side of the rest stop. As for other vehicles, he was the only one in sight. He rolled into a parking lane and cut the engine.

After hours of loud rumbling, his ears were ringing. He popped his neck and climbed out of the truck, then reached his arms over his head and stretched as far as he could, hearing stiff joints pop and snap. The air was still, not even the slightest breeze. He glanced around, taking note that aside from the ringing in his own ears, there was no sound. Something about the place sent an icy chill down his spine. He pulled out his phone and opened the map. The closest town was Sierra Diablo. Something about the name felt oddly familiar. It hung there like a distant memory from something learned in his past.

He pinched and pulled the screen, taking note that the town of Toyah was awfully close as well. Growing up in rural Texas, he knew that name well. The stories were prolific, from black-eyed, demonic children, to hitchhiking demons and even something about coyote shapeshifters. There were lots more, he just never bothered to listen to them. Colter was never a big fan of horror movies. But now, standing alone in this desolate stretch of highway, surrounded by the west Texas mountains, with no civilization in sight, he couldn't help but feel slightly exposed.

Shadows in his peripheral vision shifted and moved. He turned his head and saw nothing. Cursing his overactive imagination, he closed the door to his truck and made his way to the men's room.

As the door swung open, the fluorescent lights flickered overhead, casting a harsh, yellow light across the dank room, the air thick with the smell of urine and mold. In one of the stalls, the toilet flushed loudly, startling him. The door swung open and a giant beast of a man stepped out. He locked eyes with Colter and gave a curt nod. "Evenin'," he said.

"Evenin'."

Without another word, the man washed his hands and left, leaving Colter to himself. He hurried up and finished his business, wanting nothing more than to leave the dank room behind him.

The sound of a truck rolling onto the highway met his ears as he walked out of the restroom. Colter glanced around, taking note that the other truck had also left while he was inside the building. He was alone.

Or so he thought.

He paused, cupping a match to light his cigarette, the flame briefly illuminating his face before he sauntered back to his truck. As he got closer, he could hear the subtle sound of a woman humming. He stepped around to the back of his truck and found himself gazing upon a mysterious young woman who was leaning against his bumper.

Colter cleared his throat to gain her attention.

She turned around, her long, dark hair cascading around her shoulders, draping low across the dark red tank top she was wearing. Her lips curled into a pleasant, welcoming smile as she stepped closer to him. "Hello," she said.

"Hello."

The woman gazed at him for an uncomfortably long period, then glanced down at the truck. "Oh! Is this yours?"

She carried herself with a subtle confidence that made it difficult for him to look away. This woman was sexy, and she knew it. Colter let his eyes crawl down her body then back up again to meet her eyes. Unfazed, the woman stared back, a slow, sultry smile playing at the corners of her lips. "Do you like what you see?" she asked.

Startled by her forward persona, Colter's mind went blank, but he quickly recovered and flashed his best country boy smile. "I do," he replied, then stepped closer.

The woman leaned against the back of the truck, turning her body in just the right angle to show off her athletic form and long legs. "You gonna introduce yourself?"

"Colter," he replied. "Colter Trask."

She closed the little distance that remained between them. "Nice to meet you, Colter. My name's Isabelle. My friend's call me Izzy."

"So, tell me, Izzy, what is a goddess like you doin' out here all alone this late at night?"

"Waiting for you," she replied coyly.

She sounded like she was telling the truth, but he knew she was just toying with him. Flirting. He glanced around at the now empty rest stop, then turned his gaze back to her. Ready to play whatever game she had in mind, Colter took a final drag from his cigarette, then tossed it to the ground and snuffed it out with his boot. "Well, then. You found me. What now?"

Izzy twisted a lock of her long dark hair around her finger, then took a quick step back, all the while grinning provocatively at him. "I was hopin' you could give me a ride." She scanned his body with her amber brown eyes. "I don't have any money to pay for gas, but I have other things I could trade."

"I bet you do," he replied, his mind swimming with the possibilities.

Truth be told, even if she wasn't as hot as she was, he wouldn't have left the rest stop without offering her a ride. It wouldn't have sat right with him to leave a woman alone in a desolate place like this. "So where are we takin' you?"

"My house is a few miles up the road. If you don't mind, I'd like a ride there."

A lone coyote called out from the hills.

"Well, we should get goin'. Wouldn't want a denizen of the desert to think we might be a good snack or anything," he said jokingly.

"Oh no, we wouldn't want that at all," she said with a strange tone in her voice.

"Home it is." He gestured to the truck. "Hop on in and we'll get goin'."

Izzy needed no prodding. With a playful wink of her eye, she spun around and climbed into the truck.

Colter shook his head, thinking how no one would believe this happened. Hell, he was living it and barely believed it himself. He climbed behind the steering wheel and turned on the engine.

"I'm just gonna apologize in advance," he said. "This old beast is pretty loud."

She slid across the bench seat until their thighs touched, triggering a warm sensation that started in his groin and shot right through his entire body. With a slender hand, she reached up and touched his dog tags hanging from the rearview mirror.

"Shouldn't you be wearing these?"

"If I was still active, I would. But, I ain't no more." He threw the truck into drive, then rolled out of the slip and onto the highway.

Izzy took the tags down and flipped them around in her hand. "Type O positive," she said. "The universal donor."

"So I've been told." He glanced out at the dark, empty road. "How far we goin'?"

"About two miles from here, there's a turnoff." She hung the tags back on the mirror.

A comfortable silence descended upon them. Colter wasn't one for small talk, from what he could tell, Izzy didn't seem to mind. She began to hum a soft tune.

Just like she said, what looked like a makeshift exit ramp appeared about two miles up the road. He glanced around, thinking he missed the exit sign, only to realize there was none.

"Turn here," she said.

Colter was no stranger to back wood Texas towns. When it came to sparsely populated places, the state was always slow to act on necessary improvements. He shrugged away the missing signage and turned onto the narrow road.

If he thought the highway was dark, it had nothing on the road they were traveling down. His headlights bounced off of the desert terrain as they twisted and turned down so many curves, he began to wonder whether he would be able to find his way back out to the interstate.

"Turn left here," she said, pointing.

He did as he was told and found himself rolling down an even more narrow gravel road. Having grown up in the country, dark, empty roads were no big deal for him, he'd spent countless nights wandering down many in his teen years. Still, something about this little side quest didn't feel quite right. He glanced over at Izzy who smiled innocently back at him.

The trees opened up, revealing a picturesque farmhouse set against the backdrop of a tall mountain that looked more like a precarious stack of rocks thrown together by a child. Serene. That was how it could best be described.

With the sound of his tires crunching on the gravel, he rolled to a stop at the base of the steps leading up to a cozy front porch. He peered up at the house, taking note of the warm glow of the lights in nearly all the windows.

"Well, here ya go ma'am," he said. "Just as promised. Home safe and sound."

Izzy leaned over and gazed into his eyes. Without breaking eye contact, she climbed onto his lap, straddling him. "And I promised to make it worth your while," she cooed as she leaned in for a slow, lingering kiss, then pulled away. "This is gonna be a night you won't forget. Come on," she said, pushing open the door.

His pulse was racing, his body was on fire. He climbed out of the truck and glanced around, taking in the oddly quiet surroundings.

Izzy pressed her body against him. So close, he could feel her heartbeat through the thin fabric of her tank top. The heat radiating from her body was intense. She kissed him full on the lips, sending shivers down his spine, then pulled away and took his hand. "Over here," she said softly. She began walking, tugging him along behind her, as they headed toward a massive red barn.

"Wait," he said, pulling back. "The house is right here."

Izzy smiled. "I said it would be a night you wouldn't forget. The house is boring," she said, flashing a sultry smile. "Which is why we're going to the barn." She winked and turned around, guiding him once again.

He shrugged and followed her lead. It wouldn't be the first time he had sex in a barn. It would, however, the first time he'd ever been led to one by such a gorgeous lady. This already was a night he would never forget, he could hardly wait to see what else she had in store for him.

Less than ten feet from the entrance, Izzy released his hand, giggled playfully and sprinted off, disappearing into the gaping, dark void of the barn.

Colter paused at the entrance and gazed inside, unable to see Izzy, or anything at all. A cool breeze wafted by, swirling and churning around him, wrapping him in the scent of fresh straw, old wood stain and the subtle odor of a decaying animal. He wrinkled his nose at the sickly sweet smell, thinking nothing of it. They were in the middle of the desert after all. Dead animals were simply par for the course out here.

Somewhere in the shadows, Izzy hummed a melodic tune. He took a step inside the barn.

A sudden sharp whistle sliced through the air to his left. Startled, he turned and found himself face to face with a blond man about his age and slightly taller. The man flashed a grin, exposing sharp canines, his eyes glowed electric blue.

"Night, night asshole," he said, then he slammed his head directly into Colter's face.

A kaleidoscope of bright lights exploded around the edges of his vision, then the world turned off.

"Wakey, wakey," said a strange male's voice, followed by two sharp slaps across Colter's face.

He shook his head, his eyes still refusing to open. His arms were numb and cold and pinned behind his back somehow. The world was spinning. Wait. He was spinning. He tried to move his legs, but they were held in place at his ankles.

Once again, Colter shook his head, this time forcing his eyes to open. He blinked and realized he was hanging upside down. His vision slowly returning, he locked onto a pair of well-worn cowboy boots standing right in front of him.

Panic threatened to wield its ugly head, but he knew better than to do that. Whoever was doing this could have dispatched him while he was unconscious. Something else was afoot.

He watched as Izzy's boots came into view, standing right behind the other set. It was a setup. Of course it was. He lifted his gaze to see his captor's face.

The blond man crouched down on one knee in front of him. "Hello," he said, wearing a malevolent grin. "Nice of you to join us." He paused as though he were waiting for Colter to say something. "What's the matter? Cat got your tongue?"

A round of laughter erupted, sounding an awful lot like the cackles of a pack of coyotes.

Colter looked around, realizing there were three more men standing nearby. His anger boiling, he yelled, "What the fuck is wrong with you people?"

"Now, now, now," said his captor. "That ain't no way to talk to a man, especially after you've gone and hit on his lady behind his back."

Colter's eyes shot up to Izzy, then back to the man. "Is that what this is all about?" He chuckled. "You can keep her. She's obviously got a lot more mileage on her than I'm lookin' for."

He felt a flicker of satisfaction as the man's eyes blazed with fury, but the feeling quickly turned to agony with the force of the man's knee slammed into his stomach. As he coughed and gagged, Colter decided it was worth it.

The man waited for him to regain his composure. "How about a little introduction," he said, jovially, as though Colter wasn't hanging upside down in his barn. "You've already met Izzy." He jabbed a thumb behind him. "That one right there is Ezra and the big fella is Bass." He spun Colter around. "And that right there is my baby brother, Pax."

The blond man twisted him around one more time to face him. "And I'm Caleb."

"I'd say nice to meet you," said Colter. "But it ain't." He grinned defiantly. "Forgive me if I don't give a rat's ass about who any of you are."

"You've got balls," said Caleb. "I like that. Must be a Marine thing." He crouched down and leaned back on his heels. "I suppose a little demonstration is in order. Just so you understand what the stakes are and where exactly you sit on the food chain."

His eyes glowed electric blue. Staring directly into Colter's eyes, his teeth grew. Not all of them at first, just the canines. As Colter watched in stunned silence, sharp fangs protruded out from between Caleb's lips. The wet, squelching sound of snapping bones and ripping flesh filled the area. He raised his hand so Colter could watch as a single large, deadly claw erupted from his fingertip.

The barn grew quiet.

Caleb reached out with a single vicious claw and dragged it across Colter's cheek.

Thick hot blood oozed from the wound, dripping into his eyes, clouding his vision. He blinked, clearing his sight just in time to watch Caleb lick the blood from his finger.

A round of coyote laughter broke out all around him.

Fear swept over Colter like an icy wave. Whatever these things were, it wasn't right. He was not up against regular people. That he could handle. This was something else entirely different. The last vestige of bravado melted away.

"Do I have your attention now?" asked Caleb. He stretched his neck and his fangs disappeared, leaving the face of a normal, average man.

Unable to do much else, Colter nodded.

"Good," said Caleb. "We can finally begin."

"I suppose you're wonderin' why we gathered here tonight." He stared at Colter as though he were expecting a response. When none came, he said, "As you have probably noticed already, there isn't a whole hell of a lot to do for entertainment in these parts." He grinned. "So when the opportunity arises, we like to play a little game out here. How it ends is entirely up to you. You ready to hear the rules?"

Colter nodded.

"In a moment, I'm gonna cut you down. You will then have exactly two minutes to get as far away from here as possible. After that, we come huntin'." He leaned closer. "You got that?" This time Caleb didn't wait for a reply. "Now, before you go thinkin' it's a done deal, I have a little caveat for you. If you can make it to the next town by sunrise, we'll let you live."

Until that moment, Colter never truly understood the phrase, staring into the eyes of death. Whatever these monsters were, they most certainly were not human. He gazed up at Caleb as he stared back at him with cunning malevolence.

Caleb stood up and pulled a long hunting knife from the back of his belt. With one swift movement, he cut the rope that held Colter aloft, leaving him to topple to the floor headfirst.

There was a tug at his arms behind his back, then suddenly his hands were free. Colter pulled himself up on all fours, struggling to regain his equilibrium.

With hardly a moment's pause, Izzy began to count in a sing-song voice. "One, two, three, four—"

"Time's a tickin' boy," said Caleb. "Best get movin'. The game ain't gonna play itself. Get on out there and find your way. Ya know, adapt, improvise, overcome and all that bullshit."

Colter pulled himself up on his feet.

"I wouldn't dally if I were you," said Caleb. "This is your only chance to survive. I won't give you a second."

Needing no more prompting, Colter bolted out of the barn. His truck was still parked over by the house. He ran for it. Inside the cab, he scoured his pockets for the keys. Of course, they weren't there. Outside, Izzy continued to count. A cacophony of coyote chatter erupted from the barn, followed by a single loud howl. He didn't have time to try to hot-wire the engine. There was no other choice than to make a run for it.

With his eyes on the horizon, Colter took off into the hills, hoping that his sense of direction wasn't off.

The sound of coyote yips behind him only helped to fuel his energy.

After six years in the suck, a run through the desert would be no issue at all for him. His confidence growing, he calmed his mind, put his confusion aside, and continued moving at a quick pace. "Hold your shit together, Trask."

A lone howl echoed through the mountains, bouncing off the stone, giving him the sensation that the pack could be anywhere. Colter glanced behind him. The farmhouse was nowhere in sight. He had successfully put a considerable distance between himself and whatever the hell those things were back there.

The moon hung heavy and full overhead, providing him with much needed light. If nothing else, he could avoid stepping into some obstacle on the ground. A cool breeze carried the scent of sage and dirt. He used to like that smell, but on this night, he would give anything for the stench of B.O. coming off his platoon mates.

Up ahead, a long line of tall green trees meandered. A stream or river! Just what he needed. Not only would he be able to take a quick break, he'd also have water and the added benefit of camouflage. He licked his dry lips and quickly made his way over.

Just as he thought, a narrow stream wandered through the center of the trees. He fell to his knees at the edge of the water and cupped a handful of the clear, cool liquid, bringing it to his parched lips. It washed down his throat and into his belly, calming his nerves, giving him a sense that all would be okay. He splashed water on his face and in his hair, giving himself a moment to orient his mind. The silence around him made him uneasy. He knew the pack was hunting him, if he couldn't hear them; it could be they lost his trail. It could also be that they were smart enough to know they needed to hide their presence.

Once again, a tinge of fear reared its ugly head.

Now was not the time to wallow in the situation. The parameters had been set. If he can make it to the next town, he would escape. That is, if Caleb was a man of his word.

Man? That was no man.

Another howl echoed through the hills.

It was time to move on.

Colton scanned the area. According to the sound, the pack was close, but not quite close enough to catch him just yet. Based on the direction the sound came from, he had only one avenue of escape. Feeling less nervous and slightly recharged, he scrambled to his feet, crossed the stream and quickly made his way through the trees. As soon as he reached the edge of the tree line, he sprinted for the nearest hill where he crouched low and studied the land for any sign of the pack.

The desert was alive all around him, playing tricks with his mind. Every trembling bush, every shifting shadow was a potential hiding spot. He pinched his eyes and told himself to get it together. The only way he would survive the night would be to keep his wits about him. He could do this.

His face stung. He ran his finger across the jagged edge of the gash on his cheek. For the first time in his life, Colter found himself fearful about infection.

The edge of the tree line moved in an unnatural way. Colter ducked low to the ground; his eyes locked on the trees. A single, large beast crept forward out of the foliage. Based on the height of the trees when he was standing next to them, one thing was perfectly clear—this thing was positively enormous. It looked and moved exactly like a coyote, but it was larger than any wolf he had ever seen. How the hell was he going to battle something like that?

As he studied the creature, it raised its giant head and sniffed the air.

Like minions stepping forward from the abyss, three more coyotes slinked out of the shadows, followed by one particularly cunning looking beast. Colter needed no confirmation. He knew exactly who that was—Caleb.

How the fuck was it even possible that a human could become an animal?

While the others cackled gleefully, Caleb scanned the area, his blue eyes carefully gliding from right and then to his left. He paused and tilted his head as he locked eyes with Colter.

Shock coursed through Colter's body as he stared back at the beast. How could he see him? What chance did he have if they could see so well in the dark for such a long distance?

The coyotes grew quiet as they gathered around the alpha. All at once, they turned their gazes to the hillside where Colter lay.

He stared back for only a second, then scrambled to his feet and took off, running as hard and as fast as his legs would carry him. His heart pounded in his chest desperately trying to move enough blood to keep him going. His lungs were on fire as they struggled to bring in enough oxygen to feed his body. He regretted every cigarette he ever smoked.

Perking up his ears, he could hear the sound of feet softly thumping on the ground. As he listened intently, the sound grew louder—closer. It was all around him. He glanced over his shoulder. They were right on his heels.

The air filled with the gleeful yips of the pack.

Why hadn't they attacked?

There was only one possible reason—they were toying with him.

His mind rushed over the words that Caleb uttered in the barn;

they were playing a game. A sick, malignant game of cat and mouse. And he was the mouse.

Run. That was what they wanted him to do. That was what they expected. It was how they entertained themselves. Anger swelled in his chest, fueling his pride. No more.

Colter stopped dead in his tracks, his fists clenched tightly as he spun around to face the pack, waiting for one of them, or all of them, to attack.

Silence.

He stared them down. They were all there, laying on the ground like a pack of dogs who were ordered to heal by their owners.

"What are you waiting for?" he shouted. "Come on!" He slammed his fists against his chest. "You want me? Come get me!"

A round of cackles broke out. They were laughing at him.

"I'm not running anymore," he said. "I ain't playing your stupid games."

Silence.

The alpha rose to his feet. He crept forward, moving closer to Colter, snarling malevolently.

Even though his instinct told him to run, Colter refused to move. His pride cemented his feet to the ground where he stood.

Caleb was now close enough that Colter could reach out and touch him if he wished.

Colter stood firm.

A menacing growl crawled out of Caleb's lungs. He moved even closer.

Fear reared its useless head, making Colter's heart flutter in his chest like prey. He inhaled and pushed it back as he stared directly into the eyes of the beast.

With snapping jaws and bared teeth, Caleb lunged forward, his snout coming inches from Colter's face.

Tiny droplets of saliva splattered on his cheeks. He wiped them away and grinned defiantly. "You're gonna have to do better than that," he said.

The beast huffed and gave a slow nod, then suddenly lunged forward and took Colter's leg in his powerful jaws.

A scream, partly of shock and partly of pain erupted from Colter's lungs.

Caleb's teeth were embedded in his calf halfway up to the knee. He yanked hard, pulling Colter off balance, sending him crashing to the hard, rocky ground.

Colter struggled and pulled his leg, but the beast's grip was too strong.

As if they were one creature, the pack rose to their feet and yipped. Their taunting laughter mixing with the malevolent sounds of Caleb's growls.

Still holding Colter's leg in his jaws, Caleb took off running, dragging him.

Rocks sliced his skin while desert foliage reached out their deadly tendrils clawing their ounce of flesh from his body, tearing away at his clothes and pulling his hair from its roots. More than once, Colter's head slammed against the rocky ground, sending shocks of excruciating pain through his head.

As abruptly as it began, it ended.

Silence surrounded him.

Struggling to regain his wits, Colter lay on the ground and waited until his vision cleared. His leg was free. He sat up and gazed around. He was alone. The pack was nowhere to be seen. Confusion washed over him. Why didn't they kill him when they had the chance? The game. They merely wanted to send a message to him loud and clear. They were going to play their game, and he had no other choice than to comply.

A single howl echoed from the hills, followed by yips and cackles. They were waiting.

Colter quickly took stock of his body. The pain in his leg was excruciating. He pulled the torn strips of fabric away to get a better look at the damage. It was bad, but not debilitating. Surprisingly enough, Caleb managed to avoid puncturing an artery. Of course he did. If Colter bled out, that would ruin the chase.

His whole body ached from the hundreds of tiny and large wounds the desert inflicted upon him. He rose to his feet and scanned the area. His eyes locked on a tiny, flickering spark of orange light. Was that a fire? He stared intently as the light danced in that familiar way that only a campfire could do. People!

Hope washed over him. If he had a chance at all, it would be there. With any luck, one of them would have a firearm. Unable to run fast, he hobbled his way along the uneven terrain, his eyes set on the orange and yellow light in the distance.

As excited as he was to see people, Colter knew better than to run right in to their midst without first checking them out as much as possible. After all, this was west Texas. A random group of campers in the middle of nowhere could be anyone—hobos, backpackers, traffickers, or cartel. Caution was necessary. As soon as he was close enough to make out the silhouettes that were sitting around the fire, he slowed his pace, crouched low among the scattered shrubs, and listened.

As far as he could tell, there were four people. Three men and one woman, all sitting around the fire, chatting and laughing the way a tight-knit group of friends would. His mind crawled back to his buddies in the Corps. He would give anything to be back among them right now.

The scent of weed wafted on the breeze. He scanned the area around them for a vehicle, only to realize they didn't have one. He sighed in disappointment, suddenly losing hope that anyone in this group would have a firearm.

The pack called out from the hills.

Colter glanced around at the dancing shadows. Whatever the reason, the pack was keeping their distance. He wanted to believe it was because they feared a larger group of humans, but his gut told him it had a lot more to do with the game they were playing than anything else.

One of the men from the group lifted his head and howled back at the hills. From their hiding places, the pack responded with a cacophony of yips.

The sound of their taunting laughter made Colter's blood run cold. These people had no clue what they were playing with. He set his sights on the campfire, climbed to his feet, and hobbled over.

As he moved closer, Colter struggled with what to say to these strangers that wouldn't make him sound like some crazed desert dweller. Help? Run? Hey there! He chuckled at the ridiculousness of his mind even pondering any of this.

So much for perimeter warnings, he thought as he managed to get well within striking distance of the group before one of them even noticed the grown man walking toward them.

A tall man stood up and took a slow step toward him. "Hey man," he said, his voice sounding cautious. "What can I do for you tonight?" He stood firmly on his heels with his right hand resting on a holstered handgun.

Colter had never been so happy to see a weapon in his life. He hobbled close enough for the man to see his face then said, "I need some help." He glanced around at the darkness that surrounded them. "In fact, I think it'd be a good idea if we all just got the hell out of here. Right now."

The man didn't move. He studied Colter with a critical eye, then slid his gaze out along the barrier of light. He turned back to Colter. "Is there something wrong?"

"There's a lot wrong. In fact, everything about this hellscape is wrong. It's all wrong," said Colter. He ran his hand down his face, struggling to remain calm. "Look, if I took the time to tell you all that's happened tonight, you wouldn't believe me. I don't really know if I believe it or not either. But please, believe me when I say to you, me and your friends need to get the hell out of here before they come."

"Who's they?" asked a second man now standing beside the first.

Without taking his eyes off of Colter, the man with the gun said to his friend, "Charlie, go check it out."

"Don't do it, Charlie," warned Colter. "Look. I know how weird this all looks, but, for the love of God, just listen to me. We have to get away from here now!"

The woman and another man stepped forward. "What's going on, Kev?" she asked.

"Stay there, Mel," said the man named Kev. "Zeke, go with Charlie to see what this asshat's on about."

"Maybe you shouldn't," said Mel.

"She's right," said Colter. "Listen to your girl. You don't wanna know what's out there."

"Shut the fuck up!" Kev's hand twitched by his side. "When I wanna hear from you, I'll ask! Until then, just stay right there." He tilted his head to his buddies. "Well? What are you two waiting on? Go check it out."

Zeke and Charlie shared a nervous glance, making no attempt to move from where they stood.

At least someone was listening.

"Maybe we should do what he says and get the hell out of here," said Zeke.

"Why?" shot Kev. "Because some asshole comes along and tells us to? He's punking us."

"Do I look like I'm pulling a prank?" Colter held his arms out, hoping that if they could see some of his injuries, they would finally take him seriously. He was trying to save their lives—his too. Why the hell was it always so hard to get people to listen?

Cowed by Kev's retort, Charlie stepped past Colter, his eyes focused out into the dark wilderness that surrounded them.

"Charlie, no," said Mel with a pleading tone.

"I'd listen to her," said Colter.

Somewhere nearby, a coyote howled; it was too close for comfort. The pack was warning them and these people were too stupid to listen. Colter needed to get them to move, or at least get the dude in front of him to give him his firearm. His throat was dry as the desert sand that surrounded him, and his leg throbbed in pain. He raked his fingers through the sweaty hair on his head.

The expressions on their faces told Colter everything he needed to know—they thought he was insane. He shook his head and just went for it. "There's, there's a pack of coyo—"

Before he could finish the word, a single giant beast launched out of the shadows. With a fury of sharp white teeth and terrifying growls, the beast grabbed hold of Charlie's leg and took off, disappearing into the darkness way beyond the light of the fire. The man's terrified screams bounced off the hills as he was dragged further away, followed by a volley of screams, cries of pain and horrifying growls. They were tearing him to pieces. Eerie silence descended. There could be no doubt that Charlie was dead.

Colter turned back to the others, only then did he realize Mel had been screaming.

Zeke, his mouth wide in shock, stumbled back, falling heavily to the ground. His face a mask of terror. Dumbstruck, he scurried backward like a sand crab until he bumped up against Mel.

Both of them were trembling with fear. Understandable. After all, who ever heard of coyotes as large as the one that just slaughtered their buddy. Say nothing for the fact that they usually don't attack humans.

Kev stood frozen in place; his eyes locked in the direction that the beast had dragged Charlie. He hadn't even pulled the gun from its holster.

Colter would have unloaded a full clip into the beast, only stopping long enough to reload. He realized if they were going to survive this, he would have to take control. First, he needed to get that gun.

"Give me the firearm," he said, holding his hand out.

Kev glanced down at his hip as though suddenly remembering he had the weapon. He swallowed nervously and shook his head, then finally pulled it free from the holster, swinging it around aimlessly at the surrounding darkness. "Fuck no!" he said. His hands were trembling.

As long as Kev had the gun, they were fucked. Colter knew there was no way he would give him his weapon. Who would? He sighed and locked eyes with him. "Then at least make sure the safety's off."

Still trembling, Kev did as Colter told him.

"Come on!" shouted Mel, as she helped Zeke up on his feet. She turned and bolted over to the fire, kicking sand to douse the flames.

The sound of swift movement erupted in a flurry all around them. It was too late. Another beast burst forth. Snarling and frothing at the maw like a rabid dog, it grabbed hold of Zeke by the shoulder and dragged him away, filling the night with his screams.

Almost simultaneously, a second beast ruptured from the darkness. Its powerful jaws clamped down on Kev's arm. A shot rang out, followed by several more. Bullets were flying everywhere, slamming into the dry earth with tiny plumes of dust.

Mesmerized by the sight before him, Colter watched as the beast jerked its giant head, pulling Kev's arm free from his body as though he were nothing more than a stuffed doll.

He could only stare in horror as the feral creature bit and tore at Kev. It showed no mercy, seemingly determined to inflict as much pain and torment as possible. Dark red blood poured out from the stump where his arm had been. With a malevolent growl, the beast reared back, then lunged and grabbed hold of Kev's leg, dragging him off into the desert, leaving nothing more than a narrow river of blood in his wake.

Screams of pain and terror filled the night, mixing with the unnerving sound of the pack yipping and growling as they tore both men to pieces.

Over by what remained of their campfire, Mel was screaming as she spun around in circles. The sound of her friends dying was all around them.

The gun! Colter glanced down at the disembodied arm laying on the ground like a Halloween prop. A momentary sense of relief washed over him when he saw that the lifeless hand was still holding on to the weapon. He leaned over and wrenched it free, then ran up to the campfire, taking a knee beside the pack where Kev was sitting. He needed to find more rounds.

"What the fuck are you doing?" shouted Mel.

She was hysterical. Useless. She would be no help whatsoever in this nightmare. All the same, Colter had to do whatever he could to help both himself and this woman survive. Oddly enough, having someone other than himself to take care of gave him a sense of calm and resolve. Without pause, he continued digging around while explaining, "I need to find the rest of his rounds."

His hand struck pay dirt in the center of the bag. Inhaling deeply, he pulled the box out along with a second clip; it was fully loaded. Unfortunately, the box had hardly any rounds in it. Colter poured what little there were into his hand and shoved them into his pocket, then rose to his feet.

The screams stopped, followed by the celebratory sound of coyote chatter.

He turned to Mel. "Run!"

A look of resolve washed over her face as she nodded her head. Without saying a word, she ran up alongside him, leaned close and pulled his arm around her shoulder.

"What are you doing?"

"I'm helping you," she said. "Come on! The road's that way." She pointed. "Just over those hills."

The pack chatter was dying down, Colter knew exactly what that meant. At any moment they would turn their attention to the last two remaining survivors. Holding the gun in one hand, he gritted his teeth against the pain in his leg and hobbled as fast as possible toward the road, hoping to find freedom and safety there.

The uneven terrain made each step excruciating.

An eerie silence descended.

His hand gripping the gun tightly, he glanced around, knowing that the pack was far from finished with them. He had no doubt these monsters had no intention of letting them go.

As much as he appreciated the help, Colter understood that as long as Mel was helping him, her chances of surviving this nightmare were slim. He stopped walking and said, "Look, Mel, you have to run. I'm the one they really want. If you run now, you have a chance." He hopped back to put some space between them.

Mel shook her head. "I'm not leaving you." Her eyes darted nervously around the landscape.

"You're not," he said defiantly. "You're gonna run up ahead, get to the road and flag down some help."

She didn't move. The determined look on her face told him she was struggling through a mix of terror, her own sense of self preservation and concern for him.

Ordering her to go on ahead wasn't going to work, so he shifted gears and tried to convince her. "If we're gonna get through this, you have to go get some help. Please. I'll be right behind you all the way. If they come up on us, I've got this to hold them back." He held up the gun, wondering how useful it could be against these things. All the same, the weight of it in his hand made him feel better.

That seemed to do the trick.

Mel scanned the horizon, then turned her head back to him. "Okay," she said. "I'll do it." She took a tentative step forward, then paused, making Colter fear she changed her mind. But rather than come back over to him, she gave a quick nod of her head and ran.

As he watched her scurry up the hill, Colter allowed himself a momentary sigh of relief, feeling as though he finally did something right. If nothing else, she would survive.

She crested the hilltop, her silhouette standing tall against the backdrop of billions of sparkling stars in the night sky.

Each step forward shot pain throughout his entire body, making him regret forcing her to leave him behind. The burning in his leg intensified. Once again, his mind turned to the possibility of infection.

A burst of activity erupted behind him.

The pack had returned.

Ready to face his fate, Colter spun around, putting the full weight of his body on his good leg. He raised the handgun and exhaled, forcing his nerves to calm in order to ensure a good shot.

The first beast appeared, followed by the others.

Rather than fire at all of them, he set his site on the alpha—Caleb. In rapid fire, with a sense of calm that surprised himself, Colter sent several shots, all of which hit their mark with stunning accuracy.

The beast yelped. Blood sprayed into the air like plumes of dust. But the beast was unfazed.

The rest of the pack charged past him. He spun around just in time to witness as they pounced—all at once, upon Mel.

Her screams filled the night, combining with the ferocious growls and barks as the pack tore the poor woman to pieces.

As he stood there in shock, he watched as the beasts yipped and cackled in celebration, then trotted off triumphantly, carrying pieces of her along with them.

Colter collapsed to his knees. He did this. The death of that woman and her friends was all on him. Had he not run into their camp, they would still be alive. A deep sense of defeat descended upon him, followed, once again, by acceptance of his fate. He turned his head and stared directly into the eyes of the alpha.

"Well?" he yelled. "What are you waiting for? Come at me!" Hot tears sprung forth from his eyes. He blinked them away, unwilling to give Caleb the satisfaction.

But the beast made no effort to move forward.

The standoff seemed to go on forever.

Why the hell wasn't he moving? Colter wondered. Then it hit him. It's all a game for these things. They want him to run so they can take him out like a coward. A steely sense of resolve settled upon him. He shook his head and let out a rueful chuckle. "No more," he said. He raised the gun and held it to his head. If he was going to die tonight, he would do it on his own terms. Closing his eyes, he said a silent apology to his family—to everyone he had hurt along the way. To Lori. He placed his finger on the trigger.

A forceful blow knocked him to the ground, as the alpha slammed into him, knocking the wind out of his lungs. His head fell against a rock with so much force, it created an explosion of tiny stars in his vision. Nausea washed over him.

He could feel the cool metal of the gun still clenched tightly in his hand. Hoping he still had a chance; he raised the weapon.

But the beast was having none of that.

It locked its powerful jaws around his hand with such force, he could feel the tiny bones snapping like thin splinters of wood. He cried out in pain, releasing the weapon, as his fingers were no longer useful. The alpha took the gun in his mouth and trotted off, the whole time laughing as it disappeared from his view.

He was alone.

Colter no longer had a choice. Slowly, he climbed to his feet. Clenching his mangled hand against his chest, he hobbled his way up the hill, pausing long enough to glance down at what remained of the woman who tried to help him.

Another one of his victims.

He scanned the area ahead. The sky was shifting to a pale blue as dawn was approaching. The road! He could see the road! Even better, he could see a sign that read, Welcome to Toyah.

Against everything he had endured on this night, a sense of hope washed over him. Could he be so lucky? He glanced around—there was no sign of the pack.

Colter took one step down the hill only to slip and lose his footing. Tumbling head over feet, he careened down the hillside, coming to an abrupt stop at the foot of the hill. Clinging to the tiny thread of hope, he scrambled to his feet and continued forward.

His eyes were filled with tiny bits of grit from the desert floor. He blinked to clear his vision, shocked at what he saw up ahead.

A lone truck sat idle just beyond the sign, and a single, lone figure stood leaning against the tailgate.

Convinced he was hallucinating; Colter shook his head and pinched his eyes. When he reopened them, the vision was still there. A cherry red glow illuminated the face of a young man about his own age.

From where he stood, Colter could hear the welcoming sound of the truck's engine idling calmly. His mind screamed at him to run for it. A rush of adrenaline coursed through his body, giving him the strength to move much faster than even he thought possible under the circumstances. He was now just a few feet away.

The sound of low growls met his ears, but this time Colter had no intention of stopping. He pressed forward.

As he made his way closer, he locked eyes with the man who took one final drag from his cigarette and tossed it to the ground. Exhaling a plume of smoke, he snuffed out the ember with the toe of his boot.

Colter reached the sign. Resting his hand upon the smooth surface of the metal pole, he let loose a hysterical chuckle. He made it! He made it to the other town!

Still laughing, he collapsed to his knees in exhaustion, raising his good hand in the air toward the hill where he could see the silhouettes of the pack standing idle. "Fuck you!" he shouted defiantly.

Someone's hands were upon him. His first instinct was to fight, but he calmed as soon as he heard the man's voice.

"Woah, woah, woah," said the man. "I'm just trying to help."

Colter calmed and allowed the man to help him to his feet. Painfully aware of all his injuries, he allowed the man to help him into the passenger side of the truck. The sound of the door slamming closed was music to his ears. He leaned back against the seat and closed his eyes.

Outside the pack yipped and howled with laughter.

He peered out along the hillside. The alpha's eyes glowed as it bowed its head, then the pack turned away and ran off into the desert. It was all just a game to them, thought Colter. And he survived.

The driver's side door flew open, and the man climbed inside behind the steering wheel. He stared at Colter with an odd expression. "You look like shit, my friend," he said jokingly.

"Brother, you don't even know the half of it."

"My name's Dylan," said the man as he put the truck into gear and pulled out onto the highway.

Colter glanced around, taking in the messy cab. A sticker covered guitar case rested on the back seat, buried beneath a trash pile of fast-food wrappers and empty cans. He sighed and replied, "Colter. Colter Trask." He gazed up at the tiny metal bass guitar dangling from the rearview mirror. "You a musician?"

"Sometimes," replied Dylan wearing a strange expression on his face. He reached behind him and pulled a bottle of water from a small cooler. After handing it over to Colter, he set his focus to the road ahead.

As the nightmare faded behind him, Colter held the bottle in his hand, the cool liquid inside called to him. Dehydrated and exhausted, he twisted off the cap, raised the bottle to his lips and drank every drop, relishing the cool sensation of the water as it poured down his throat, quenching his thirst.

A heavy sensation washed over him. His head was spinning. Something was wrong—terribly wrong. With his vision blurring, he gazed down at the empty bottle in his hand. Drugged. He's been drugged. He shifted his gaze over to the now blurry man seated beside him.

Dylan glanced at him apologetically and said, "Sorry about that. Nothing personal, just following orders." Then he seemed to shrug as if to say—it is what it is.

As consciousness drifted away, the world around Colter went completely dark.

To Be Continued in Crossroads, Volume 3

FERAL

KOSOMA, OKLAHOMA – FIFTEEN YEARS AGO

CHAPTER 1

The soft thud of her boots on the damp earth vibrated through her legs. A horrifying, guttural scream, the final breath of her brother, echoed in her ears, a raw, visceral sound that clawed at her sanity as she ran, the air around her thick with the smell of fear and blood.

Keep going! Don't look back! She commanded herself.

Clutching the toddler close, Maggie raced through the forest. The child's small body trembled in her arms; his sobs muffled against her shoulder. "Mama!" he cried.

"Shh, shh, shh," she whispered as she scanned the dark forest that surrounded them. She couldn't keep running aimlessly. Panic swelled in her chest as she realized she had no idea where she was or where to go for help.

From the dark, dense pines surrounding her, a coyote's sharp bark cut through the stillness, the sound echoing eerily through the trees. All around her, the forest was alive with movement. The coyote's sharp bark was answered, and then another joined in, until a symphony of wild yips and howls filled the night. The pack was closing in.

Nightmare visions of the horrible barn swam forward in her mind. She must keep running. If they catch her, she would suffer the same fate as all the other poor souls who stumbled into their compound.

She ran.

Her heart pounded frantically in her chest; each beat a deafening pulse in her ears. She could almost feel the beasts breathing down her neck.

Headlights! There must be a road up ahead!

Keep running! Don't stop!

The toddler squirmed, his small body twisting and turning against her grip, a muffled whimper escaping his lips.

She clutched him tightly. Shh, shh, we're almost safe. We're almost there.

A gentle blue-gray, tinged with the faintest rose of sunrise, gradually spread across the sky above, whispering the promise of a new day. She'd never felt such relief at the break of dawn.

She pushed herself to keep going.

Up ahead, she could see a dark ribbon of asphalt through the trees. Hope exploded in her chest. The road! A jolt of energy, like an electrical current, shot through her, revitalizing her weary legs and urging her forward; the forest floor seemed to spring beneath her feet.

Coyotes barked and chattered all around her.

She tumbled from the trees, landing hard on the pavement with a jarring thud, the impact jolting her arms and making her grip on her precious cargo even tighter. The rough pavement scraped her skin. The child wailed, obviously terrified.

The sharp, insistent blare of a horn sliced through the night, making her whip her head up just in time to see a pair of headlights rushing toward her. A screech of metal on metal, the acrid smell of burning rubber, and a cloud of dark smoke erupted as the eighteen-wheeler's brakes locked up.

She glanced behind her. A large beast hovered in the shadows, its eyes glowing ominously. It lunged forward, a blur of brown fur, deadly teeth and hot breath washing over her as it missed her by inches.

Seizing the opportunity, she scrambled to her feet and ran to the passenger door of the truck, yelling, "Help me! Please!"

From the dark woods, a pack of snarling coyotes materialized, their teeth bared in a terrifying display. They surrounded the truck, their hot breath steaming in the cool morning air.

She flung the door open and found herself staring into the face of a confused middle-aged man. "Please," she begged as she climbed inside the cab and slammed the door closed. "Go!"

A piercing, chilling howl, sharp as shattered glass, sliced through the air, followed by a heavy, unnerving silence.

"What the fuck?" whispered the man under his breath. "Nah," he muttered, "fuck this." He threw the machine into gear then roared the engine.

The beasts refused to move.

He blew his horn.

Nothing.

"Please, just go!" she shouted. The toddler's cries filled the cabin.

With a grunt, the man pushed the gas pedal, the vehicle jolting forward with a sudden surge of speed.

One of the beasts launched into the air, landing with a jarring thud on the truck's hood. The impact sent vibrations through the cab. The creature lunged again and again. A snarling, frothing mess of gnashing teeth and deadly claws scrabbled at the glass in a frenzy. Its hot, fetid breath steaming the windshield.

A cloud of dust erupted from the rear tires of the truck. Its engine roared like a ferocious beast as it plowed through the pack of coyotes, sending them scattering in a panicked flurry of fur and high-pitched yelps. Once he'd driven through the pack, the driver slammed on the brakes, the screech of tires a jarring counterpoint to the thud of the large beast crashing against the windshield, sending it flying into the air before tumbling to the ground.

With no hesitation, the driver slammed the accelerator once more, a blur of speed and the engine's roar filling the air as they sped down the road.

A shiver of exhaustion ran through her entire body. Held in her arms, the toddler's wails cut through the air, his small body shaking uncontrollably, his face blotchy and stained with tears. His cries for his mother were laced with desperation. The poor child had no idea his mama was dead. Another body dangling in the barn on meat hooks alongside Maggie's brother James, her best friend Elyse and her husband, Drew.

Her thoughts shifted to her brother. His sacrifice had bought her escape. But at what price?

She gazed down upon the child sitting on her lap, his breath hitching in his chest as he clutched a worn stuffed animal. What was the reason for keeping him in that old house? They killed his family, so why did they leave him alive? For how long had he been a prisoner of those wretched beasts?

He struggled against her grasp, again calling for his mother.

Maggie rested her cheek atop his head and whispered, "Shh, shh, we're safe now."

Feral - Coming in September

ALSO BY N.L. MCLAUGHLIN

Signed copies are available on my website

www.nancylmclaughlin.com

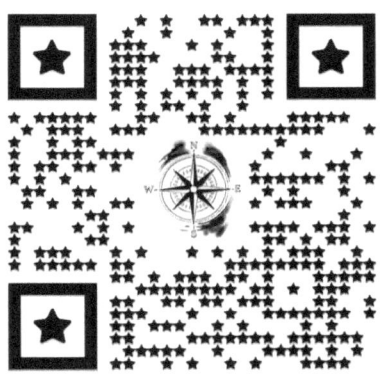

Crossroads Volume 1

Crossroads Volume 2

American Nomads

Lost Boys

Imaginary Dragons

True North

American Nomads - The Complete Series

ACKNOWLEDGMENTS

First of all, I want to thank my husband, Robert. He's always been my rock, my best friend and road trip partner. He listens to my rants and ravings, all the while, offering input whenever he can. He will always be the love of my life. When I say none of this would be possible without his endless support and love, I mean it.

My kids, Brenna, Connor, Meagan, Shannon & Rory and their significant others, aka my bonus sons, Cody and Logan. I spent two decades supporting and cheering them on to pursue their dreams and now these wonderful human beings are doing the same for me. Seriously y'all, I have the best kids.

And finally, I need to take a moment to thank all the fans of horror out there. I hope, with all my heart that you enjoy reading this book as much as I enjoyed writing it.